DEAD OF WINTER

DEAD OF WINTER

STEPHEN MACK JONES

THORNDIKE PRESS
A part of Gale, a Cengage Company

GALE
A Cengage Company

Copyright © 2021 by Stephen Mack Jones.
An August Snow Novel.
Thorndike Press, a part of Gale, a Cengage Company.

**LIBRARY OF CONGRESS CIP DATA ON FILE.
CATALOGUING IN PUBLICATION FOR THIS BOOK
IS AVAILABLE FROM THE LIBRARY OF CONGRESS.**

ISBN-13: 978-1-4328-9058-2 (hardcover alk. paper)

Published in 2021 by arrangement with Soho Press, Inc.

Printed in Mexico
Print Number: 01   Print Year: 2022

For the strong, brave women who have often picked me up, patched me up, dusted me off and pushed me forward: my mom, Evelyn Louise; MK + Lauren + Christina; Mars; Karen B.; Aunt Sadie; and, of course, Viva La Valentina!

Also for Dr. Marc Lindy & the artist Nan Capogna . . . the best of humanity

1

My house is quietly becoming Franken-stein's monster.

Carlos Rodriguez and Jimmy Radmon, my good friends and partners in the business of flipping houses in the southwest Detroit neighborhood of Mexicantown, have for the past several years used my house as a laboratory guinea pig for features they'd like to integrate into our renovations. Several months ago, it was "smart house" features: light switches, door locks and thermostats I could operate through an app on my smart-phone.

"It's seamless technology, boss man," Jimmy told me. "You don't even need no key or nothin'!"

"What if I drop my phone in a gas station toilet?" I said.

"Then you're kind of screwed, boss," Carlos said. "You don't want to reach inside a gas station toilet. Toilet snakes are poison-

7

ous, man."

"*Toilet* snakes?" Jimmy said.

"He's yankin' your chain, Jimmy," I said.

"Don't be *doin'* that, man!" Jimmy said, punching Carlos in the shoulder.

Without my having given them my permission to install it, or even a key to the house, a vented gas fireplace log (with remote) appeared in my living room. I hadn't used the fireplace since I'd moved back to the house, my late parents', after my $12 million wrongful dismissal dustup with the Detroit Police Department. Every Michigan winter since then the hearth had seemed like a sad waste of a hole in the wall.

In the winters of my childhood, my parents would sometimes sit in front of the fireplace staring at a wood log burning, my mother swaddled in a wool throw blanket, my father's strong arm around her shoulders.

"What are we doing?" I'd ask after a while, not understanding how something with no plot or exposition could be so interesting.

"Thinking," my father once answered.

"Or *not* thinking," added my mother.

It's quite possible I hadn't used the fireplace for exactly this reason: remembrance of those long-ago times with my beloved parents might prove a bit difficult on top of

8

whatever moderate Afghanistan-induced PTSD I brought with me here back in the world.

I was even less keen on the new-tech voice-assistant pods: The wonderful women in my life hardly ever listen to me anyway. Why add the disembodied female voice of a robot to the mix?

"I've got an idea," I said, when I came home to find the pods installed. "How's about this, guys? Maybe you could install door locks on my house that even *you guys* can't pick?"

Carlos and Jimmy exchanged a look, then burst out laughing.

"Ain't no such luck with no such lock, Mr. Snow," Jimmy said.

Begrudgingly, I let the boys work on the house. Mainly because when I saw them these days, I felt guilty: what had looked like promising employment for a kid with no future (Jimmy) and a Mexican immigrant not authorized to work in the US (Carlos) had come down to one last house to renovate and flip on Markham Street. Certainly, there were other properties in Mexicantown, but with Detroit's recent renaissance, more suburbanites and real estate companies were buying up properties with a solid promise of a 300 percent return on investment. Instead of a one-and-a-half-square-mile lower-to middle-income working-class brown-and-Black "ghetto," Mexicantown was quickly becoming the hipster, urban-chic place to be. I couldn't find properties fast enough, and when I did, I was outgunned on fair market price.

My real estate agent (who is, I suspect, part-time Oracle of Delphi) had warned me this day was coming five years ago.

"What was lost, abandoned and forgotten all them years will be found again, young Snow," Miss Jesse had told me over hibiscus tea and gingersnaps at her 6,000-square-foot Neo-Renaissance Louis Kamper-designed Indian Village home. "Everybody done forgot about the '08 mortgage melt-down. The pirates are soon to find your little island nation of Mexicantown, and they will spread they money like cancer."

Had I known I'd be responsible for the livelihoods of two good men, I would have listened a bit harder to Miss Jesse.

"You guys haven't touched anything in the kitchen, have you?" I said.

They were tinkering with the personal-assistant pod on my fireplace mantel.

"No, on account we know you like it just like it is," Jimmy said.

"And somehow that didn't translate to the

rest of my house?"

Carlos and his family, who had been chased out of the US by white nationalists wearing federal badges, were now hardworking, taxpaying, poutine-and-hockey-loving Canadian residents living only fifteen minutes south of Mexicantown (via the US/Canada bridge across the narrow churn of the Detroit River) in Windsor, Ontario. He'd started a heating-and-cooling business that was struggling but promised growth if he could just hold on for another year. A bridge pass made for easy commuting to this side of the Detroit River for Carlos to work on my flip jobs and collect cash infusions.

I'd convinced Jimmy to take a few college classes between his reno work, karate lessons at Club Brutus and video game nights. He'd been sure he would fail. His first term at Wayne State University he'd brought home a 4.1 GPA for a course load including Introduction to Electrical Engineering and Mechanical Engineering 101. Still, we were down to the last house on Markham, and I had no dependable employment to offer him. He was worried because he had become a homeowner. And as every middle-to upper-middle-class working stiff knows, money is how you keep a home running. I'd told Jimmy he didn't need to worry. I'd be there for him.

"Boss," he'd said, "I don't mean no disrespect, but a grown man don't want no charity. He wants his shot. He wants what he earns."

Hard to argue with that.

"Okay, Mr. Snow," Carlos said. "Check it out."

"Check what out?"

"Ginger! Your personalized home assistant," Jimmy said. "Go ahead! Ask her something."

"Ginger," I said reluctantly, "can you make a Guadalajara-style mole sauce?"

The pod on the mantel of my now-functional fireplace lit up. After a second, the pod said, "I'm afraid I can't make a Guadalajara-style mole sauce. I did, however, find a number of recipes for mole sauce. Would you like to hear the top five? Or shall I print them for you?"

"Hey, Ginger," I said, "who do you like more, Smokey Robinson or Marvin Gaye?"

"Both were award-winning musical artists signed with music impresario Berry Gordy's Motown record label in —"

"Ginger," Carlos interrupted, "what's today's temperature — in *Celsius*?" Carlos smiled and gave me a sideways glance.

"That's what we use in Canada."

"Socialist," I said with mock disgust.

"Today will have a high of seven degrees Celsius," the pod said.

"She plays chess and *Jeopardy!*, too, Mr. Snow!" Jimmy said.

"Be still, my beating heart," I said feeling fairly creeped out by the prospect of having more data points collected on me. "Guys, I'll be honest with you — I'm not too keen on having some machine connected to an eighty-acre corporate server farm listening to my every whisper, fart and flying fornication."

"I told you," Carlos said to Jimmy.

"You can turn it off anytime!" Jimmy said.

"Then what's the sense in having it in the first place?" I said.

"But you can order food for delivery, boss," Jimmy said with a tinge of desperation. "You don't have to go out or nothing!"

"When I get that hungry or lazy, shoot me. Ginger ain't my kinda gal, guys."

"Doggone it," Jimmy said as he fished a five-dollar bill from a pocket and handed it to Carlos.

"Yep," Carlos said, accepting the money. "Told you."

"You mind if I go to Windsor for a couple days to help Carlos out, Mr. Snow?" Jimmy said as the two men collected their tools. "Drywall for this last house ain't coming in until Friday, and Carlos got a restaurant heating job."

"Help Carlos out," I said.

The two men unplugged and boxed up the three personal assistant units they had installed in the house. Then Jimmy scrubbed any memory of Ginger from my router before both men left, one of them five dollars richer.

I was in the middle of steam cleaning my face by hovering over a pan of chicken, shrimp and oyster paella (no mussels — too much work for too little return) when my phone rang.

"Octavio!" Elena said. "Do you have a moment?"

"For you," I said to my beloved godmother, "always." I sprinkled a bit more cayenne pepper into the aromatic mix.

"You think perhaps you could come with me tomorrow morning to Authentico Foods to meet with Mr. Ochoa?"

"Old man Ochoa?" I said. "What's going on?"

"He has some sort of business proposition for you," Elena said. "Plus, Jackie will be there. You remember Jackie."

14

I did; she was my unrequited middle- and high-school crush and a teen-in-heat top of the list at Saturday confession.

"I'm sure you'd like to see her."

"I'd love to see Jackie," I said, slowly stirring my concoction. "But to be honest with you, Elena, I'm not much on expanding the Snow business empire, or investing in someone else's."

"He's dying, August," Elena said with sincere gravitas. "Por favor."

"I'll drive," I said.

"No, querido," Elena said. "*I'll* drive."

2

When I was a kid, the only reason I liked Mr. Ochoa was that my mother liked him.

Or rather, she "understood" him.

While my cop father patrolled the pot-holed streets of Detroit, my mother — during my school hours — had worked as a batch mixer at Mr. Ochoa's corn and flour tortilla business in Mexicantown. Between my second and eighth grades, Mr. Ochoa's business grew from a cramped Mexican-town storefront mom-and-pop to a major Midwestern-restaurant supplier of tortillas, restaurant-branded salsas and specialty blended tomato-and-queso white sauces — all organic because Mr. Ochoa didn't know any other way.

My mother, having worked for Mr. Ochoa and his wife, Esme, since the beginning, was promoted to a quality assurance position, watching over a small team of bakers and packagers, ingredient inventories, cooking

16

equipment and Ochoa family recipes, which she both protected and executed like a culinary guardian angel.

"He's from the old days," my mother used to say to my father, who had little regard for Mr. Ochoa. "Not as enlightened as one would hope. Not as bad as one might think."

Truth is, Mr. Ochoa was never very fond of Black people — mayates — even though his unflappably loyal director of accounts billable for thirty years, Francine Evers, was a petite, rail-thin Black woman with thick-lens glasses and a shy demeanor. He told my mother Francine was an exception; she wasn't like the rest of *them*. Apparently, my father was another exception to the mayate rule, since he had married into the greater Chicano family and was a cop who had chosen to live in Mexicantown. My mother believed Esme, Ochoa's late wife, had been the quiet catalyst behind her husband's growing list of exceptions to the myths and assumptions about the mayate.

Now, twenty years later, I sat across from Mr. Ochoa in the second-floor Authentico Foods, Inc. office, still located in Mexican-town on a city-block-long stretch of Vernor Highway a mile east of the I-75 freeway. With me was my godmother, Elena Gutierrez, wife of my godfather and best friend, Tomás.

To Mr. Ochoa's right was his beautiful, dark-eyed daughter, Jacqueline. When I'd known Jackie in middle and high school, she had always been nice enough, but distant. Fifteen years later, she still inspired a quickened heartbeat and electrified hormones. For college, she had gone away to USC. I had mended my broken heart by going to Wayne State and chasing other girls who might have resembled Jackie.

Standing next to her like a sentry in a snappy suit was Daniel Antonio Romero, Esq. Danny was the Ochoa family lawyer and a self-inflated, insufferable prick. I'd known him since middle and high school, too. A snake-skinned bully, moderately talented football jock and ladies' man, who, not unlike myself, could never get next to the one love of his life — Jackie Ochoa. Even now, when he had one hand gently placed on Jackie's shoulder, it was easy to see he wanted to impress her. At one point she looked up at Danny and dispassionately assured him she was quite all right. Reluctantly he removed his hand. Clearly, Danny was a horse with a bit in his mouth and saddle on his back.

To Mr. Ochoa's left was Francine Evers,

frailer than I remembered her, cradling a stack of thick, overstuffed binders.

"It's good to see you, Octavio," Mr. Ochoa said in a strained voice. "You served our country just like our beloved Norberto." Save for Jackie, we all made the Sign of the Cross. "And your mother — she was a wonderful woman. A woman of God. Like my Esme. My heart was broken when she went home to Jesus." He paused to suck in a long breath of oxygen through his nose-mounted breathing tube.

Mr. Ochoa had suffered through two bouts of throat cancer. Chemo, radiation and two surgeries had left him a gaunt, ashen man with a whisper-thin voice. Now he was succumbing to lymphoma, which wanted what scraps remained of him.

"Thank you for your kind words about my mother," I said in the tone one uses to respectfully address the dying.

"That painting," he said, gesturing to the large portrait of his younger self that hung behind his desk. "Your dear mother painted that. I've always loved that painting. She captured a spirit I never quite saw in myself. A spirit that I've tried to live up to over the years." The painting was centered on the wall behind his desk. It was flanked by numerous high school and army photos of his son, Norberto, and a shadow box displaying his assortment of ribbons and medals, including a Purple Heart. He had been KIA in the Uruzgan Province of Afghanistan. He was twenty.

The British hadn't been able to hold it.

Neither had the Soviets.

Now it's our turn to bleed out in the same sand where other empires have gone to die.

At the bottom right of Norberto's memorial wall, a single high school graduation picture of Jackie was barely noticeable. Nothing that indicated she'd achieved an MBA from the University of Southern California, had authored two bestselling business books, and was often the number-one photogenic choice when Bloomberg News, Reuters TV, CNBC or Cheddar needed a brown face for stories on female entrepreneurs.

Mr. Ochoa coughed. Jackie, who had been beautifully stoic save for the occasional smile sent my way, patted him on the heaving bones of his back and offered him water. He waved it off with a skeleton's hand. "Your father," Mr. Ochoa rasped. His daughter held a water bottle for him, and he consented, taking birdlike sips. "He looked out for us. A good man. A police officer. There were things I said that I should never have said —"

"Señor Ochoa, forgive me for interrupting," I said. "I'm not a priest, so may I suggest you save your confession? None of us has ever truly been the person we could have been — maybe *should* have been. I know I'm not. But I have the feeling that when God weighs your soul on His scales, He'll find yours to be the exact weight of an angel's feather." His daughter mechanically patted one of his hands while Miss Evers gently held the other as if it were a piece of priceless china. Danny Romero just glared at me. "You've given people in this community good livings for over thirty years. When neighbors couldn't afford food, you fed them. When their kids walked to school in worn-out shoes in the dead of winter, you put boots on their feet, gloves on their hands and scarves around their necks."

"I've — said things —" he croaked.

"The LEGO Air Tech Claw Rig," I said.

Everyone in the room looked at me as if I'd just floated a shiny non sequitur midair during a deathly serious moment.

"The — what?" Mr. Ochoa said.

"I was eight when my mother brought home the LEGO Air Tech Claw Rig," I said. "A 954-piece toy semi-truck with a working pneumatic crane. *You* bought that for me as

21

a Christmas gift. For over two weeks, me and my dad lay on the living room floor putting that model together in front of the fireplace. You gave me an incredible two weeks with my dad. Sometimes what a man *says* doesn't truly represent who the man truly *is*."

Mr. Ochoa lowered his head. "Thank you, Octavio."

Elena spoke up. "Octavio, Mr. Ochoa wanted to see you because he needs to ask you something. Something you might want to take a bit of time to think about —"

"But not too much time," Mr. Ochoa said with a wheeze. "I don't think there's a road back for me this time."

"There's always hope, Mr. Ochoa," Danny said in Spanish.

"No," Mr. Ochoa said curtly, "there isn't."

"Anything I can do, it's done," I said.

"August," Jackie said, her voice raising my pulse a bit, "Papa wants you to consider buying the company."

I sat in shock for a moment before I found my voice. "I don't know the first thing about running a company. I barely know how to run my own house," I said. "Plus, Jackie's your daughter. Your blood. Why not her?"

"Because I don't want it, August," Jackie said brusquely. "I've worked hard to build my own life. A life outside of the frozen prairies and plains of the Midwest. Outside of my hero brother's memory. And one that definitely does not include selling tortillas and cheesy whatevers."

Then they told me what was *really* going on: They'd been approached by a real estate speculator who went only by "Mr. Sloane." Sloane — described by Francine Evers as an instantly forgettable skinny white man with male-pattern baldness and wire-rim glasses — claimed to be working on behalf of Detroit's resident billionaire, Vic Bronson, a man who'd made his fortune selling mortgages and collecting adjustable-rate mortgage balloon payments in an overleveraged housing market almost twenty years earlier. Since moving his empire's headquarters from suburban Birmingham to the revitalized Guardian Building in the heart of Detroit, Bronson had purchased thirty buildings through his Sextant Properties Group.

Now, it seemed, his larger-than-life shadow was falling on the edges of Mexicantown.

"He wants to demolish this place," Danny said. "Turn it into some sort of boutique 'ethnic destination' shopping mall: tapas restaurants, avant-garde shops, an art gallery, ten to twenty high-end flats above. 'Casa Nuevo Sol.' "

"Vic Bronson and this Mr. Sloane know everything about acquisition and possession," Francine Evers said, "but they don't seem to know boo about appreciating another person's history or cultural heritage. A gentrified Mexican theme park is what he's talking about. Ride the giant sombrero down the waterfall. Makes about as much sense as cornrows on a white girl."

"No doubt," Danny began, "this area *could* benefit from a large capital infusion and some forward-thinking development, but —"

Jackie cut her eyes up to Danny. He stopped speaking.

They told me how much Sloane had offered for the building.

I might have whistled.

"Even had the nerve to bring it up in here! In *cash. Showed* us!" Francine said. "Two big ol' suitcases stacked on a luggage dolly!" She gave a shiver. "Gave me the midnight willies 'cause you just know that kind of cash don't come from no good."

"Folks," I began, "I've got a lot of money. Frankly, more than I'll ever need. But comparatively speaking, I don't have *that* much. I'm sorry. I just couldn't —"

24

"We'll sell it to you — *everything,* Octavio! — for a third of his offer," Mr. Ochoa pleaded. "Just — just make sure my people — I've got to take care of my employees. Francine. And Jacqueline."

"I can take care of myself," Francine said. "Don't you worry about me, you old fool."

"Ditto," Jackie said. "Do whatever you want, Papa. But the clock's running on the offer. *And* you."

"I'm sure this is a lot for you to think about, Octavio," Elena said. "But every day, the character — the history — of Mexican-town is being eaten away. Please. Promise me you'll think about Jackie and Mr. Ochoa's proposal."

"For the record," Danny said, puffing out his lawyer's chest for all to see, "I think this is a grave mistake — and not very good business sense — to make this offer to Snow."

"Wow," I said. "It *speaks!*"

Danny took a step my way. "Hey, at least I didn't get booted off the police force like your scrawny ass."

"Scrawny?" I laughed. "Adonis-like, yes. But 'scrawny'?"

Jackie smiled. An unexpected and much appreciated checkmark in the win-column for yours truly.

"He may have conned a good deal of money out of the city. And he may have renovated and flipped a few houses. Any third-rate grifter could do that. But he's no businessman," Danny said, keeping me in his steely glare. "You put a dirty ex-cop in this company's driver's seat, and Authentico's sold for parts in three months."

"As much as it pains me, I have to agree with Danny," I said to Mr. Ochoa. "Except for the dirty cop part. You've got a very rich offer on the table from Vic Bronson through this Sloane guy. An offer that could take care of your employees and leave Jackie sitting prettier than she already is."

"It *is* a handsome offer," Jackie said.

"Let's just leave things at I'll think about it," I said. "That's all I can promise, Señor Ochoa."

"One more thing before you go, Mr. Snow," Francine Evers said. With a trembling hand, she offered me a forest-green file folder.

"Oh, Jesus," Danny said. "Is this really necessary?"

"Danny?" Jackie said. With just his name, Jackie had pulled his reins.

I flipped through the paperwork in the folder: spreadsheets, profit and loss statements, accounting mumbo jumbo, a simple

26

breakdown of Sloane's offer, how the offer would be paid out, an unsigned contract.

"The last page, Mr. Snow," Francine said in a soft voice.

A list of amounts of money.

And a name that instantly injected ice water into my spine.

"Gambling debts," Mr. Ochoa said quietly. "*Old* gambling debts. I'm embarrassed. Sick about it. I've paid most all of it back to the company. To my employees. *And* to that loan-shark."

"Why would Vic Bronson, of all people, feel it necessary to introduce this . . . information into an introductory business negotiation, Mr. Snow?" Francine said in a trembling voice. She knew the language of money. She was now acquainted with the terror of a personal threat presented as a spreadsheet.

I was still staring at the loan-shark's name on the sheet of paper.

"I'll get back to you on that," I said, feeling the need for a shot of bourbon.

And a very large gun.

3

People who drive it seem to love it.

The Toyota Prius.

Me?

I don't quite trust any car that (1) can't accommodate my height and muscle mass and (2) doesn't make a sound.

With me as her passenger, Elena drove us home from the meeting at Authentico Foods, Inc., in her blue Prius. I wished Elena had taken me up on my offer to drive us in my refurbished silver '68 Oldsmobile 442 — a thank-you gift from Jimmy and Carlos.

"The male version of a steel vibrator," she'd called it, permanently damaging my pristine image of my godmother.

We turned south off Vernor Highway onto Clark Avenue, driving slowly past Mexicantown's Clark Park, its multitude of trees showing off their array of fall colors. I thought about how much I'd loved the park

as a kid: Baseball and soccer, Saturday barbeques, Sunday walks with my mom and
dad, eating lemon ices from the crazy-eyed
vendor parked outside of Most Holy Re-
deemer Church. Attempting to smoke stolen
cigarettes, making out with Gina Rojos
while fantasizing I was tongue deep with
Jackie Ochoa.

Now, in anticipation of an early and snow-
packed winter, the owners of the local
Mexican grocery store, Honeycomb Market,
were busy setting up the skating rink they'd
donated to the park.

Who says Black and brown kids don't play
hockey?

"There's no way you could see yourself
buying the business, Octavio?" Elena said
as we hummed/levitated through Mexicantown in her Prius.

"I don't know anything about running a
business. I don't *want* to know how to run
a business. I don't even know how much a
half gallon of milk costs."

"If only you drank milk, Octavio," Elena
said. "Of course, I'm sure you know how
much a single malt whiskey costs."

Touché.

Then she said, "You already run a suc-
cessful business turning over houses."

"*Flipping* houses," I said. "And I'm just

the paymaster. Jimmy and Carlos do the heavy lifting. Besides, they're both moving into other things. Jimmy's enrolled at Wayne State in electrical engineering, and Carlos has a running start on a heating-and-cooling business in Windsor."

"And of course you're funding both." Elena issued the kind of sigh that only godmothers seem capable of, one that speaks leather-bound volumes of profound disappointment. It wasn't that Elena disapproved of the way I spent my money. It was simply that she feared I might someday be living out of the trunk of my car, eating Lucky Charms from the box and waiting for a nice spring rain so I could shower.

"A fool and his money are soon parted," my father used to say as he handed me my dollar-a-week allowance. "Don't be that brand of fool, son."

I've tried not to be.

Especially since my wealth came at the cost of a portion of my soul.

"Maybe it's just time, Elena."

With sad resignation, Elena nodded.

"What concerns me is why this Mr. Sloane would feel the need to introduce dirt on Mr. Ochoa as leverage so early in the negotiating."

"I very much doubt there's any

'negotiating,' " Elena said. "More of a hostile takeover strategy. Maybe he thinks Mexicans know nothing about business and are easily intimidated."

"He'd be wrong on both counts," I said.

We were quiet for a moment. Then Elena said, "Maybe you could find out who this Mr. Sloane is? If he really represents Vic Bronson? Maybe reason with him? You're very good at those things, Octavio."

I smiled at Elena. "I don't much like being handled. Even by exceptionally smart, extraordinarily beautiful, immensely savvy women. Are you trying to handle me, Elena?"

"Maybe," she said with a quick, demur smile and an ingenue's innocent shrug. "Un poco. Tatina seems to have had some success 'handling' you."

"Ouch."

When we stopped in front of my house, I said, "I'll see what I can shake loose about this Mr. Sloane. But in all honesty, it sounds like this guy takes a lot of pride and extreme caution in being the ghost of an agent provocateur. I'm not very good at finding ghosts."

"Maybe not," Elena said. "However, it seems they're very good at finding you."

Before getting out of her miniature spaceship, I asked if Tomás was home. Elena said he might be by then, but the last she knew he had gone to the post office to see if there were any new collectable postage stamps he could put away for their granddaughter, June. He'd been collecting full sheets of special stamps since June's birth six years earlier.

Having known my godfather for as long as I had, I knew buying collectible stamps wasn't the singular and true objective of his solo outing.

Once Elena and her Prius had scooted off, I retrieved my car keys from the house and made my way to the shed out back.

"Hello, gorgeous," I said, laying eyes on my beautiful '68 Olds 442. "Miss me?" I apologized for smelling like environmentally conscientious electric-car betrayal and fired up the four-hundred-cubic-inch Rocket V8 engine. Three hundred ninety steel stallions ready to stampede . . .

Unfortunately for my 442, the ride was a relatively quick one that didn't involve flexing her steel-and-iron V8 muscles. About five minutes away from Markham Street and east across the hellacious expanse of I-75 was an abandoned one-story post office. Loosely draped across the boarded-up windows was a banner: COMING SOON!

SALON MARITA — HAIR, MANI-PEDI, DAY SPA! Apparently, Marita's financing had fallen through; the banner, faded by summer sun and shredded by winter winds, had been hanging there for the past three years.

I parked in the rubble-strewn back lot, got out and took a spectator's seat on a stack of crumbling bricks.

"You got a minute?" I said.

Tomás had a young man backed up against the building, one fist in the air. The punk's face was already bloodied.

"Yeah," Tomás said. "What's up?"

Another man was on his knees and moaning, his head lolling on his thick neck as he slobbered blood and saliva into his cupped hands, which held what I assumed were several of his teeth. A third man, skinny and wearing a pair of the worst Chinese knockoff Air Jordan basketball shoes I'd ever seen, was crawling toward a discarded 9mm handgun. I quietly bet myself that he wouldn't make it.

"You hear anything about Vic Bronson using an intermediary to buy Authentico Foods?" I asked.

Tomás jackhammered his fist into the young man's face.

Nighty-noodles, punk.

"Yeah," Tomás said, turning to kick the

kneeling man in his missing teeth. "Don't smell quite right."

"If it was Bronson, it would be all over the news," I said. " 'Sextant Properties Group Buys Mexicantown Block, Rolls Out Two-Year Development Plan.' "

Tomás pointed to the man within arm's reach of the gun. "And when were you gonna tell me about this?"

I smiled and said, "Smart money's always on you, mi amigo."

"Thanks for your fucking support, pendejo."

Tomás delivered a kick to the man's ribs that could have launched him from Ford Field's forty-two-yard line cleanly through the goalposts. The man was now in the fetal position, weeping and soiling himself. Tomás picked up the 9mm, ratcheted a bullet out of the chamber, let the magazine fall to the ground, then hammered the grip on a stack of cinder blocks until it was no more.

"So, I take it you have a dispute with these gentlemen?" I said.

"Yeah," Tomás said, pointing to a collection of plastic baggies and foil packets strewn on the cold ground. "Name it: coke, heroin, fentanyl lollipops, Mexican and Canadian Oxy knockoffs, bath salts, hemp vaping cartridges. Even got what looks and smells like Cambodian sticky-brick hash. Guess where I found these yahoos?"

I picked up one of the foil packets and looked at the cartoon sticker keeping it sealed. Our spongy friend who lives in a pineapple under the sea.

"I'm thinking near Detroit Cristo Rey."

"What kind of a sick fuck sells drugs to kids who just learning algebra?"

"Apparently, these kinds of sick fucks." I tossed the packet to the ground, put my shoe heel into it and gave a twist. "You done here?"

"Just about." Tomás knelt by the man holding his ribs. Grabbing a fistful of the sobbing man's bright chartreuse imitation Polo Ralph Lauren bubble coat, Tomás raised him so they were face-to-face. "I see you or your girlfriends hangin' around Mexicantown again and I'll wipe my ass with your faces. You understand me?"

"Yeah," the man managed to say.

"I didn't get that," Tomás said, giving the man a hard shake. "What?"

"Yessir!" he said, then added in menacingly accented Spanish, "Sí, Señor El Sepulturero!"

Tomás released the man and stood.

"Still trying to get people to call you 'The

Gravedigger'?" I said as we walked to my car.

"It's a cool nickname," Tomás said. "Not so much in English, but in Spanish it's bad-ass."

"You're a man in his late fifties who wears custom-made orthotics and plays tea party and Candy Land with his granddaughter every chance he gets," I said. "Why do you need a 'badass' nickname?"

"Does Tatina know what a buzzkill you can be?"

"Second time today a Gutierrez has brought up Tatina's name," I said. "You guys know something I don't?"

"Nothing other than the fact that she loves you and you're too much of a pussy to admit you love her back."

"I want you to take a ride with me —"

"Yeah, but first you and me's going out to Royal Oak to see Duke Ducane," Tomás said.

I stopped and turned to Tomás. "You need to see Duke Ducane? Why?"

" 'Cause them three fuck-bags I bloodied up said they got their shit from him."

"Funny," I said, seeing absolutely nothing funny at all about visiting Duke Ducane. "I was just on my way to see Duke myself. He's been blackmailing Mr. Ochoa."

36

"Up jump the devil."

"Yep," I said. "Up jump the devil."

4

Marcus "Duke" Ducane had reached the dubious status of legend in Detroit's criminal underworld. Forty years ago, his multimillion-dollar empire spanned gambling, prostitution, loan-sharking, drugs, money laundering and human trafficking. Lawyers and judges, state legislators, city council members, cops and at least two mayors had all benefited from Duke's weekly and monthly payouts. He had beaten two extortion and racketeering trials and a two-year-long FBI investigation for wire fraud.

After wreaking decades of havoc on Detroit and across five states, Duke Ducane was finally collared for extortion and sent away by a young, eager Detroit Police detective lieutenant — me. Duke got a paltry five years in a minimum-security slam, a prison where he could perfect his golf swing and make new friends in banking and investment portfolio management. I suspect he handed the prosecution the win in a byzantine scheme to retire from a criminal underworld that he felt had become an impersonal, multinational, venture capital machine indistinguishable from any other craven corporate enterprise.

Now, two years after his prison release, he was the proprietor of a high-end recording studio in the northern Detroit suburb of Royal Oak.

"I'm surprised you didn't want to make a stop at your gun locker before heading out to see Duke," I said as I brought the Olds 442 to a stop in the small parking lot at the south side of SoundNation Recording Studio.

"If the guys I put a beatdown on were telling the truth, then I want Duke to get the same up-close-and-personal intensive care."

"What about the Compton twins?"

"You handle 'em," Tomás said, getting out of the car.

I'd tried handling Duke's mammoth, psychotic bodyguards all by my lonesome a while ago. The result had been three fractured ribs and a face that resembled beef tartare. Maybe I should have stopped and bought a dozen roses for the twin goliaths. Or at least a twenty-ounce steak they could tear at in the lobby like Cerberus with a fresh soul.

The lobby of SoundNation Recording Studio was no longer the vomit-inducing Jackson Pollock fever dream it once had been. Now it had softly illuminated purple and magenta walls where projections of recording legends — Marvin Gaye, Tammi Terrell, John Lee Hooker, the Supremes, Jack White and Eminem — alternated with photos of a revitalized Detroit and corporate logos. From all indications in that lobby, Detroit was an extremely happy place populated by good-looking people of all ethnic, racial and religious stripes.

Sitting at a frosted glass desk in the shape of a baby grand piano, beneath a chandelier fashioned after a fifties B-movie flying saucer, was the receptionist — an attractive white woman in her late forties, early fifties, with spiked red hair, large round red-frame glasses and a red leather bodice barely able to contain her freckled breasts. She was not the impossibly white-skinned Goth woman Ducane had been employing as receptionist-cum-gargoyle last time I'd been by. Still, she was a woman you could look at in anticipation of hearing a uniquely entertaining life story.

"Where's White Girl?" I said to the new

receptionist.

She grinned, revealing rather large, perfectly aligned planks of luminous white teeth. "She's touring with her band, Sapphire G-String!" she said with an easy southwestern drawl.

I extended my hand and said, "I'm —"

"I know who you are, Mr. Snow," she said, resolutely holding her grin. Calmly she folded her hands on the desk; each long fingernail was painted a primary color different from the ones beside it. "I got a long-barrel Smith & Wesson in my desk drawer. Pearl handle. Belonged to my granddaddy, then my daddy, now me. Unlike White Girl, I've been shootin' since I was six and have no compunction about it. Shoot the furry balls off a squirrel at a hundred yards. So. We gonna engage in the Alamo two-step or what, Mr. Snow?"

"I find myself at a disadvantage," I said, extending my hand again. She didn't take it. "What may I call you?"

"TB."

"Like — tuberculosis?"

"Like Terri-Sue Boudreaux," she said, sitting back in her chair, casually rocking and revealing meaty, freckled thighs. My synaptic interpretation of what I was seeing fluctuated wildly between a middle-aged

41

lady dressed as Wonder Woman for Comic Con and a Japanese anime rendering of a big redheaded cowgirl from Texas.

"What's your take on the Lions, TB?" I said.

"They need receivers who can actually catch the ball," TB said. "Ain't had that since they ran them little legs off Barry Sanders and squeezed Calvin 'Megatron' Johnson dry. And they need a defensive line that ain't afraid of getting their feelings hurt. Other than that, I don't give a shit. I'm a Cowboys girl."

I turned to Tomás and smiled. "I like her."

Tomás was unmoved. "Your sad excuse for an asshole boss in?"

"Sir," TB said, "I'm not sure I like your attitude."

Tomás appeared to be done with his wan attempt at diplomacy. "And I ain't too sure I like standin' here flappin' gums with some West Texas scrub shovin' all her bra's business in my face."

"You remind me of my second husband, God rest his soul," TB told him sweetly. "A mule-kicker in the sack. Dumber than a bag of dollar-store hammers."

"See?" I said to Tomás. "I *like* her!"

"Thanks, TB." Duke Ducane had appeared from around a corner. He was wearing a lavender suit, dark purple shirt and purple Puma Adreno soccer shoes. He may have been as old as the dirt on Jesus's sandals, but he carried himself like an OG ready to pop at a nanosecond's notice. "I got these assholes."

"You're sure, Mr. Ducane?" she said.

"Yeah, TB." Duke stared unblinking at Tomás and me. "Maybe someday I'll give you the go-ahead to unload on these wastes of time and space. But until then, just keep her locked and loaded."

Duke nodded for us to walk with him. I had to slow Tomás down with a hand on his shoulder as we followed Duke down a studio hallway. In one of the studios was Detroit's reigning white-boy king of rap spitting rhymes into a microphone. Me, I'm not much for rap, but the kid's all right.

"Jesus, Duke," I said. "Your new receptionist. What do your recruitment ads look like? 'Must know Microsoft Word, PowerPoint, Smith & Wesson'?"

Tomás — impatient and ready for a taste of blood — jerked my hand from his shoulder and grabbed Duke's upper right arm. Shoving his massive chest against the one-time Black *capo di tutti i capi,* Tomás looked down at the shorter Ducane and said, "You sellin' drugs in Mexicantown, pendejo?"

"I ain't sold drugs in thirty years, pendejo," Duke said, pushing back against Tomás's chest with his own. "I'm a hundred percent legit. I do, however, *take* a lot of drugs: Metformin for type 2 diabetes. Lisinopril for my blood pressure. Prozac 'cause it's depressing as mothafuckin' hell living the life of a Black man in Ameri-KKK. And metoprolol for something called 'essential tremors.' Guess it's karma's way of getting back at me for all the drugs I *did* sell. Now, since yo breath smell like you been nursin' on buffalo balls, back the fuck up off —"

"I just beat the living shit outta three punks claimin' you supplied 'em," Tomás snarled, undeterred.

"Like I said, ya big dumb wet mothafucka, I ain't got the time, patience or inclination for that game no more," Duke said. "Unreliable people. Margins too thin. Pharmaceutical companies got a thousand times more juice on the street than I ever had. If them punks said it was me, then they lyin' they asses off."

"And I'm supposed to believe that bullshit?"

"Onliest thing you supposed to do is take a bath every Saturday, go to church on Sunday, be brown and die," Duke said.

44

"Aside from that I don't much give a shit what you want to, have to, supposed to or shoulda done. You believe me? Fine. You *don't* believe me? Cool. Couldn't care less."

"You all right, boss?" I heard one of the Compton twins say in a subwoofer mountain-troll voice.

They were standing outside of a large conference room; paused on the sixty-five-inch flat-screen TV was the face of Hercule Poirot as played by David Suchet. At the end of the conference table were two large salads.

"We coo," Duke said.

"You guys eat *salad* now?" I said.

"Can't have my protection lookin' like no chicken-'n'-biscuit niggahs," Duke said. Then to Fergie and Fin, he said, "Go on, boys. Finish your lunch."

"You sure you don't want us to hurt 'em?" either Fergie or Fin asked.

"I'm sure," Duke said in a calming voice. "Go on now." The two giants returned to the conference room and Hercule Poirot. Then to Tomás, Duke said, "You got about two seconds to push off me, ya chupacabra-lookin' mothafucka."

I shouldered my way between Tomás and Duke. "I suppose you don't have anything to do with blackmailing Mr. Ronaldo Ochoa with old gambling debts?"

Duke adjusted his expensive suit, brushing what he could of Tomás off him, and furrowed his eyebrows. "Ronaldo who?"

"Ronny Ochoa," I said. "Owns Athentico Foods in Mexicantown. Came to you maybe twenty years ago for a loan to cover some gambling debts. Says he paid you off with interest. And I know your interest rates are about as reasonable as Wells Fargo's."

Duke searched my eyes and Tomás's before he said, "Somebody out there usin' me as a cutout. Sleight of hand for suckers — and it looks like y'all done been played." Duke gave me a hard, unblinking look. "When have you ever known me to be that damned obvious? God, Allah, Buddha and yo momma as my witnesses, I ain't sellin' no damn drugs, and I ain't squeezin' no old brown dude for his last peso."

After a moment, I said, "God help me, but I believe you."

"Seriously?" Tomás said incredulously. "You believe this piece of shit?"

"I do," I said.

"Look," Duke said. "I'm bein' fo real, awright? Punks trading on my name don't do my new brand no good, because the day five-oh stops surveilling me and the news media stops doggin' me is the day both be

46

sure I'm dead. So, listen up; I'll pay you —
both of you — to find out who's throwin'
shade on my name."

"And if we find out, what then?"

"Let's just say y'all step out; I step in."

"You are just shitting me, right?" Tomás
growled at me. "You're gonna take the
devil's money to prove he's a freakin' angel?"

"You awright, boss?"

It was TB. Standing, she was an imposing
woman: tall, full-figured and strapped with
her Smith & Wesson long barrel. Her star-
spangled cowboy boots added to the effect.

The Compton twins had joined us in the
hallway again, ready to pounce.

"Everybody just take a breath," I said.
"This is just a spirited negotiation, not Saint
Patrick's Day at the Old Shillelagh, okay?"

August Snow, UN peacekeeper.

"We're not taking a dime of your money,"
I said to Duke. "For whatever reason, I
believe you. That being said, if I find out
you are in any way, shape or form playing
me, I will come back here and kick you so
hard in the nuts you'll have three Adam's
apples."

"You can fo damn sure try," Duke said.

I had to physically turn Tomás by his thick

47

shoulders and push him through the front
door of SoundNation.

5

The drive from Royal Oak back to Mexicantown was uncomfortably quiet and palpably tense. I had believed Ducane when he pleaded innocence. Tomás, on the other hand, wanted a collection of Ducane's teeth stuck in his calloused knuckles.

I thought a nice *capricciosa* pizza and a couple Valentine Vodka martinis at Bigalora would appease the beast.

"Fuck that," Tomás said. "And fuck you. Just take me to my truck."

"Don't forget to buy stamps."

"Eat shit, cabron."

Ten icy-silent minutes later, when I brought my car to a stop by the abandoned post office, Tomás finally said, "You was a marine, right?"

"Once and always."

"And a cop, too, right?"

"At least for a minute. Where's this —"

"Then you must be old enough to know

49

tigers don't change their stripes and leop-
ards don't change their spots. And that goes
double for old gangster motherfuckers like
Duke Ducane."

I started to reply, but Tomás got out of
the car — not bothering to close my passenger door — climbed into his truck, hit
the gas and, tires squealing, headed home.

I just hoped he remembered stamps.

There are certain things one should consider when attempting to rebuild a picture-
perfect childhood neighborhood from memory, most important of which is this:
memory is almost always fragmentized,
sanitized, demonized or wholly fictionalized
by its constant travel companion and fickle
lover, imagination.

Take for example the house next to my
family home on Markham Street in Mexicantown: Long ago, it belonged to the
Alvarez family. The children — Antonio
(Tony), who was the same age as me, and
his younger sisters, Alma and Antonia —
were my playmates. The Alvarezes had had
a scruffy-looking dog named Roy and a
parakeet.

On Saturdays, the Alvarez kids were
homeschooled in Hispanic history and
culture by Mrs. Alvarez for two hours before

they were allowed to play. My mother, much to my disappointment, adopted this practice when I was five or six.

The Alvarezes had been the first to welcome my parents, an interracial couple, to the house on Markham Street, bringing over homemade tacos, seasoned beans and rice. A much-appreciated gesture, considering Blacks and Mexicans haven't always been the best of pals.

The Alvarez house was a quiet one; they were generally a fairly quiet family right up to the day they moved to Houston for work. Now, years later, the house, which I revitalized with some of my DPD settlement money, serves as something of a postmenopausal hippie sorority. Its occupants — retirees and longtime friends Carmela Montoya and Sylvia Zychek and their much-younger buddy Lucy Three Rivers, a Native computer whiz from Michigan's Upper Peninsula — each blast their respective preferred music (classic rock, Tejano and polka, EDM and Native flute). They also laugh loud and argue loud. All of which is often fueled by medical marijuana brownies or the occasional box of middling rosé wine.

I imagine the volume emanating from the house is predicated on the fact that Carmela and Sylvia left their good hearing behind a couple decades ago and Lucy is simply making an effort to effectively communicate with her half-deaf, moderately high, generous and loving landlords.

I was unlocking my front door when I heard Lucy's shout from the kitchen next door. "You *never* listen to me! I *told* you this would happen! What the *hell* is the matter with you bitches?"

Against my better judgment, I went over.

"Seriously," I said once Lucy flung open the door, "you guys sure you don't need a couple nice, shiny new bullhorns? 'Cause, I mean, I don't think you're getting maximum screech volume."

"Oh, ha ha," Lucy said sarcastically. "*You* try dealing with these knuckleheads!"

I invited myself in.

Carmela and Sylvia sat next to each other on their cranberry velvet Victorian sofa, their faces twisted in pain. Carmela had her left leg elevated on the ornate coffee table; she was gingerly pressing a freezer-storage bag filled with ice to her knee. Sylvia had a freezer bag full of ice pressed to her left hip.

"Let me guess," I said, looking at the two of them. "Mixed martial arts cage match with a cashier who wouldn't accept your Kohl's Cash?"

Lucy, her arms folded tightly over her

chest, paced back and forth in front of her landladies. "*This* one," she said, thrusting a forefinger at Carmela, "refuses to wear her knee brace. Her expensive, custom-fitted, high-freakin'-tech knee brace!" Lucy turned the forefinger on Sylvia. "And *this* one refuses to get her hip checked out by an actual doctor of medicine instead of some blond-dreadlocked, natural remedy shaman who's been high since the age of five!"

"Don't get old, Mr. Snow," Carmela groaned. "It's no fun."

"Amen, sister," Sylvia said.

The ladies bumped arthritic fists.

"May I see you in the kitchen, Lucy?" I said.

"Oh, what?" Lucy snapped. "Now *you're* gonna give me some big badass adult wisdom?"

"Something like that," I said.

"I'm not done with you boneheads," Lucy said to the old girls on the sofa icing their aching bits and pieces.

In the kitchen, Lucy planted her fists on her narrow hips. "Go ahead, Sherlock. Tell me what a rotten little brat I am for yelling at my elders."

"Actually, I was gonna say the exact opposite," I said, feeling myself smile. "I'm actually kind of proud of you."

"Really?"

"Really," I said. "I mean, yeah, sure, you could bring the volume down a notch, but it shows me you've finally got some personal investment here. You don't get mad like that at people you don't care about."

Lucy leaned against the refrigerator. "The old broads didn't have to take me back in. They been real good to me. Like — like moms doin' whatever work my mom left behind, if that makes any sense."

"Perfect sense," I said.

Lucy had boarded with Carmela and Sylvia a while back. After an especially traumatizing experience at a Detroit River freighter service pier, Lucy had decided to revisit her Upper Peninsula roots. She'd hoped kneeling by her mother's graveside would provide the guidance and wisdom she so desperately needed to know her place in an often confusing world.

Only the quiet, lonely expanse of Upper Peninsula wilderness persisted.

And then there was the question of a certain retired and dogged sheriff's deputy with damaged pride and one testicle who had an outstanding score to settle with her . . .

Carmela and Sylvia had welcomed Lucy back with opened arms.

"The girls just make me so fucking mad sometimes!" After a moment, Lucy gave me a glance and said, "Sorry about the yelling."

"Welcome home, kiddo."

"Oh, don't get all mushy on me, Sherlock," she said, pushing past me. I followed her back into the living room. "You ladies want an outing? I'll *give* you an outing! I'm making doctor's appointments for *both* of you, and there's no way you're wiggling out of 'em. You behave, I'll buy ya lunch. You don't and I'll have you committed to an old folks' home — or worse, have your kids take you in."

"Oh, Jesus Lord, Madre María!" Carmela said.

"What if —" Sylvia began meekly. "What if — the doctor says I need a hip replacement?"

"Then you *get* a freakin' hip replacement!" Lucy said. "They actually make spare parts for humans these days."

"Okay, ladies, I'm heading home," I said. "But for the love of God, the apostles and all the saints — let's put a cap on the shouting for today, okay? Dogs eight blocks away are starting to complain."

Sylvia leaned into Carmela and whispered, "Wha'd he say?"

"Get 'em to an audiologist, too," I said to Lucy.

"No shit, Sherlock," she said. She pushed me toward the door. "Go! You're done here, dude."

56

6

First snow of the season.

A gentle, drifting, Hollywood-set snow. The kind that lovers strolling in the park pause to kiss in, dogs bound and frolic in and kids in puffy snowsuits attempt to catch on the pointed pink tips of their tongues.

Of course, this being Michigan, the first snow is also the psychological harbinger of the frozen apocalypse to come: The wasteland months of isolating grey days with temperatures plummeting to subzero. Mountainous snowdrifts suffocating any and all hope. The creaking, jostling and groaning of sturdy houses against relentless freezing winds that infiltrate the smallest concrete crack, the tiniest fissure in mortise and tenon.

And the heating bills!

Jesus.

I gave brief thought, as most Michiganders do, to moving south. Equatorial south.

Then I remembered: it's either suffer this deep freeze temporarily or relocate to a southern land soon to be made uninhabitable because of the crap humans have vomited into the air and oceans.

I was in my kitchen celebrating my Black heritage by making one of my father's favorite dishes, baked macaroni and cheese with barbequed pulled pork topping (my mother always added chopped jalapeños because, well — Mexican). I was trying not to think about the dying Mr. Ochoa and his perishing business. Shamefully, my thoughts settled mostly on Jackie Ochoa's legs, shapely and California tanned. I hadn't been able to tell if her stoicism during our meeting at Authentico had been the emotional depletion of someone grieving her father's slouched march to death or the impassivity of someone who had long ago left the unloving patriarchy of her family behind.

All I knew was I could still hear the way she'd laughed as a kid. See her dimpled cheeks when she smiled. Feel her secret voltage.

There had been no evidence of any of those at the Authentico meeting. Okay, maybe a bit of her secret voltage, but then that could very well have been just me . . .

I was about to mince four large cloves of garlic — no garlic powder for me; there's a staleness to it I can't get past — when my doorbell rang.

Since thieves, killers and zombies rarely use the doorbell, I answered with relative confidence I wouldn't be mugged, beaten or eaten.

Jackie Ochoa, swaddled in an expensive and so very politically incorrect three-quarter-length mink. "Mind if I come in?" she asked.

"Not at all," I said. "In fact, you might want to get in here fast before one of my neighbors calls PETA."

She laughed and came inside.

Dimpled cheeks . . . secret kilowatt voltage . . .

I was about to offer her a hanger from the front closet, but she'd already tossed her dead animal coat with elegant disregard on the back of my forest-green leather sofa. It slid to the floor, and I, being a good manservant, quickly brushed it off and hung it in the front closet.

"Seems you landed on your feet, August Octavio Snow," she said, running a hand along the length of the sofa while giving my fireplace and collection of books a casual once-over. "Decorated marine. Hero cop. I mean until you *weren't.*" Her eyes rested on my mother's painting of Federico García Lorca. "And now gentleman millionaire and neighborhood hero — depending on who you talk to."

"Who have *you* been talking to, Jackie?"

"Papa," she said, turning to me. "And Danny."

"Hence the divergent views," I said. "Can I get you something? Coffee? Tea? Juice box?"

"I think we're a few years beyond juice boxes." She laughed.

There . . . those dimples . . .

"You strike me as a single malt man," she continued. "Would I be right?"

I pulled two Waterford tumblers from a kitchen cabinet and poured us each a bit of Royal Lochnagar. Before I could hand Jackie her glass, she stood on tiptoe and kissed me. It was everything thirteen-year-old me had dreamed it would be. Of course these days I suspected ulterior motives and dark intentions from most people. A hangover from having been in Afghanistan, aka "the sand."

"I face that temptation every day in the bathroom mirror," I said, finally handing her the tumbler of whisky. "But what was that for?"

60

"Curiosity."

"And has your curiosity been satisfied?"

"It may take a lot more than that to satisfy my curiosity." She took a seat on my sofa. "Just like a man! A giant, stupid TV over a fireplace."

"*Both* with a remote," I said, sitting down next to her. Showing off, I grabbed the fireplace remote and turned it on. Frankly, I was taken by how relaxing and mesmerizing it was to stare at the glowing logs and feel their warmth. Not to mention how romantic it felt in the company of a beautiful woman. I was beginning to understand my mother, swaddled in a wool throw, staring at the flames with my father's arm around her. I'd have to remember this when Tatina was in town. "So, what brings you around, Jackie?"

"You've done wonders with the neighborhood, Octavio," she said. "Papa told me you've been renovating Markham Street house by house, but I never expected this. It's beautiful! I was tempted to knock on the door of my old house, but, well, that would just be weird, right?"

"Not really," I said. "One of the guys who works with me, Jimmy Radmon, lives in your old family house. Good guy. Talented. I'm sure he would have been glad to give you a tour, but he's in Windsor right now."

"God," she said, "why didn't we ever hook up?"

"Frankly, I didn't think you even considered me a contender," I said, a bit flustered. "Plus, Danny Romero was always running pass interference."

"Danny meant well. At least, he used to."

"The guy's one turd shy of being a flushable load, Jackie."

"He's mostly served my father well," she said, minus any conviction. She took a sip of her whisky and seemed to admire its color.

" 'Mostly?' "

"That's what brings me here, Octavio," Jackie said. "I'm not so sure we — my father and I — can trust Danny to handle things quite the way they should be handled. He's a good lawyer —"

"Jury's still out on that one," I said.

"— but I know more about the business world than Danny ever will." She issued a theatrical sigh, then took a sip of her scotch. "But no matter what I do, my business experience, acumen and success mean considerably less than my goddamn ability to procreate and make enchiladas. Our culture —"

"Keeps pretty little Mexican girls with

mostly Spanish blood from mixing with 'mayates'?"

Her eyes locked onto mine for a second or two before she said, "I know better now, August."

"What do you want from me, Jackie?"

"I'd like for you to watch Danny," she said. "Need you to, really. I think he's desperate enough to — I'm afraid he'll — do something — that won't be advantageous for my father."

"Or you?"

"I'll be burying my father soon enough, August," she said. "I just want this ugly business settled so I can get back to my life somewhere that isn't a goddamn frozen wasteland three-quarters of the year." The knife's edge glint in her eyes softened for a moment. Then she leaned into me. Kissed me again. Longer. Deeper.

I let her.

This time I felt a different electrical impulse shiver through me. The kind that tells you to move fast when a shadow not your own twitches in the dark.

I pulled out of the kiss and said, "I'll think about watching Danny for your dad. And you. But a good kiss isn't a signed contract, Jackie."

"Only 'good'?" she said. "I must be losing

63

my touch."

"Somehow, I doubt that."

She downed the rest of her drink, then stood and donned her fur coat. "I'm staying at the Westin Book Cadillac Detroit," she said. "Just in case you'd like to discuss anything else at length, August."

"Good to see you, Jackie," I said, opening the door for her. "Don't be a stranger."

Then she was gone.

"It's not nice to spy on your neighbors, Lucy," I said. She was covered head to toe in snow from the pile she'd jumped into to avoid detection.

"Yeah, well, it's not nice to cheat on your girlfriend either! I don't care how far away she lives!" Lucy said, shaking and stomping the snow off in my small foyer.

"These are hardwood floors, Lucy!" I kicked as much of the snow back outside as I could. "Come on!"

"You were kissing that chick!"

"She was kissing me."

"I fail to see the distinction." Lucy folded her arms across her chest as she made her way to my kitchen. "Was your tongue in her mouth?"

"Listen." I drew in a slow, calming breath. "I'm not going to debate with you. Before you ducked behind a snowbank, what did you want?"

"The name of your lawyer," Lucy said. She was checking out my fridge. The mac and cheese with pulled barbeque pork didn't interest her. The leftover paella did. "The girls want to revise their wills or some creepy shit."

"Tell you what," I said. "I'll give you the name of my lawyer if you do something for me."

"Oh, yeah?" Lucy said, spooning the cold paella into her mouth. "And what would that be, Mr. Gigolo Snow?"

I handed her an American Express charge card.

The name on the card was Jacqueline E. Ochoa.

7

City Councilwoman Nadine Rosado, District Six, southwest Detroit/Mexicantown representative, had been lobbying the city for a DPD substation anywhere along the Vernor Highway business corridor. Nothing that left a policía Estatal jackboot footprint, since a great number of her constituents were personally familiar with what pathetically passed for law enforcement in Mexico, Nicaragua and Colombia. What she wanted was more like a twenty-four-hour rotation of four to six cops (at least one Spanish speaking) and the commitment of one patrol car. Flowers in the lobby, suckers for the kids and maybe a bright sign in the window that read, AQUÍ PARA AYUDAR, TODOS LOS DÍAS! (Here to help, every day!) She'd even secured a small, empty storefront that the owner would gladly lease to the city for five years at half of its fair market lease value.

The chief of police was on board.

The police commissioner loved the idea.

City Council President Lincoln Quinn had one very public and one very private problem with the proposal: Publicly, he was bombastically vocal about the costs of establishing and maintaining such a substation. He argued that if there were going to be more neighborhood DPD substations, a nonpartisan study should be commissioned to establish which Detroit neighborhoods most needed them (in ranking order by number of residents, per-capita crime stats and types of crime).

Privately, Quinn knew Mexicantown was where I lived.

Several years earlier, he had argued vehemently against my $12 million wrongful dismissal award. When the TV news lights were shining and the newspaper ink flowed like the Detroit River he had spared no amount of vitriol in denouncing me as a "parasite," a "moneygrubbing media whore" and an "enemy of the poorest amongst us."

My attorney, David G. Baker, had urged me to sue Quinn for defamation.

"Somebody needs to shove a used jockstrap down that asshole's throat," G had said.

Exhausted from my lawsuit and trial, the

immeasurable harm it had caused my already dying mother and the 24-7 media circus surrounding it all, I'd urged G to drop the whole thing so I could just get on with using the money to slowly kill myself via cirrhosis of the liver in a world tour of high-class boozeries and deeply funky foreign dives.

Now, while the corroded gears of the city government continued to grind in a pitiable effort to move Detroit forward, Tomás and I devised our own "neighborhood watch" plan for both Clark Park and Authentico Foods: For the next two weeks, we would surveil both locations, three hours during the day, two or three hours at night. If we were lucky, maybe one of us would spot any wannabe drug kingpins or the illusive Mr. Sloane, which would offer Tomás and me the opportunity to lean on either. If nothing popped up in two weeks, we would sum everything up as either a hiccup or someone somewhere (Duke Ducane?) having gotten the message that we weren't fucking around.

Not much of a plan but more than what had been on the table.

Tomás was still pissed that I'd taken the word of an old gangster like Ducane over his rather sizable reservations, but he begrudgingly agreed to my two-week surveillance plan.

"You do, of course, know you're dumb as shit," he said as we drank beer at my kitchen island.

"Yeah." I took a slug of my Negra Modelo. "I know."

Neither of us thought our neighborhood-watch self-assignment merited a trip to Tomás's gun locker. My Glock and his S&W 610 revolver would be enough to scatter any rats or roaches we might encounter.

I'd been on a number of stakeouts during my career as a Detroit cop, and I'll say this much: for all the wacky bullshit Hollywood tries to sell you when it comes to cop movies and TV shows (Black-white buddy cop comedies, cowboy-cop-in-the-big-city stories, precinct musicals, vampire detectives, etc.), there's one thing they do manage to get right — stakeouts are the closest thing to actually, truly being bored to death.

A cold November week had passed with me huddled inside my Oldsmobile 442 and Tomás hunched over a thermos of hot coffee in his classic Ford F-150. Elena — not a fan of our late-night/early-morning surveillance scheme — usually packed Tomás an enviable cooler assortment of sandwiches; soft-shell chorizo, beef and fish tacos; tortilla chips; and hot green salsa, all of which she commanded him to share with me.

Which he didn't.

At least, that is, until the end of the first boring week of surveilling, when he drove past my tree-shrouded spot on Clark Avenue near Porter. He slowed down enough to toss two lovingly wrapped fried-egg-and-bologna-on-toasted-challah sandwiches out of his passenger side window and onto the hood of my car before driving off to a parking space near Authentico Foods.

I called him around midnight. "Thanks for the sandwiches."

"Don't think I ain't still mad at you for taking Ducane's word over mine, tu pequeña mierda," Tomás said.

"You don't get over things easily, do you?" I said.

He disconnected.

For the next thirty minutes, the only activity I observed was a young couple steaming up the windows and testing the shocks of a rusted blue Chevy Impala. Tatina and I had done the car thing once in the middle of a Norwegian winter just outside St. Hanshaugen Park. She has a MINI Cooper. I got a two-day charley horse, and my back was out for a week. Still, I think I performed admirably.

I was about to call it a night when a DPD patrol car, lights flashing, raced west the I-96 on Vernor Highway.

Then another whipped past.

My stomach muscles clenched, and a chill shot through me.

I followed.

Both patrol cars were stopped at angles on Vernor in front of Authentico Foods.

I got out of my car just in time to see one of the blues kneeling by the prone body of a man.

Tomás.

"This is eight delta eight! Officer Hennesey!" the cop shouted into his shoulder walkie. He cradled Tomás's head. "I need an ambulance at — Jesus! Where the fuck is this?"

"Eight seven nine one five West Vernor Highway!" his partner shouted.

I took a knee by Tomás.

He'd been shot twice, an ugly wound in the shoulder, the other in his side near his hip. His blood steamed as it pooled on the cold concrete sidewalk.

The back of his head was bloody.

"One white male —"

"He's Mexican-American," I said absently.

"Who the hell are you?" the cop cradling Tomás's head shouted at me.

71

"I'm his friend, goddammit!"

"You do this?"

"No."

Tomás's breathing was shallow.

"Sir," the cop's partner said, his hand resting on the grip of his holstered weapon, "I need you to back off —"

"He's my godfather!"

"I'm not asking."

An eternally long four minutes: I thought about losing my parents. Losing friends in Afghanistan. The possibility of losing my godfather on what was nothing more than a fool's errand. The recoil of every gun and every bullet I'd ever sent, every bomb's shock wave that had rippled through my body, every drop of blood seeping into sand. I thought about Elena and the fallacy of a widow's forgiveness. All as I watched Tomás lying on a cold street, dying.

After four minutes another patrol car and an emergency medical transport came to a stop in front of Authentico Foods. I crowded the EMTs as they belted Tomás to the gurney and loaded him into the ambulance.

"How's he doing?" I asked.

"No fucking clue," an EMT said as she strapped an oxygen mask over Tomás's nose and mouth. "If I had to guess, not very good. Who the hell are you?"

"His — friend."

"Looks like maybe you should take better care of your friends," she said, closing the doors of the ambulance. Lights flashing, siren blaring, the emergency medical transport sped off, my friend — my godfather — inside.

"We're gonna need a crime scene tech," someone behind me said. "We got a stiff upstairs."

8

He was in emergency surgery at Henry Ford Hospital for an hour, which was how long it took to dig the bullets out of his shoulder and his hip, the one in the latter lodged dangerously close to his liver.

The doctors would have tried to do more in surgery, but Tomás had taken blunt force to the back of his head, and there was swelling of his brain. Once his bullet wounds were addressed, they put Tomás in a medically induced coma in the hope that the swelling would abate. The human body is, for the most part, an amazingly resilient machine.

The human brain? Not so much.

In his hospital room, Tomás — unconscious, breathing through a tube and connected to all manner of beeping, dripping and eerily glowing machines — was handcuffed to the side rails of his bed. A DPD patrol blue stood dispassionately at the door.

"This is bullshit," I told Detective Captain Leo Cowling. We were standing near a nurses' station.

"What's bullshit?" Cowling calmly blew steam from his cup of vending machine coffee. "That I had to leave a hot piston pumping to come down here and talk to yo high-yellow ass? Is that what you mean by 'bullshit'?" He was wearing a tan car coat over a black cable-knit turtleneck sweater, expensive jeans with creases that could carve beef and black Reebok trainers. The only thing he was wearing that didn't look quite right was a gold detective's shield on his belt.

"They checked his gun at the scene —"

"*And* yours."

"Neither one was fired," I said.

"So, you think old man Ochoa shot your running buddy before he turned the gun on himself?" Cowling said calmly. "What are the chances of that?"

"You've got a gold shield," I said, irritated with Cowling's smug attitude. "Figure it out, goddammit."

"Oh, you can bet your ass I am *well* motivated to find out what's going on," Cowling said, "since you and the Cisco Kid were strapped where the dead man's business was broken into."

Unnerved and exhausted, I heard myself say, "He — Tomás — he's my godfather."

"I got me an uncle," Cowling said, leaning against a wall and contemplating the steam rising from his cup of coffee. "Uncle Theo. Little spit of a niggah. Can't be no more than five-six, five-seven. Funniest man you'd ever wanna meet. Have you fall out laughing in five seconds flat. Everybody in the family loves Uncle Theo. Bad thing is you never get a trigger warning with that crazy mothafucka. Spent eight months in Fulton County Jail in Atlanta on account he beat the living shit out of his runnin' buddy, Tooty Howard, 'cause Tooty hadn't paid him back the five bucks he lent him six months prior. See what I'm sayin'?"

"Yeah," I said. "Yeah, I think I do. You're saying you're a useless loaf of dog shit with a badge pinned to it."

I started back to Tomás's room.

As I approached, Elena emerged looking pale, haggard and confused. She was accompanied by Tomás's surgeon, a stocky Indian-American man with an Albert Einstein shock of salt-and-pepper hair.

"We'll know more in the next sixteen to twenty-four hours, Mrs. Gutierrez," Dr. Jack

76

Gupta said. "Just trust he'll get the best care possible in the meantime. And I so deeply apologize for the handcuffs" — he shot the DPD cop at the door a nasty look — "which are *totally unnecessary* given his current status." Elena just stared vacantly at the doctor, nodding as he spoke. "You should try to get some rest, all right?" He took both of her hands in his. "Please. Do get some rest."

As Gupta attempted to walk past me, I caught his arm. "Is he going to be okay?"

"Are you police or a relative?"

"I — He's my godfather."

He nodded toward Elena. "Then you'll have to ask the lady, who is, I assume, your godmother. Confidentially, he's critical. If I don't see a considerable reduction in the swelling of his brain in sixteen hours, he risks permanent brain damage — or worse."

" 'Worse' meaning —"

"Yes," he said, acknowledging the unspoken word. "That's generally what 'worse' means in any hospital, sir."

He continued on to the nurses' station, where I heard him give Cowling a blistering earful about the handcuffs on his comatose patient.

"I am —" I began. "Jesus, Elena, I am so —"

Elena looked up at me with wet, swollen red eyes.

"Always with you two," she said. "Playing cowboys."

Then she slapped me.

Twice.

And walked away.

"Popular as ever," Cowling said with a self-satisfied grin as he passed me.

I considered grabbing Cowling's service Glock out of his hip holster and pistol-whipping him half to death with it. Unfortunately, we were in one of America's premier hospitals, and they probably would have had him up and kicking his heels in no time.

Some people just deserve to suffer.

I decided to go home, soak my liver in tequila and plan my escape from everyone, including myself. Maybe find a place in the world where names didn't matter, the rubble of my history meant nothing and the night could swallow me whole.

On my way out of Henry Ford Hospital, I saw Jackie Ochoa and the Ochoa family pet/lawyer, Danny Romero. Danny was gently holding Jackie by an elbow, just in case she should become overwhelmed by the vapors of grief and require a strong man to lean her pliant body against.

"I'm sorry about your dad," I said to Jackie. "He was a good man."

"Tonight, tomorrow, a month from now — what's the difference?" Jackie said with dry-eyed indifference. "He's gone and as such so is the business."

"You don't sound too broken up about either," I said.

"People process grief differently, Snow," Danny said. "Why don't you just —"

"Do I — *did* I love my father?" Jackie interrupted. "Of course. Did he love me? Probably, in his way. Did I deserve more — *much* more — from him? You'd better fucking believe it." She took a breath. "I'm selling the business, August. It's mine now and I'm selling it. I don't need you as a partner anymore. Sloane's made a very generous offer on behalf of Vic Bronson. All cash. Then I'm gone. Back to California, where my power and presence are my own."

"Something's not right with this Sloane guy, Jackie," I said. "You should —"

"She should what, Snow?" Danny said. He took a daring step into me. A jock twenty years past his prime, a bully without a good right hook, a rib cage begging to be broken. "Wait around and twiddle her thumbs because you've got a washed-up cop's dollar-store hunch? God! You are so full of yourself! Maybe you've got a lot of money, but you're still a classless hood rat, mayate piece of shit."

I looked past Danny to Jackie and, holding my thumb and pinky finger to my ear like a phone, said, "Give me a call when you're ready for a lawyer who doesn't smell like Cheetos and cheap beer."

"Fuck you, Snow," Danny said, backing off. "Let's go, Jackie."

Danny ushered Jackie away.

"I hope you know Tomás had nothing to do with your father's death, Jackie," I called to their backs.

Jackie turned to me.

Smiled.

9

A good drunk is like a bad vacation — you may have gotten away for a while, but in the end, it was expensive and not nearly as enjoyable as you'd hoped it would be.

I was halfway through a fifth of Cava de Oro Extra Añejo tequila that I'd purchased as a birthday gift for Tomás. The tequila's refined and complex notes of cinnamon, vanilla, caramel and nutmeg, with a finish of toast and maple syrup, were lost on me by about an hour into it. I did, however, have a very keen interest in its muscle- and mind-numbing 40 percent alcohol-by-volume content.

Nearing Earth's atmosphere-escape velocity, I decide to drunk-dial longtime family friend and probably the world's oldest living Franciscan priest, Father Grabowski. He had taken a week off from his duties at St. Aloysius Church on Washington Boulevard downtown to attend some sort of a

Catholic convention in — of all places — Las Vegas.

"How much have you had?" the old priest said with a sigh. In the background I could hear whooping, hollering, clanging bells and electronically synthesized chimes.

"Well, that doesn't sound at all like Vatican City," I said.

"How much?" he repeated.

"More than you could handle, old man."

"Kabul again? That little boy?"

"No," I said. "But thanks for bringing that one up."

My phone became my confessional: I somehow managed to ramble, stammer and burp through what my recent nightmare days had been like. My complicity in Tomás's life-threatening injuries. The loss and harm I had visited upon the dearest of family and the closest of friends.

While I slurred my way to the edge of incoherence, someone in the background on Father Grabowski's end yelled, "Fuckin' A! Now that's what I'm talkin' about!"

I assumed whoever had yelled this was white since I have never in my adolescent or adult life heard any Black or Hispanic of any age say, "Fuckin' A!"

"Ya know, Father," I said, "God can be a real nasty fucker sometimes."

Father Grabowski sighed again. "Getting mad at God for the hell men put each other through is like pissing at the moon: the only thing that's gonna get wet is your shoes." Then he said, "Put the bottle down, August."

"Right." I tossed another tequila shot down my gullet. "Done."

"I know you're probably too wasted to understand this," he said patiently, "but the love of God is all about how we lose and how we take the loss. Not about pursuing and celebrating the win. I mean, come on — who needs mercy, guidance or grace when you're shooting sevens and the house is paying four to one? The word 'mercy' — from the Medieval Latin *merced,* or 'price paid' — only applies to our darkest days, the days we're suffocating inside our loneliness. When we're hurt, hated and hunted. Those are the times when we most need to risk our hearts on what we know is right, full well knowing the track is muddy and the footing unsure. Those are the times we most require God's mercy. The times we should expect — demand! — God's grace."

Even in my tequila stupor, Father Grabowski had thrown me a lifeline. A lifeline that may have fallen a bit short of my drunken reach . . .

"You still there?" Father Grabowski said.

"Isn't having a Catholic convention in Vegas a little like preaching abstinence in a brothel?"

"Makes me regret not converting and going to rabbinical school," he grumbled. "I'll tell ya, August; priests should be allowed to marry, including same-sex! *And* we should have mandatory six-month psych evals! I feel like I'm walking through a goddamn Hieronymus Bosch painting!"

I laughed.

Then I tossed a third of my earlier lunch up on the area rug in front of my fireplace.

"Go to bed, son," Father Grabowski said. "I'll keep Tomás and Elena in my prayers. You know, I still believe you to be one of God's most gifted earthbound angels."

"Or one of the devil's own," I said.

"You'll find peace in bearing this burden, August," the old man said. "You always have."

"Yeah, sure," I said. "A Carthaginian peace, padre."

The next day, after waking up slumped over at my kitchen island in front of my open laptop with Thor's hammer sparking on the anvil of my head, I decided to make the Herculean effort to rejoin the better angels of the human race.

84

Never once in my time as a marine sniper or my time as a Detroit cop did I ever evade the detailed, always-painful situation reports on how an enemy combatant or a comrade in arms was injured or died. For better or worse, I felt that if an accurate death or injury record was dependent on my word, then my word should be as complete and truthful as humanly possible, even if the truth cost me a hash mark or the loss of a friend or job.

Maybe the Michelangelo-fresco-style image of my soul standing before the interstellar judgment of God had been drilled into me a little more deeply than necessary by my devout Catholic mother. (My agnostic father, meanwhile, had thought acknowledging and embracing thorny or bloody truths was a necessary obligation of living an "honorable man's life.")

Tomás lying in a hospital bed because of my half-assed surveillance plan was somehow different. Weightier and more grueling. A hard-edged, indisputable guilt that, if looked at directly, threatened to turn me into a pillar of salt.

It was an altogether too-intimate shame coursing through my veins and reaching into the marrow of my being. I had failed a loved one, perhaps fatally.

Sackcloth, ash and flagellation were not enough to vanquish such shame.

It was for this reason I had not made an effort to talk to Elena about why Tomás was now weightlessly languishing somewhere between the earth and all the rest.

While I had indulged my guilt with drink, Elena had spent the last day at his bedside, praying the rosary, updating him on neighbors, reading articles from the local Spanish-language newspaper and sleeping curled up in a bedside chair. The nursing staff had given up on trying to persuade her to leave after visiting hours, choosing rather to make her as comfortable as possible with a blanket, a pillow and, when needed, fresh coffee and cookies from the nurses' station.

Dr. Gupta had admonished her to go home, or at least to her daughter's house in Ferndale, to get a full night's rest. He had assured her the swelling of Tomás's brain had gone down and all indications pointed to normal functioning. News that he had mistakenly hoped would alleviate at least some of her worries.

In my cowardice, I could not bring myself to face Elena. I slunk past her in the Henry Ford Hospital lobby, where she was waiting for her daughter to drive her home after the evening's visit. I sat next to the machine keeping track of Tomás's heartbeat and blood oxygen and read him a poem by Antonio Machado.

As I was finishing the poem, Tomás's daughter, Manolita, called me. She had just dropped her mother home.

"You know she's angry with you," Lita said. "Jesus, God in heaven — *I'm* mad at you! But — in my heart, Octavio, I know none of this is your fault. It's just the way you two idiots are made up."

"Thanks for those kind words."

"No, I mean it," she said. "You and Papa are just a couple of stupid little boys who never stopped wanting to be gauchos. Riding dusty trails in your floppy cowboy hats and leather chaps, dispensing open-range justice that no tin star could. And to be honest, I've always kinda admired that — that spirit — in Papa. *And* you. Listen. Momma's madder at herself than you, Octavio. She's mad at herself for decades of having bought into the myth of you and Papa's invincible machismo. It's why we love you. And why we fear for you." In the background, I heard Tomás's granddaughter, June, ask if momma was talking to abuelo. "You wanna make things right, Octavio?" Lita said.

"Yeah," I heard myself say quietly. "More

than anything."

"Then get off your ass and make things right."

She disconnected.

After a moment, I stood, squeezed Tomás's hand and whispered, "No te mueras, hijo de puta. Te amo y te necesito."

Then I left.

I have a hunch my real estate agent, Miss Jesse Yolanda James, is on her fourteenth or fifteenth reincarnation as a Nubian oracle high priestess whose fingertips are without prints and glowing with generations of hoodoo. Her skin is as dark and smooth as obsidian glass, her cheekbones high and angular, and her eyes shaped like large almonds. The fact that she's still tall and straight-backed at nearly ninety years old further fuels my supernatural speculation, as does how swell she looks in a flowing gold, orange and rust-colored silk caftan.

Truth of the matter is, she's nobody's "magical Negro." She's just another example of the mental and spiritual acuity, tenacity, fearlessness and fathomless hope it takes Black folk to live a long life in a country that, in every vein of its deformed body, prefers we die with their knee on our neck.

"Tell me why I knew you was soon to be

here, son?" she said at the ornate oak-and-brass door of her Indian Village home. I very much doubt she knew I was coming to see her. But it's just good manners not to question an elder's self-woven mythology. With her hair up in a complicated purple silk wrap, she looked like a million World War II savings bonds. "Come on in. Let me put the kettle on."

It was always a pleasure to visit Miss Jesse in her home, where grandeur and intimacy waltzed in a design by legendary architect Louis Kamper. She fixed herbal tea, preferring to carry the large silver service herself to a drawing room where the light of a warm fire gave the fireplace's silver-blue and seafoam-green Pewabic Pottery tiles an otherworldly shimmer. Perhaps that was the portal from which she emerged every day. The room's tall leaded glass windows gave the ebbing and flowing winter landscape outside a Currier & Ives coziness instead of showing it for the ravenous frigid beast it truly was.

We sat in floral Jacquard-upholstered wingback chairs facing the fireplace, the tea service between us, listening to a recording of Detroit's own Xiao Dong Wei's ethereal erhu music. While she poured, I took in her numerous pieces of art: montages by Carole

Morisseau and Carol Morris; paintings by Madge Scott, Peter Williams, Paulette Gassman, Bowen Kline, Tylonn Sawyer and Gail Borowski; found-art creations by Nancy Rodwan; and photography by Rachel Timlin and Lesa Ferencz.

While Miss Jesse may have possessed some extraordinary pieces of art, only one commanded my full attention: a portrait of Miss Jesse done forty years earlier by my mother. Miss Jesse sold my parents our Mexicantown family home at a time when no other real estate agent in Detroit would touch a brown or Black neighborhood.

"That was when I looked a whole lot different, young Snow," Miss Jesse said, handing me a cup and saucer. "She was a beautiful lady, your mother."

"That she was," I said. I took a sip of tea: some sort of lavender-mint concoction with a touch of ginger. Not bad.

"Sorry to hear about Tomás," she said.

"You heard?"

"Baby boy, ain't much I don't hear," she said. "Been steppin' and stompin' these parts since before they paved over Black Bottom." She narrowed her eyes at me. "Here's what's syncopating, vibrating and oscillating in the air these days in your neck of the woods: Some third-party deep pockets mystery man named Sloane wants to buy up some *almost*-freed-up real estate in Mexicantown. All cash. Word is he's using Vic Bronson as a cutout. But since when do some billionaire real estate mogul need a one-man front on the down low? And what does an all-cash transaction say to you, young Snow?"

"Dirty money looking for a wash and wear."

"But let's suppose that money's *already* been laundered two, three times. Let's say that money's as clean as a wealthy white baby's fresh cotton nappy? *Then* what?"

"Dirty hands holding a stack of clean bills."

"And what them hands want to latch on to?"

I thought for a moment. "A way to churn money through a property investment. Real estate used as clean gears in a dirty machine."

"You *half*way there, son."

"Halfway?" I said. "You mean I'm not as smart as I think I am?"

"Hardly anybody is, boy." Miss Jesse smiled at me, perhaps the same way she had smiled at King Menes of the first Egyptian dynasty. She took a sip of tea, long, elegant pinky-finger out. "Rumor has it the Purple

Gang owned themselves a thirty-acre ceme-
tery just outside of Lansing, ninety miles
northwest of where you sittin'. Paid some
toothless, one-mule cracka whiskey and
cash to groom the grounds, wash the bird
shit off the headstones. You think the Purple
Gang owned that graveyard and paid a
drunk, dirt-farmin' peck-a-wood in order to
make a dollar? Or maybe they knew — just
knew! — the last place on God's green earth
the po-lice would look for a body was in the
one place that had a whole mess of 'em?"

Staring into the fire, I slowly turned her
words over in my mind.

"Of course, you know you're freaking me
out, right?" I said to Miss Jesse.

"Oh, son, I don't mean to." She laughed.
"Give it another twenty years. Hardly
anything will freak you out. You'll have seen
nearly all the really weird shit twice, three
times by then. *Especially* the electoral damn
college."

10

I wasn't quite sure if it was the beginning of evening or if the sun had just given up after a valiant midafternoon fight to break through Michigan's undulating grey blanket of snow clouds. Whatever time it was when I left the warmth of Miss Jesse's Indian Village home, the remains of the day were cold, damp and monochromatic.

After a brief stop at Schmear's Deli for coffee, half of a turkey Reuben sandwich and light conversation with owner Ben Breitler, I pointed the Olds 442 in the direction of home and gingerly accelerated that way. (A big-block, 350-horsepower engine powering rear-wheel drive isn't exactly ideal for Michigan winter driving.)

Parked in front of Carmela and Sylvia's house was a two-year-old white Chevy Tahoe with a temporary plate. The only reasons I took note of it were the bumper sticker that read, I WAS HERE BEFORE YOU,

WAABISHKIIWED! and the bejeweled dream catcher that was hung over the rearview mirror.

After parking the 442 in my shed, I went over to Carmela and Sylvia's to stick my nose into the business of whose SUV was parked out front.

Sylvia answered the door wearing a pair of those disposable rectangular sunglasses optometrists give patients who've had their eyes dilated. She pointed a rigid forefinger at me, and in her version of an Austrian accent, she said, "I'll be *bach*!"

Then she laughed and invited me in.

"So, what's up, Sylvia?" I said.

"Oh, we've just had the most *wonderful* day, Mr. Snow! After we picked up Carmela's new hearing aids, we got our eyes checked! And I'm getting a new hip!"

"You're excited about that?"

"Oh my goodness yes," Sylvia said, gesturing for me to join her on their sofa. I demurred. "I was, of course, apprehensive at first, but Lucy convinced me a brand-new titanium hip would make me unstoppable. Like a cyborg!"

"Like the Terminator."

"Yes! Exactly!" she said. "Now, you know how much we love Jimmy. It was great when he lived with us. But I have to say — we

94

absolutely *love* Lucy! She doesn't pull punches, but she takes wonderful care of us. Like — you know — *family.*" Then, without my having to ask, Sylvia said, "Did you see the car out front?"

"Yes, ma'am," I said.

"We got that for Lucy!" Sylvia clapped and bounced in her seat like a six-year-old girl seeing her candle-lit birthday cake for the first time. "My son-in-law manages a Chevy dealership, so we got it dirt cheap. He had his mechanics go over it three times, stem to stern."

"I didn't think she had a driver's license," I said.

"Yes, she does," Sylvia said. "Well, honestly — no, she doesn't. I mean, she has three, but you know — they're fake. But the car's in my name, and once she does have her license — her *real* one — it's hers!"

"Where are they?" I said. "Carmela and Lucy?"

"Oh, they're at *your* house," Sylvia said. She took my left hand in both of hers and squeezed. "We know you've been having a bit of a time lately, what with your godfather in the hospital and everything. So, we got you some sweets from Sister Pie and some good beer bread from Avalon Bakery. And Lucy made her delicious chili!"

95

Once again, I would have to talk to Jimmy about improving the door-lock security of my house. Maybe electrostatically triggered C-4 plastic explosive charges in the keyholes.

I gave Sylvia a hug, thanked her for her concern, then I left.

When I entered my house, Lucy was descending the staircase from the second floor. For a moment she looked at me like a deer caught in an eighteen-wheeler's headlights. Then she said, "When ya gotta go, ya gotta go."

"You know there's the downstairs bathroom," I said.

"Yeah, but I *hate* the wallpaper in there," she said. "It's like a psycho-crazy-drugged-out-hippie coloring book. Besides, who does wallpaper anymore?"

In all honesty, she was right. The wallpaper in the cramped downstairs bathroom was one of the few things I hadn't changed. My mom had thought it was festive. My father had (confidentially) thought it was obnoxious and dizzying. I never much minded it, primarily because I never saw it; I usually hit that bathroom first when I got home from school and always spent my time on the can eyeballs deep in the latest primary-color Spider-Man, Batman or Thor comic book.

Carmela was seated on my forest-green leather sofa; she had just stuffed a greeting card into a large blue envelope.

"I wanted to finish this so it would be a surprise," Carmela said, looking up at me. "But, well, arthritis being what it is. Here!"

She handed me the envelope, and I opened it. On the front of the card was a photo of three kittens hanging by their front claws from a tree limb. Inside, the card read: "Good friends always hang in there with you!" It was signed — "With Love!" — by Sylvia, Carmela and Lucy.

There was also a five-dollar Subway sandwich gift card.

"We love you, Mr. Snow," Carmela said. "Don't we, Lucy?"

"He's awright, I guess."

"And we want you to know," Carmela continued, "anytime you need a friend or help with something — *anything*! — you can call on us. Even when *Jeopardy*! is on!"

I was genuinely moved even if I, by implication, took a back seat to *Jeopardy*!

I gave Carmela a kiss on her cheek.

We talked for a moment about her new hearing aids, and how Lucy had marshaled them from one appointment to the next with nary a cuss word, and Lucy's new SUV, which Carmela said came with a special "double-premium" three-year parts and power train warranty plus free transmission fluid and oil changes courtesy of Sylvia's son-in-law.

Then Carmela left.

It was nearly time for *Jeopardy!*

"You know you need a Michigan driver's license," I said to Lucy, grabbing a flavored seltzer from my fridge. "A *real* one."

"Hey," she said defiantly, "if five-oh checks any of the ones I've got against their rickety old NDR or NMVTIS databases, they'll see a model citizen who goes to bed praising Jesus for her virginity and wakes up singing 'The Star-Spangled Banner.' "

"You need a *real* one," I said sternly.

"Whatever."

Having been the recipient of approximately eight hundred million of Lucy's "whatevers," I interpreted her inflection on this particular one as a decisive win for me.

She wanted to talk about Tomás.

I didn't.

"That bottle of Tylenol PM you've got on your bathroom vanity? And the empty bottle in the trash?" she said. "Does that help you sleep?"

"You shouldn't snoop, Lucy."

98

"Yeah, well, just so you know, Sherlock, Tylenol is a liver killer. You need to watch it with that stuff."

"Thanks for the advice."

"You want me to smudge your house?" she said. "I know how to smudge. I mean *really* smudge. Not the colonizer's tie-dyed-flower-child way. The *real* way. The *Native* way. I got some sage sticks and —"

"That's all right, Lucy," I said, not quite trusting Lucy to light a botanical fire in my house. "Save the smudging for another time."

Someone awkwardly, loudly clambered onto my front porch. Instantly, my right hand settled on the handle of my Glock, secured by my belt in the small of my back. Military muscle memory. An ex-cop's fight-or-flight instincts.

A fist banging on my door.

"Stay there," I said to Lucy, pointing to the space between my kitchen island and stove.

I brought out my Glock and concealed it by my right thigh before I swung the door open.

A thick pink and purple knit mitten slapped me.

"*No*body breaks up with me via Skype!

*No*body!”
Tatina.

11

I stood in the doorway slack-jawed for a moment as Tatina — wearing a silver bubble coat, pink and purple knit scarf, black tights and snow-encrusted black knee-high boots — pushed past me, dragging her overstuffed wheeled luggage.

I gathered enough of my senses to close the door behind her and say, "You might want to go home now, Lucy."

"And miss *this*?" she said. "No way!"

"Who are *you*?" Tatina said, pointing an accusatory mitten at Lucy. "Who is *she*?"

"I'm Lucy. Lucy Three Rivers." Lucy offered her hand. "Maybe the big dude's mentioned me?"

"Oh, my God, *yes*!" Tatina instantly switched from angry, jilted girlfriend to BFF. The women embraced, with Tatina giving the two-cheek continental kiss.

"Holy shit!" Lucy said. "You're *beautiful*! I mean, it's like you're photoshopped or something — only in *real freakin' life!*"

"So are you! Oh, my God, I *love* your hair!" Tatina said, laughing. "August is always going on about how smart you are, what a good person you are, and how you keep him honest. 'That's one smart kid,' he always says."

"Seriously?" Lucy said, cutting me a look.

"Don't let it go to your head, kid," I said.

"And you *broke up* with her?" Lucy said to me. "By *Skype*? Are you *nuts*?"

"Lucy —"

"He was drunk," Tatina said with theatrical disgust. "Talking about how I deserved better than him and how everybody he gets close to gets hurt."

"Well, statistically," Lucy said, "there's, like, a five point three percent likelihood of that actually happening, yeah."

I was starting to feel a schoolboy's sense of shame and embarrassment flush my cheeks.

"Oh, rubbish!" Tatina said. "And *then* I ask him what's going on, and he says it's best I don't know. Like I'm a child! *Then* he has the grotesque audacity to burp and hang up!"

"You *burped* at her?" Lucy said trying not to laugh. "Jesus, Sherlock!"

"Lucy, I swear to God —"

"Well," Lucy said, "looks like from the old clock on the wall I should be getting home." Then in a mock aside to Tatina, she said, "Cut him a little slack, okay? Been kinda rough for the big guy lately." Passing by me on the way to the door, Lucy whispered, "Oh, you are in such deep doo-doo, bro."

Tatina and I stood facing each other for what felt like a long, awkward time.

Not knowing exactly what excuse I could pull out of my ass, I said, "Listen —"

"Before you go any further," she said sternly, "I just need you to know my original flight was canceled. The next best flight I could get was from Oslo to Berlin, Berlin to Boston, Boston to New York, *then* here. I've been in a very bad mood for the past seventeen hours. So. I'm not in the mood for any bullshit. Understood?"

"Understood," I said, walking to her.

Then I kissed her.

She abruptly pulled out of our kiss, and said, "Don't kiss me when I'm mad at you. It's just rude."

I sat at my kitchen island watching Tatina pour my liquor stock down the drain, including a barely touched bottle of Redbreast fifteen-year-old Irish whiskey.

"Don't you think that's a little extreme?"

103

I said, interrupting my own twenty-minute confession of shortcomings, failings, transgressions and sins. "Shouldn't you, as a former bartender, see how senseless that is?"

"It's *because* I'm a former bartender that I can see the urgent necessity of this," she said. Luckily she didn't touch any of the Negra Modelo in the fridge. She didn't often drink beer, but she loved the flavor of Negra Modelo. And, for whatever reason, the way it made her burp also made her laugh. I like it when she laughs.

Watching her dump the remaining half of a fifth of WhistlePig rye down the drain was painful, but I finally, in my confession, was addressing the things that were and had been tying my guts into a million strangling knots.

"People get hurt around me," I said. "That's the way it was in Afghanistan. The way it was at the DPD. And now . . ."

"People are *saved* because of you, August," Tatina said. She'd stopped pouring my booze down the drain. What a party that would be for the sewer rats of Detroit. "And don't think for a minute I don't know *who* you are, *what* you have done and *can* do. You're not that good of a liar, and I'm not that naïve. Neither of us has any rightful claim to innocence."

"I — I just don't want to risk you getting hurt," I said.

"And when did you get it into your head that you were my appointed protector?" she said. "*Min Gud!* I could swear you were more evolved than that!"

"Save for a little hair on my knuckles, I am. But —"

"But nothing, August!" Tatina laughed. "I'm a grown woman! I'm half-German and half-Somali — which half do you think is the feckless maiden in limp-wristed distress?"

"Tatina, listen —"

"My father — a thoracic surgeon in Berlin — volunteered to treat men, women and children caught in the cross fire of a never-ending Somali civil war. My mother shielded, fed, fought and buried brothers and sisters, aunts and uncles, while dodging bullets, machetes and gang rape. And I can break down, clean and oil, then reassemble your Glock 17 blindfolded. So again, Mr. August Octavio Snow — tell me why I need *you* to be my valiant knight in shining armor?"

I thought about saying something snarky to break the tension.

Then I thought again.

"There are only three places I can see where you haven't displayed courage," Tatina said. "You know the first. We've talked about it before. The second is making what peace you can with Elena. And the third is finishing this new business so that nobody else in Mexicantown gets hurt." Sitting near her, I felt stronger. Listening to her, I felt forgiveness. "We are the outsiders, my love. The half-breeds who embrace our anomalies. Our curious histories and unique abilities. The legacy of duty we have inherited down generations. What you feel right now, August, is what every outsider feels from time to time: the weight of having cared too much for a world that cares so little. In these times we crave warm shadows. But you know as well as I — the shadows are not where we belong. They are not our destiny."

After a moment of looking into her eyes, I said, "How'd I get so lucky?"

"I have absolutely no idea," she said with a smile. "However, *my* standards must be slipping."

"Think I can get you into bed if I feed you?"

"All I've had in the past seventeen hours is a grisly piece of bratwurst with pickled pearl onions and a glass of vinaigrette salad dressing masquerading as a cabernet," she said. "You could get me into bed with a cheeseburger, small fries and a Coke."

"Wow," I said. "I think my luck's about to change."

After ten well-stuffed and brightly decorated soft-shell tacos at Taqueria El Rey (me six, Tatina four) and two soul-satisfying margaritas (me zero, Tatina two), it was easy to see she was fading. Still, she insisted we end the evening with a visit to Elena.

"She's probably not home from the hospital," I tried lamely.

"Avoidance isn't an answer," Tatina said. "She's your godmother. I was never so blessed."

"You're pretty good at this laying-out-guilt thing, aren't you?"

"I have a doctorate, love."

Much to my disappointment, Elena was home. She was wearing Tomás's huge purple-and-burgundy Everlast satin boxing robe, his name emblazoned on the back. She'd given the robe to him several Christmases ago, and a morning rarely saw him without it. He'd even worn it flipping hamburgers and turning hot dogs at backyard barbeques. The robe nearly swallowed her whole.

"Tatina!" Elena said as the two women embraced.

Elena looked haggard and exhausted. Her eyes were darkly circled, bloodshot and sunken.

She came out of her embrace with Tatina, looked at me, then hugged me tightly and wept into my chest. I held her and kissed the crown of her head. In her hair, she had carried home the scent of sterilized hospital hallways and recently administered pharmaceuticals.

I apologized profusely for everything.

Elena apologized for blaming me for Tomás's injuries.

We tumbled over each other in the colors and passion that are the Spanish language with tearful apologies and heartfelt declarations of love and forgiveness without condition. At one point, through tears of the pain, hope that family members feel when in full embrace of each other's faults and failings, Elena and I laughed, apologizing to Tatina for speaking rapid-fire Spanish.

"Está bien," she said with a slight shrug. That's okay.

In our luminescent moment of reunion, Elena and I had forgotten Tatina spoke fluent Spanish. And Norwegian. And German, French, Italian and Arabic.

Elena's phone, sunk deep in a pocket of the robe, began ringing and vibrating.

Our hearts stopped. She dug the phone out from the deep well of the robe's pocket and, with a trembling hand, said, "Hello?"

The hospital.

After a few seconds, she began weeping.

Jesus, this can't be, I thought. *It just can't —*

Overwhelmed and shaking, Elena handed the phone to me.

"Hello?" I said.

"Octavio?" Tomás said. "Jesus, where'd Elena go?"

"I think she's busy weeping tears of joy and thanking Baby Jesus right now," I said holding back my own tears. "I have to say — I'm pretty happy to hear your voice, too, old man."

"Yeah, well, I hurt like a sonuvabitch," Tomás said, "but that's something I can live with. Being dead ain't something I could live with, you know?"

"I hear ya, mi compadre."

"Hey, listen," Tomás said, "I could eat the ass out of a galloping stallion! All they got here is a prefabricated turd floating in some kind of brown sauce and fuckin' green Jell-O. You think you could get me some tacos or tortillas? *Both!* Get me *both!* And for some reason I got a taste for Doritos. The ranch dressing kind. I fuckin' hate

109

Doritos, but can you bring me a bag? Not the *small* bag! The *big* bag!"

Someone in the background (a nurse?) cautioned him that visiting hours were over and if he wanted something to eat, it would have to be "the brown turd and the green Jell-O."

I promised I'd stop by first thing fully loaded with tacos, tortillas and a big bag of Doritos.

"Somebody conked me on the head and shot me in the back, Octavio," Tomás said in a low growl. "And that somebody's gotta pay, comprendes?"

"Sí," I said. "Understood, mi amigo."

Then I handed the phone back to Elena, who was cradled in Tatina's arms, interrupting her fifth Hail Mary in thanks for Tomás's return.

Neither Tatina nor I wanted Elena to be alone. I offered to take her to her daughter's house. Or she could stay with Tatina and me, I said. Elena declined, saying that she could breathe again, and having her breath and faith back, she wanted only the bed she shared with her husband.

"His scent is on the pillows," she said.

For the life of me, I couldn't imagine what that scent was.

At around midnight, it began snowing.

Normally, the drive from Tomás and Elena's house was five minutes tops in the winter. With the '68 Olds 442 growling and ready to rip and run, it was a ten-minute fishtailing adventure.

"You know your car is — how you say? — stupid for the snow, *ja*?" Tatina said as I escorted her upstairs. She was asleep on her feet and reverting to broken English.

I undressed her, tucked her beneath the sheets and brought my thick down comforter up around her shoulders.

"So — we are not of the breaking up?" she said, her eyes closed.

"No," I said. "We're not broken up."

"Det er bra," she said. *"Det er veldig, veldig bra."*

Then she was out.

I was about to cuddle in with Tatina when I heard a timid series of knocks on the front door. Knocks at an hour and in weather in which only amateur thieves, first-time murderers, drunk lovers and elderly priests timidly knock.

Wearing only boxers and hugging the shadows of my house, I made my way downstairs — Glock in hand — and peeked through the living room window.

I opened the door.

111

"Sorry 'bout the hour, ma brotha. You got some coffee or somethin'?"

12

There's a man I know who wears the skin of this city, and he lives in the humid shadows of its writhing subterranean strata . . .

He is listening . . .

. . . always listening . . .

. . . taking four-dimensional mental notes . . .

. . . breathing when he needs to . . .

. . . holding his breath when he has to.

His name — or rather one of the names I've known him by — is Sweets.

Sweets is one of a number of itinerant intelligence operatives working the streets of Detroit. When alleyways get too cold and the streets too hot, he perches at a barbershop headquarters on 7 Mile Road near the Lodge Freeway where both the valiant and the villainous seek information one folded C-note at a time: Smitty's Cuts & Curls.

He was dressed for a much harsher winter

than had been forecast for southeastern Michigan: Canada Goose navy overalls topped off with a Canada Goose Wyndham Parka with fur-lined hood and midcalf Sorel Caribou wool boots. The kind of winter garb one wears to mush a sled-dog team along the Iditarod Trail.

"Sorry if I woke you, ma brotha," Sweets said after a sip of coffee, black, two sugars. "Or, you know, if you was in the middle of somebody."

"No problem," I said. "Since when do you make house calls?"

"Since I'm on my way outta town," Sweets said. "For good. Retired."

"Comox, British Columbia?" I said. "In the middle of winter?"

"Best time to get to know a place," Sweets said, stirring his coffee with a thumb, then sucking the coffee from it. "Plus, Comox don't hardly get the winters Michigan gets hammered with. I'm just dressed for the drive, man. Got my little eighteen-hundred-square-foot shack, Lund Pro-V fishin' boat, reels, poles, lures and line, 'bout three-hundred books, my grand-daddy's huntin' rifle and enough Courvoisier and Coke to start my own niggah nation — which ain't gonna happen, since I am true to my heart sick to death of Black folk, country-ass crackas, them racist-ass DC swamp rats and everybody inside and outside them three."

I tried to keep from laughing, since Tatina was upstairs doing a grand jeté through the land of Nod. "So, what brings you by on a night not fit for man or beast?"

"Thought you might like to know 'bout some brothas just rolled in from Jersey," Sweets said. "Seems they got a big blue-vein hard-on for you."

"Any connection to Duke Ducane?"

"Not as far as I can tell," Sweets said. "What's weird is they ain't locally connected, but they rumored to have a nasty track record in Jersey City, Brooklyn and Cape Cod —"

"Cape Cod?"

"Yeah," Sweets said after a slurp of coffee. "Word has it they East Coast troubleshooters for off-book real estate deals. I mean *big* shit! Mansions with no addresses, high-rise apartment complexes with no numbers, beach houses with no latitude or longitude. You know what kind of juice it takes to flip a blacksite real estate deal for any of that shit?"

"Major."

"Mighty, *mighty* major," Sweets said. "You gotta butter everybody's bread on that one: tax rolls, politicos, police, power and water hookups, inspectors — even the goddamn US mail!"

"Hello?"

Tatina on the staircase.

Sweets didn't know whom to gawk at — me or the beautiful woman with the long caramel-brown legs. She was wearing one of my Wayne State University T-shirts. Sweets settled on staring at Tatina. Who could blame him?

He rose awkwardly from his stool at my kitchen island and said, "Ma'am."

"Sorry if we woke you," I said.

"You didn't," she said, descending the steps with the same élan as Venus displayed emerging from her clamshell. She took a seat next to a mesmerized Sweets. "I turned and you weren't there."

"You can close your mouth now, Sweets," I said.

"Your name is Sweets?" Tatina said.

"Uh — yeah — yes, ma'am," Sweets said. "Least that's what some folk call me."

"Nice to meet you, Sweets," Tatina said, shaking Sweets's hand. "You two are friends?"

Sweets and I exchanged looks, assessing what exactly we were to each other: Associates? Friends? Confidential informant and client? Seller and buyer?

116

"We go way back," Sweets finally said. "When he was a beat cop and then a detective."

"What was he like back then?" Tatina said.

"Careful, Sweets," I said, "or your coffee gets poured into a to-go cup and you are to-gone."

"Truth, ma'am?" Sweets said with a slight laugh. "He was a cocky young smartass who thought he walked hand in hand with truth, justice and the American way. He was also fair, generous and respectful. Had him a kind of, you know, insight — a wisdom — about folk. *Real* folk."

"I take it there's more," a very astute Tatina said, "but you're being cautious around me. Which you needn't be. Right, August?"

This appeared to be a deceptively simple final-exam question for the recent lesson Tatina had given me on honesty. She was smiling at me, but her unblinking brown eyes told me I was under cross-examination.

"Right," I said.

"Dang, girl," Sweets said with a laugh. "Where that sexy accent from? Virginia?"

"Norway via Somalia and Germany," she said.

"Daaaang!" Sweets said. Looking at me, Sweets said under his breath, "You drivin' imports now?"

117

"So, what's going on?" Tatina said. "*Really* going on."

After a moment, I nodded to Sweets, indicating he had the go-ahead for full disclosure. Frankly, I don't know how anyone, least of all me, could resist even the slightest interrogation from Tatina.

After five minutes and a coffee refresh, Sweets had clued Tatina in to the fact that men had recently arrived in town with the mission to kill me. After another ten minutes, and I had filled in the background: an increase in drug pushers in Mexicantown, who were using former criminal Duke Ducane as a "false flag" for the drug supplier; a mystery-cloaked real estate broker named "Mr. Sloane" and his interest in buying the city-block-long Authentico Foods; Mr. Ochoa's suspicious death; and how everything seemed to circle back to Sloane.

"Sorry, Miss Tatina," Sweets said. "Looks like your boy here got himself a talent for gummin' up the works when it comes to mothafu — unsavory types."

"There's an old German saying," Tatina said, rising from her seat at the kitchen island. "A hero is just a dumbass who doesn't know when to quit." Then she leaned over the kitchen island and gave me a quick kiss on the lips. "You're my hero."

"Gee, thanks," I said.

She made her way back upstairs like a slow-motion dream of a conquering warrior goddess.

"Boy, I ain't lyin'," Sweets said, shaking his head. "I'd crawl a mile over broken glass —"

"Do *not* finish that sentence."

Sweets had no idea where the killers were staying in town. He doubted, however, they were the home-invasion type of contract killers, which eased my mind a bit. No, these boys seemed to like making a front-page show of their demented work. The Brooklyn real estate broker they had allegedly murdered had been found hung from the beam of a multimillion-dollar high-rise apartment. The only reason she hadn't been written off as a suicide by the NYPD was the fact that she'd been beaten with a baseball bat like a piñata, then shot three times.

A real estate broker on Cape Cod — a rather corpulent fellow, as the story goes — had been force-fed ice cream, fried clams and lobster rolls until he suffered cardiac arrest. But it wasn't the heart attack that had killed him: ultimately, it had been one of three bullets fired down his throat following his gorging.

Jersey City had been a murderous abomination that made the previous two hits look like evenings of cotton candy at ice-skating escapades.

"Well, you can't say they don't enjoy their work," I finally said.

"Yeah," Sweets said after a sip of coffee. "Maybe a little too damn much."

A quiet moment passed between us. Then Sweets said, "Comox, BC, ain't but a couple days' drive. Got plenty of room in the truck for you and your lady. Pitch in for gas and —"

"Thanks, Sweets," I said. "Think I'll stick around."

"You gonna be awright on this one?"

"Sure," I said. "Easy peasy."

"Your boy is out of commission," Sweets said, referring to Tomás. "And I don't know who you got for backup, but that big Mexican dude had to be the every-time, all-the-time choice for a second gun."

"Still is," I said. "Just got a little healing to do."

"Well," Sweets said, finishing his coffee and standing, "I'd best be gettin' on the road. Got four, maybe five days of driving ahead of me."

"What do I —"

"You don't owe me nothin', Snow," Sweets

said. "On the house. You always treated me with respect — not like some of these ashy back-alley ghetto rats sniffin' for a piece of cheese."

We shook hands.

"Took smarts and guts to do what you did for as long as you did it, Sweets."

He reached into the chest pocket of his insulated bib coveralls, pulled out a business card and handed it to me.

"I only had six of these things printed," Sweets said. "So, don't be losin' it, okay?"

"Delmonico Firenza?" I heard myself say as I stared at the name on the card.

"Yeah, I know," Sweets said. "My grandmomma was Italian. My granddaddy liked her last name so much he took it legal."

"Safe journey, ma brotha."

I watched him get in his used Toyota 4Runner and drive off toward the glow of the US/Canada bridge.

Didn't know him all that well.

Wish I had.

Visiting hours at Henry Ford Hospital didn't start until noon. For whatever reason the thought of three ruthless punks on their way to kill me felt less urgent than taking Tatina to Eastern Market, the largest and one of the oldest public market districts in the US, where the city mixed and mingled as people searched for the perfect fresh zucchini, heirloom tomatoes, apple butter, handmade seasonal wreaths or specialized vendor treats such as individually prepared mole and barbeque sauces. Thousands of aromas from the world's dinner table permeated the air, even after hours: saffron and cinnamon from Vietnam and Thailand, halal lamb and fish, kosher beef and kugel, roasted peanuts and cashews.

A couple summers earlier I'd taken Tatina to Vivio's, one of my favorite Eastern Market restaurant haunts, a neighbor-hood-style bar and grill where suburbanites and urban folk sat shoulder to shoulder, hunched over huge sandwiches, arguing sports stats, laughing at bad jokes and washing down their muffalettas, spicy buffalo wings and lobster rolls with a variety of ridiculously large Bloody Marys. (Try the Stacked Bloody Mary, the only drink where roasted asparagus, celery and a kosher dill peacefully coexist with a strip of thick-sliced applewood bacon.) We'd had tickets to see some rap musical about one of America's slave-holding founding fathers. We missed the play, opting rather to enjoy a few more Bloody Marys. Tatina gave some new friends free how-to-cuss-in-Norwegian language lessons.

Today, though, we were on a shopping mission.

"Aren't you concerned those men might try to hurt you?" Tatina said, inspecting a stalk of broccoli.

"Naw," I said. "Murderers don't eat vegetables."

By ten o'clock that morning, Tatina had filled the house with the warm and seductively spicy aroma of Moroccan lentil and chickpea soup. While I usually enjoy being the XO in my own kitchen, I didn't mind at all taking the position of sous-chef (chopping celery; measuring cinnamon, coriander, cumin, paprika and rice; chopping onions and draining chickpeas).

Halfway through cooking, I teasingly said, "You're sure you know what you're doing?" She raised her wooden spoon out of the simmering soup and made a threatening gesture with it. "Just checkin'," I said.

Since it was going to be a big pot, I braised about three pounds of diced lamb (modest seasoning of salt and pepper, splashes of beef broth) until the chunks were medium rare. Their time in the soup would slowly cook them through while infusing them with the mixture's warm, zesty flavor.

We ladled six servings of the Moroccan soup into a large Tupperware container and, with paper bowls, plastic spoons and festive paper napkins, headed out to visit Tomás.

"You should think about getting a winter car," Tatina said, throwing a lightning-fast verbal jab into the solar plexus of my ego, my beloved Olds 442.

"You drive a MINI Cooper," I reminded her.

In Tomás's hospital room, we were greeted with smiles and embraces by Tomás and Elena.

Lita had just left with her husband, Josh, and daughter, June. Taped to a side wall of Tomás's room, surrounding the nursing-staff-duty whiteboard, were several crayon drawings June had presented her abuelo, my favorite being of Tomás riding a unicorn.

"Oh my goodness," Elena said as Tatina took the lid off the plastic bowl. "That smells *delicious*!"

Tomás, his head still wrapped in white gauze, quietly grumbled, "It's soup."

"It's Moroccan lentil and chickpea soup with lamb," I said.

"It's still *soup*."

After scarfing down two bowls, Tomás looked at Tatina and gave her an approving nod of his gauze-turbaned head. "You made this?"

"Yes, I did," Tatina said. "With a little help."

"Jesus, and you're wasting time with this cabron?" Tomás playfully jutted a thumb my way.

"Sí. He has his charms," Tatina said. "Mostly."

After another bowl, Tomás said to Elena and Tatina, "You mind giving me and muchacho a minute, ladies?"

The two women gave each other a knowing look, then left the room.

"Somebody shot me in the back, Octavio — the fucking *back*!" Tomás growled. "I see old man Ochoa slumped over his desk, brains blown out, hear something and before I can turn I got bullets in me. So, I hope you ain't been sittin' on your ass, sucking your thumb."

"I've got a pretty good idea who," I said. "But right now, I've got bigger problems."

"What in hell could be more important than jamming up the gilipollas who shot me in the back?"

"Putting down three guys from Jersey sent here to kill me," I said.

"Oh, shit," Tomás said. "Sorry, man. You win."

125

I filled Tomás in on who I suspected had shot him and why. Then I told him about the larger combat scenario that was starting to play out and what I suspected was the reason for this latest criminal conflagration. He asked me if I had any backup for the play. I said no but that I didn't think I'd need any. The grotesque showmanship of the three killers told me they liked to play with their food first. Arrogance of beginners.

Tomás gave me a sideways look. "Or seasoned pros bored with quick efficiency," he said.

I didn't tell him my backup might come in the form of someone he strongly disapproved of. Telling him that may have made him bust his sutures.

"You are your father's son, Octavio," Tomás said. "I know you love and revere your momma" — he made the Sign of the Cross — "but you are your father's son. He laid it all on the line for people he loved and people he didn't even know. Guys like me. Even when he was on the job and didn't no other cops have his 'six.' That's a lonely, hard place to be. A place I think you're at right now. But that's who we are. And good luck trying to back away from your own shadow. You're your father's son, Octavio.

And that's a helluva lot more than most people can ever claim to be. So do what you gotta do, and be done with it."

My eyes filled.

I gave Tomás a hug.

He hugged me back, even though it must have hurt like hell.

In the time and space of that hug, thoughts flashed through my mind of the men and women I'd seen through a sand-blown haze, bloodied and bandaged on stretchers in Afghanistan. Those torn and tattered brothers and sisters who gave all for goddamn nothing. I thought about those solitary three days I was held under arrest for breaking my commanding officer's nose when he laughingly referred to my single sniper shot (a speck of sand in the eye, a blink that should not have been) that had killed a Taliban leader and his ten-year-old son as a "twofer." Three days to wallow in the roiling hell of having mistakenly killed a child. Three days to curse God and harshly examine the material of this vessel that my parents had poured their lives into . . .

Until the expertise of my trigger finger was once again requested to clear a path for British Special Air Service (SAS) soldiers under Taliban siege.

When Tomás and I released from our hug,

Elena and Tatina were standing in the doorway of his room, smiling.

"This," I said, "goes nowhere."

"Men," Elena said with a laugh.

Tatina convinced me that I was not doing my beloved Oldsmobile 442 any special favors by driving her in the snow. "And the *salt*!" she said. "*Min Gud!* How much salt do they put on the roads in Michigan? Is it like they actually *want* your auto to be eaten?"

After a couple phone calls, I found a climate-controlled storage unit in the north-west suburb of Farmington Hills that I felt relatively comfortable with and told my beloved classic muscle car, "Nos vemos en la primavera, mi amor." Lucky for me, the storage unit was a stone's throw away from a GMC dealership where the saleswoman looked as if she'd won the lottery when she sold me an SUV for cash in less than five minutes.

I hate quibbling, bartering or begging.

Especially when it comes to cars.

Or sex.

Next thing you know, I'm driving off the dealership lot, and I'm on my phone through the SUV's Bluetooth with my lawyer, David G. Baker.

"What do I know about Danny Romero?" G said, his voice filling the expansive cabin of the Yukon. "I know he's a slime-ball who cheats his clients and lives way beyond his means. He's mostly estate settlements, Social Security disability and big-money divorce settlements. He settled an old lady's estate last year; the old lady's son and daughter got half a mil between them. He walked away with two point three mil in every kind of fee and hourly rate adjustment you can think of. The old lady's kids are in their second year of contesting his fees, but my guess is he's burned through most of the money. I've come up against Danny a couple times. And I always feel like I need a hot shower in holy water to get his stink off me."

"So, Shakespeare was right about lawyers?"

"Except for me, wiseass. Why you askin' about Danny Romero?" G said.

"Knew him in middle and high school," I said. "He was a self-inflated, skinny prick then, and he's a professional skinny-ass prick now. I have the feeling he's just stepped into shit that's bigger than him and dead granny's money. I just wanted to know how far up his bunghole I should plant my foot."

"My suggestion?" G said. "Get a pair of waders."

I disconnected just in time to see Tatina craning her neck, looking back in wistful amazement at the rear passenger seats and storage space of the Yukon.

"There are villages in Norway smaller than this," she said. Turning her gaze to me, she continued, "When I said you needed something for winter driving, I meant something sensible like a Subaru or a Volvo. Not — not this *monstrosity*!"

"Yeah, well, this is America, baby," I said. "And you know what we say in America —"

"Ja, ja, ja," she said in a mocking tone. *"Gå stort eller gå hjem!"*

Go big or go home.

13

Tatina, whose family included her mother, two uncles, an aunt, a niece and a young twin brother and sister all living under the roof of a modest rented Oslo house, was used to efficiently and deftly organizing activities, schedules, holidays and dinners. Tatina was the well-tuned turbocharged engine that kept her family running smoothly. No small feat, and she had kept it all up while she was earning her doctorate in cultural anthropology and now teaching at the University of Oslo.

I had by happenstance spent Syttende Mai (May 17, Constitution Day) with her big, embracing, kinetically charged family earlier in the year. With the bravado of General George S. Patton commanding the Seventh Army in World War II's Mediterranean theater, Tatina had marshaled us through a day that included a chilly morning in Oslo's city center to watch and cheer on the colorful children's parade, followed by both church *and* mosque services where prayers of thanks were offered to God/Allah for His continued protection of immigrants in this strange northern European land. Exhausted from prayer on empty stomachs, we all sat at a longboard restaurant table for a Norwegian lunch of lutefisk (choking down lutefisk was proof of the immigrants' willingness to assimilate), pickled herring, *kumla,* lefse and cheeses and later ate an evening traditional Somali family dinner (mostly to kill the taste of the lutefisk).

So it should come as no surprise that in the twenty-five minutes it took to drive home from the car dealership in Farmington Hills, she had, by phone call and text, put together a ladies' night at my house with Elena, Carmela, Sylvia, Lucy and three of Elena's neighborhood organizer buddies, including Mexicantown city council rep Nadine Rosado.

"Should I be on bail alert?" Tatina said as we walked into the house.

"I don't expect it to be elevated to that," I said. I was going downtown to have a word with Danny Romero, whom I suspected of putting two slugs in my godfather's back. Truth is I was kind of hoping Danny would throw the first punch, justifying my crumpling him like a used tissue. Might be a nice warm-up for the three guys coming to put me down.

"Okay," she said, "I'll be on bail alert."

This, of course, annoyed the hell out of me, if only because it served as yet another example of how well Tatina was getting to know me.

While uninformed outsiders might think of Detroit as a barren, postapocalyptic boneyard populated by ravagers, marauders and murderous tribes, the city actually offers a wealth of surprising civility and beauty.

Take 645 Griswold Street.

The Penobscot Building.

Situated in the Detroit Financial District, the Penobscot Building was designed by Art Deco architectural master Wirt C. Rowland and opened in 1928. Inside, the forty-seven-story building is resplendent with decorative flooring, colorful tile wall murals and stone artifices simultaneously honoring and appropriating Native Penobscot tribal art. Dramatic lighting transports you back to another era, and an assortment of restaurants pay tribute to both modern, on-the-go appetites and those of well-mannered forties fine dining.

The one hideous feature of the Penobscot

Building was its twelfth-floor occupancy by the law offices of Daniel Antonio Romero, Esq.

A single turd floating in an otherwise beautiful cut-glass punch bowl.

Danny's modest square footage included a small yet stylish reception area with glass entry doors, a narrow conference room and three back offices, the largest of which was, of course, his. The smaller offices were periodically occupied by this junior partner or that paralegal, until this junior partner or that paralegal discovered the sky-high bounce of his checks and what an absolute fuck knuckle Danny truly was. There were plants in the small lobby that required only occasional light dusting, art prints on the beige walls that didn't give a damn whether you looked at them or not, nicely framed photos of Danny posing with a few used-to-be celebrities and an ornately framed law degree, which I suspect had been special ordered from Malaysia.

The most striking feature of his office was the receptionist, a zaftig, spray-on-tanned blonde in a squeeze-me-tease-me yellow floral dress.

Come for the bad legal advice; stay for the freckled cleavage.

"Hello," the receptionist said brightly.

"Welcome to D. A. Romero Law. My name is Skye. And would you be Mr. Sloane?"

"No," I said. "I would be Olaudah Equiano. Call me Ollie."

"Wow," Skye said, giving me a sideways look, "that's amazing. I mean you have the *exact* same name as an eighteenth-century Nigerian slave who became a celebrated British abolitionist and literary phenom before his death in 1797." She winked at me. "Bad luck for you, I have a master's in English lit. Now, may I ask: Who are you *really,* sir?"

"August Snow," I said, offering a hand. We shook. *Nice knuckle-cracking grip, this one.* "And that's the first time in five years that hasn't worked."

"Local constabulary?"

"Involuntarily sent to pasture," I said. "And if you don't mind my saying, all the leaves are brown, and the sky is grey — but you're a sight for sore eyes on a cold winter's day."

She laughed. "I find wearing bright, happy colors during the dreary days of winter helps me abate the usual Michigan seasonal affective disorder." There were flecks of gold in her wide blue eyes. "Xanax helps, too. Do you have an appointment, Mr. Snow?"

"No," I said. "But I think Danny'll want

135

to see me before Mr. Sloane arrives." Then, casually sitting on the edge of Skye's desk with all the self-confident panache of a detective from one of my father's sixties gumshoe novels, I said, "It's a case involving real estate fraud, aggravated assault, attempted murder and, I suspect, actual murder. And let me guess, Skye — he's already in conference with Ms. Jackie Ochoa?"

"You seem to know more about what's going on around here than I do," she said, narrowing her fascinating eyes.

"Trust me," I said. "I do."

Standing and smoothing her formfitting yellow dress, Skye donned a short white North Face bubble coat and exchanged her bright yellow high heels for calf-high fur mukluks. As she gathered up her belongings, she said, "I think I'm going to take lunch. Maybe hand deliver some résumés. Please tell Mr. Romero I'll be back in an hour. Or not. Depends on whether or not his check clears."

"Wise choice, Skye."

It might have been helpful if I'd taken Dramamine before I watched Skye walk out of the office and to the elevators some forty feet away. I've always considered the female form movable, if at times lethal, art.

Danny Romero was none too pleased to see me as I made my way into his conference room.

"What the fuck are you doing here?"

He jumped up from his seat at the head of his conference table and charged me. He tried to push me back through the door.

I gave him a half-power right cross to his jaw, knocking him back into a leather swivel chair.

"Hi, August."

Jackie Ochoa, looking beautifully bored and unimpressed by the brief altercation.

"Hey, Jackie," I said. "What's shakin', kiddo?"

"You fucking piece of shit!" Danny bellowed. He tried to stand, but I slapped him hard across his left cheek, which settled him back in his chair. No man likes to be punched. Every man *hates* to be slapped. It's just damned emasculating.

"Quiet, Danny," I said. "The adults are talking."

"I'd hoped you and I could have a quiet moment together before I left town," Jackie said. "Maybe over a nice dinner, exceptional pinot noir and Egyptian cotton sheets."

"Sorry, Jackie," I said. "Girlfriend's in town. Besides, I think I'd be stuck with more than just the bill. Did a little digging.

137

You're up to your expensive cut-and-color in debt. Defaulting on two business loans in Sacramento and one in LA. Expensive condo in Carmel that's in foreclosure. You're bleeding money, Jackie. You *and* this sack of shit."

"I'm calling the police," Danny said, rubbing his left cheek and pulling his phone from his suit jacket.

"Go ahead," I said. "Ask for Detective Captain Leo Cowling, homicide. He'd *love* to put me away! He'd also love to hear about a lawyer living beyond his means and in need of a big, fast payday. A hack whose obsession, Jackie Ochoa, had a solution to his problems and hers — namely, her own money issues *and* setting fire to the family tree. Being a woman in a culture that often prizes only male progeny takes a toll, doesn't it, Jackie?"

"It does indeed, August," she said. "Put the phone away, Danny."

Locked in Jackie's steely gaze, he obeyed after a long moment of hesitation.

"You had to know what your father's last wishes were, Jackie," I said. "And I'm guessing in the event of his death, you knew the majority of the business would be handed over to his employees. To keep it running or to sell it for a modest retirement. He loved his employees. Loved Mexicantown. Oh, sure, you'd get a small share. But not enough to pull you out of the financial abyss you're in. *Both* of you are in."

"I don't have to listen to this!" Danny said, attempting to rise from his chair.

I slapped him hard.

"Yes," I said. "You do." Danny flopped back in his chair, looking like a child who'd been caught with a dirty hand in the cookie jar. "You've got a way with men, don't you, Jackie. You always have. Hell, even I felt the tug of your gravity pulling me into your orbit for a second or two. I'm betting Sloane's on his way here to settle with you. And Danny? Sorry, pal. You're what you've always been; a shit-outta-luck jag-off."

"Jackie?" Danny said.

"So how long did it take to convince Danny forge a new will, then put your father down like a dog?"

"A mediocre dinner, a disappointing wine and fifteen minutes in bed," Jackie said. She was dressed in a black couture pantsuit accented with what I suspected was a belt of Swarovski crystals. She uncrossed her legs, smiled at me, then methodically recrossed them. Outside, it was beginning to snow heavily.

"*Fifteen* minutes?" I said. "Jesus, Danny!

I'm just getting warmed up after fifteen minutes."

"Trust me," Jackie said. "It was quite enough."

"Jackie," Danny pleaded sheepishly.

"So, the plan was for Danny to pop the old man in the head, make it look like he chose to go out on his own terms, right?" I said, leaning against the wall and folding my arms. "Nobody's the wiser. Not even you, Danny. Which hand did you put the gun in?"

He didn't answer, so I gave his left shin a kick.

"Right," Danny said. "The right hand."

"Brilliant!" I said. "The rheumatoid-arthritis right hand that he couldn't lift a cup of tea with. Both of you knew the old man was the first one in and the last one out of building. You didn't make sure the main entrance door wasn't closed behind you, right? You hear somebody coming upstairs from the production floor to the business offices. You panic, hide behind the door. That somebody was my godfather, Tomás. And you shot him in the back twice and watched him fall downstairs. Crawl out into the street and — and —"

I punched Danny in the face until strands of his blood and drool splashed against the

140

wall, carpet and window.

"Stop."

Jackie was holding a short-barrel .38 and pointing it at me.

"There's nothing you can do now, August," she said. "Sorry, Danny. It's time we said goodbye."

"You — you said we'd go —" Danny slurred.

"Oh, you poor thing," Jackie said. "I've never really been good with sharing. But you can have the gun back once the cops are done with it, right, August?"

"I don't give a shit about turning you pieces of shit over to the cops," I said. "Right now, I've got bigger problems — like Mr. Sloane and three killers he's set loose on me. I am, however, betting Sloane sprints like a white-tailed deer with an ass full of buckshot when he sees me here. Then you get fuck all."

A look of panic washed over Jackie's usually stoic face.

She stood and said, "It's time for you to leave, August."

"And miss the look on your face when millions go up in smoke?"

"*Shoot* him, Jackie!" Danny said. "He's an intruder. *Shoot* him!"

"Oh, she's not gonna shoot me, Danny," I

141

said. "She's always liked me more than you."

"And I like financial independence quite a bit more than either of you," Jackie said, cocking the .38's hammer. "So, move to the goddamn hallway."

The ding of an elevator reaching Danny's floor.

A slight, balding white man in his forties wearing a black car coat and towing a reinforced wheeled suitcase stepped out of an elevator and headed toward Danny's office. He saw the three of us.

Saw *me.*

He ran back to the elevator.

"No!" Jackie screamed.

I wrestled the gun from her. Gave her a hard push. Landed another right cross on Danny's already-bruised jaw. He tumbled onto Jackie.

I ran for the elevator.

Too late.

Mr. Sloane was in the wind.

14

"It needn't have gone this way, Mr. Snow," Sloane, having somehow acquired my mobile number, said through my new SUV's speakers. He may as well have been explaining why a particular stock in my portfolio was down an eighth of a point. "You could very easily have enjoyed a bit of profit yourself. A finder's fee, if you will. Your personal investment in business that isn't yours seems less than rational."

"You hire some showboating guns out of Jersey to smoke me?" I said. "Does *that* sound rational to you?"

"No. It does not," Sloane said. "Unfortunately, that was not my decision."

I was navigating the tonnage of my new GMC Yukon through slush, drifting snow and hipsters in North Face in search of the perfect cappuccino. Tatina was right about my new ride; I felt as if I were driving my living room.

"So, what's the endgame here?" I said. "You buy a lot of real estate for cash — so what?"

"I generally don't speak business with a dead man," Sloane said. "However, I'll indulge you for a moment: it's the purchase of peaceful anonymity. Surely a disgraced officer of the law can understand and appreciate that."

"And Authentico Foods?" I said.

"Condos," Sloane said. "Upscale. Secure. Discreet."

"You don't really work for Vic Bronson, do you?" I said. "In fact, *you're* working *him* somehow."

Sloane said nothing.

"Jesus," I heard myself say, beginning to see light in the maze of shadows I had been groping my way through. "Safe houses. You're building Londongrad without the bombast and perfumed putrefaction?"

"Goodbye, Mr. Snow," Sloane said. "I do apologize for the men coming for you. But you brought this on yourself."

"Goodbye, Mr. Sloane," I said. "And may karma fuck you like a sonuvabitch."

Detroit had always been a pirates' cove with its history of logging barons, slavers, whiskey runners, drug kingpins and developers.

There wasn't much the city hadn't seen in dark alleyways, dimly lit halls of government and boardroom-backhander deals. But this was different. This was a lethal infection to a body that was barely back from the dead. Honest people didn't need the secrecy, anonymity and redoubled security of safehouses. In Kandahar, Afghanistan, I'd known of such off-the-grid places. Places where quiet CIA and US contract security company deals were struck over mountains of American money and fifths of Johnnie Walker Blue for one murderous Taliban leader to terminate (with extreme prejudice) another such murderous Taliban leader aligned with Russian or Saudi interests.

I navigated the Yukon toward the 14th Precinct to hand off Jackie's short-barrel .38 to Detective Captain Leo Cowling. Maybe he could pull something from the gun. Maybe not.

"So, how's it hangin', Leo?" I said. We were standing in the lobby of the 14th Precinct.

"Well, things *was* just peachy," Cowling said. He was wearing another Irish cable-knit turtleneck — this time in deep purple — jeans that had been tailored and tan Red Wing Iron Ranger boots. "Then here come *yo* ass."

"Thought you might be tired of flogging the dolphin on taxpayer time." I took the handkerchief-wrapped .38 revolver out of my coat pocket. "So, I brought you a little something to professionally occupy you."

I unwrapped the pistol. Cowling's eyes lit up.

"What's this?" he said.

"A gun," I said. "Surely you've come across a few in your line of work."

"You know what the fuck I mean."

I told him it belonged to Jacqueline Ochoa, and how she and Danny Romero were involved in the death of Jackie's father and the attempted murder of Tomás.

Cowling squinted at the gun, then said, "Well, I guess that completes the set."

"What are you talking about?"

"The gun the old man killed himself with was part of a set," Cowling said. "Some dead old woman's son and daughter held an estate sale in West Bloomfield couple years ago."

"And of course you're checking out who bought the guns?"

Cowling laughed. Then he said, "Estate sales ain't known for stellar accounting, Snow. Cash and carry. Or pinch and carry. Either way, I ain't got the time, inclination or manpower to chase down some two-year old suburban estate sale receipts."

"Just take a closer look at both goddamn guns, Leo —"

"Hey, whoa, slick," Cowling snarled. "This ain't no damned Subway sandwich shop. You don't get to march right up to the counter, put your order in, snag a bag of chips and a mothafuckin' cookie, then walk out."

"Sorry," I said. "Romero shot my godfather, Leo. I just want —"

"Revenge," Cowling said. "See, I get it. But you need to get *this:* just because you ain't got not an ounce of respect for *me* don't mean you just walk yo ass up in here — *my* house, the *14th* — without no respect, no reverence. You feel me?"

"Yeah," I said. "I feel you."

Cowling took the gun from me and said, "If anything shakes out — which I doubt — you'll know. If it *don't,* you'll know that, too. Now get the fuck up outta here."

I did as he so kindly suggested.

As I was about to push through the front doors of the 14th, my phone vibrated.

A text.

DUCK DUCANE WANTS A WORD. 11:30 PM. EASTERN MARKET, SHED 3.

Duck?

Jersey boys, come to collect their thirty

pieces of silver.

I texted back: WHAT SHOULD I WEAR?

No answer.

Assassins are so serious these days.

I called Tatina at my house. In the background were the overlapping, cacophonous sounds of women indulging in too much wine and enjoying one another's company. I briefly imagined my beloved mother among them, her lilting laugh taking wing, her eyes reflecting the glow of the moment's camaraderie.

"So," I said, "just a quiet night in with a hot toddy and Netflix?"

Tatina excused herself from her guests and went upstairs to my — *our* — room.

"Are you okay?" she said.

"Yeah," I said. Then, nervously, I added, "I may not be home until late —"

"Bail?"

"No," I said with some irritation. "I do *not* need bail."

She sighed with relief, then said, "That other business?"

"That other business."

"Anyone who can help?"

"Shouldn't be too hard," I lied.

"Come home," she said. "I'll fix you something."

"No," I said. "Have fun with the ladies.

148

When I get home, maybe you and I'll have fun."

"Then let me come with you," she said. "I can handle myself."

I knew what she meant. I swallowed the confusion of fear and anger I was feeling and said, "No."

Then I said what she wanted to hear — and what I truly felt. Which made both of us unreasonably happy. And awkward. A confusing entanglement of gravity and weightlessness.

The early evening menu at Schmear's Deli in Campus Martius doesn't vary much from the lunch menu. That being said, you can find a few special dishes that resemble dinner more than lunch. Like the porcini risotto with smoked chicken. Or calamari in saffron rice with diced plum tomatoes, roasted garlic and parsley. Or the lemon and garlic linguini with chopped hot pastrami (don't knock it till you've tried it).

"How's the linguini tonight?" I asked Ben Breitler, second-generation owner of Schmear's.

He gave a theatrical shrug. "Good if you're used to disappointment."

"I'll have the risotto and calamari."

"Both?"

"Yeah," I said. "And how 'bout three

149

fingers of that Buffalo Trace rye you keep in your office?"

"Big night ahead?"

"Yeah," I said. "Big night."

15

After a contentious phone call, which included amalgamations of profanity that shocked even my cavalier sensibilities, I made my way down to Eastern Market's Shed 3. The last vendor had probably left two hours earlier, leaving me alone inside the ghostly lit twenty-nine-thousand-square-foot structure.

A two-man security team in a tricked-out Ford Escape SUV would slowly patrol the expanse of Eastern Market — south on Riopelle, turning west onto Adelaide, then north on Russell. But on a cold late-November night with more snow expected, they would probably stay in their patrol car, listen to 92.3 FM and warm themselves with a thermos of spiked coffee or cocoa.

I was about an hour and a half early for my date with the Jersey boys, giving me plenty of time to tactically assess the shadows and run a few if-I-were-going-to-kill-mc

151

scenarios.

At 11:40, an eastside shed door creaked open.

A rush of subzero air.

Whispers.

Wrapped in the velvety shadows draping the shed's large announcement platform, I said a quiet Hail Mary and watched as three figures slowly spread out with one on point. They held weapons at the ready; I recognized one in silhouette as an Uzi with a suppressor.

"I don't like this," one of the shadowed figures whispered.

"Shut the fuck up!" another answered harshly.

Using just a touch of reverb, I said, "Red rum! *Red rum!*" into a mic connected to the PA system.

One of the men screamed, spun to face the bandstand and put three slugs into a pair of two-thousand-watt speakers.

One of the speakers was dead.

I wasn't.

"See, here's the thing," I said through the microphone. "If you're gonna tell somebody to show up at eleven-thirty so you can kill 'em, you need to be here by eleven. That's what a professional would do."

"Come on out, mothafucka, so we can

show you what a professional would do."

"Fair enough," I said.

I made my way to a patch of pearl-grey light thirty feet behind the trio and said, "You should ask yourselves two questions: One, which one of you am I gonna kill first? And two, why do giraffes still make me giggle? Frankly, I'd focus on the first question."

Knowing I had the drop on them, they each turned just in time to see a figure emerge from the darkness behind me and into my patch of light.

"Who's this OG niggah?" the thin Black man in the middle of the three said. He was wearing one of those god-awful oversized Pelle Pelle leather coats, low-rider jeans with his underwear puffed out above the belt and Timberland Radford boots. His cohorts were dressed equally ghetto fabulous.

"This is the man you claim to be working for," I said. "Mr. 'Duck' Ducane."

"It's *Duke* Ducane, ya fuckin' morons. Learn how to goddamn text," Duke snarled. He turned to me. "You called me for *this*? Jesus, God in heaven, Snow. Just *shoot* two of these low-rent shit stains and sweat the third turd."

"I called you to verify your relationship with these gentlemen," I said.

153

"I ain't *got* no relationship with these fools!" He pointed to the one with snake-slanted eyes and the one who looked as if he was about to pee his pants. "Them two are dumber than my hairy left nut, so put them down first."

I was losing patience. "My better angels — who, by the way, are becoming fewer by the minute — tell me *we* are not gonna shoot *anybody*. *You* are walking outta here fully confident that all is well with the goddamn universe."

"You do, of course, know these ashy gin-'n'-juice niggahs plan on killing you, right?" Duke said.

"Fuck dis shit," the punk with the Uzi mumbled. "I'm gettin' paid."

Just as he was about to level the Uzi, Ducane and I unloaded four shots center mass into the punk.

"You were saying something about your 'better angels'?" Ducane said as the dead man toppled over and hit the floor. "While we at it —"

"No," I said. "I need these two for questioning."

Duke said, "Your funeral. Don't say I didn't warn you." Then, turning his attention to the remaining Jersey boys, he said, "If'n y'all diseased-ghetto-rat mothafuckas

154

do manage to eight ball this brotha, then know this: I will find you and kill you slowly and uniquely. Yo mommas will have to bury the sponge I use to clean up the last little bit of you. Make book on that, you jizz-monkey bastards." Then Duke yelled, "Okay, boys! We *out!*"

From the dark corners of the shed, the Compton twins materialized, holding the two remaining Jersey boys in their gun sights. The jaws of the Jersey boys dropped. Fin and Fergie stopped in front of the two Jersey boys and held out their large hands. Without a word, the punks handed the twins their guns. Then the twins stood over the dead punk and fired them into the remains of the fallen man until the clips were nearly empty.

"There ya go," the Compton twins said, handing the guns back to their owners.

The Jersey boy to the left began weeping. Then he peed his pants.

The Compton twins followed Duke out. Fin or Fergie — who the hell knows? — stopped behind me and said in a mountain-troll rumble, "I'da paid to see them punks cap you, Snow."

"And I'd pay to see you drop twenty pounds, ya chicken-'n'-biscuit-eatin' bitch,"

I said, not in the mood for sass from Sasquatch.

Duke and his crew faded into a bitter cold Michigan night.

"Now," I began, still training my Glock on Low Rider and Pee Pants, "tell me who hired you to off me, and maybe I'll let you scurry back to your hidey-holes unharmed."

"You tell him and we both eat a bullet!" Pee Pants said before wiping his snot-glazed lips and chin.

"Since when we run scared of some Chinese Bruce Lee wannabe? I ain't a-scared of that mothafucka!"

"Chinese?" I said. "Not a white guy named Sloane?"

Silence.

Pee Pants, in full emotional-breakdown ·de, said, "I never wanted *any* of this shit! nted to go to *art school,* goddammit!"

suddenly made a run for an exit door. ∟ let him go. The door clunked open, and Pee Pants sprinted out into the cold. Then it was just Low Rider and me.

"If it ain't us, it'll be somebody else," Low Rider said defiantly.

"Always is," I said. Then I gave the bridge of his nose a crack from the butt of my Glock and brought him to his knees. I walked behind him and pressed the barrel of my gun to the back of his head. "Tell me who this Chinese gentleman is."

"*He'll* kill me if *you* don't," Low Rider said.

"Then you got nothing left to lose."

Low Rider finally capitulated, telling me everything he knew about the Chinese man: young, lean, fairly tall, nice suits. Knew him as Mr. Xiang. Xiang had used the trio three times before in the killing of a female real estate agent in Brooklyn, a male real estate developer in Jersey City and a male real estate agent on Cape Cod.

"I don't think he's no boss or nothin'," Low Rider said. "Delivery boy be my guess."

"Why do you say that?"

"He sound like some wannabe British bad boy. Or Irish. Scottish. Shit, I don't know! Mothafuckas all sound the same!" Low Rider said. "I axed him if he was the boss and he gets all mad 'n shit. Points a finger at me and says, 'Your business isn't who the boss is, mate! You take the money, you do the job! Simple enough, *eh*?' "

"And you don't know anything about a middle-aged white guy named Sloane?"

"Mothafucka, I done *told* you I don't know no damn Sloane! And you broke my fuckin' nose!"

157

"I did?" I said innocently enough. "Let's see?"

Low Rider held his head up for me to take a look at his broken and bloodied nose.

I hit it again with the butt of my gun.

"Now, then," I said. "Is this Chinese/English/Irish gentleman here? In Detroit?"

Through his pain, Low Rider laughed. "If he ain't, he sho as hell *will* be if you keep pokin' yo nose into business that ain't yours!"

"And what business would that be?"

"Who buyin' what property for whatever reason in this beat-to-shit city," Low Rider said.

"You're from Jersey," I said. "Watch your fuckin' mouth."

"You don't even know 'bout your money-bags hometown hookup!"

"And who would that be?"

"Fuck you," Low Rider said before spitting blood at me.

Duke Ducane was right — what "better angels"?

After a sixty-second pistol-whipping that left Low Rider a few teeth short and with a busted and bleeding left ear, he finally consented to tell me who the hometown connection was. And it wasn't Vic Bronson.

It was my turn to be wide-eyed and gob-

158

smacked.

"Thanks for the rotten memories, punk," I said before bringing the butt of my Glock down hard on the back of his head. He collapsed face forward, unconscious. I took out newspaper clippings citing the three real-estate-related murders from my inside coat pocket and let them flutter through the brisk air until they found Low Rider's back. With a gloved hand, I grabbed his gun and burner phone from his pants pocket and dialed.

"Nine-one-one," the operator said. "What's the nature of your emergency?"

I fired off the last three rounds from his gun, then dropped it and the still-connected phone onto Low Rider's back.

Then I walked out of the shed, into a wicked cold early morning.

I've given up on football.

Not just the Lions (who perpetually break my heart) but the NFL in general: Millionaire babies taking to the field to shuck, jive and juke for elderly billionaire plantation masters. The players who *do* take a stand by kneeling are vilified, nullified and ostracized. And fans continue to subsidize this *cirque du soulless* in some publicly funded, corporate-owned stadium with the audacity to charge ten dollars for a cup of warm beer, eight dollars for cold hot dogs and ninety dollars for jerseys bearing terminally concussed gridiron legends' names and numbers.

Dear God.

Never mind the fact that the rules of a once-simple sport have become so complicated that it takes a team of Harvard Law professors to unravel them during a two-minute time-out or a video penalty challenge.

Football's not a game anymore.

It's two-hours of Wall Street traders, stock analysts, happy-ending-massage-parlor escapades, drug addicts and wife-beaters bashing helmets.

It's *Spartacus* without the honor or drama.

The morning after tangling with the Jersey boys, I gave up on my usual black coffee and *SportsCenter*. Tatina had asked me if there was any news on ESPN of Stabæk recruiting Undagu from Strømsgodset. I told her she might be suffering a stroke because she was speaking gibberish. She punched me hard in the forearm. She's in quite good shape. Rather than hurt myself trying to understand Norwegian "football," I dressed and Tatina and I went shopping for ingredients for my father's chili. Our shopping took us to Eastern Market, where the cops still had an overwhelming presence at Shed 3.

"You?" she said as we drove past the shed.

"Me," I answered.

Tatina kept her questions concerning my previous evening's activities short. I obliged her with answers that were equally succinct. I was certain Tatina had seen the unimaginable in Somalia. She was no stranger to blood. And as such, a few details were all she required to form a full and telling picture.

Her one question that I had no simple answer to was: "Is it over?"

After a few seconds of thought, I said, "I don't think so. I'm not sure."

"If you're not sure," she said, "then it isn't over."

At about noon, Tatina and I made chili from my father's recipe: coarse-chopped jalapeños, coarse-chopped Vidalia onion, a healthy amount of smoked paprika, ground beef, stew beef (sautéed in bourbon, which I wasn't allowed to drink, molasses, butter and coarse-ground black pepper), thick-chopped applewood-smoked bacon and just less than a cup of brown sugar. Instead of adding my father's usual two bottles of Guinness stout, I poured in one bottle of New Holland Brewing's Dragon's Milk for no other reason than I liked it better.

The thought was to take some to Elena and Tomás, who was home and making Elena's life as a caregiver miserable.

"Why is it men make the absolute worse patients?" Elena had said. "Little whiny babies, every one of you! Tough guys who would faint from a hangnail!"

I thought it best not to remind Elena that

two slugs in the back was not a "hangnail."

After dropping off the chili, Tatina and I decided it was a pajama day. One of the ways for people around the world to learn American English is to watch American movies, and it's no different for Tatina. Feeling she had a way to go to speaking English more naturally and fluently, she barely convinced me to forego watching Michigan State basketball to watch *His Gal Friday* with Cary Grant and Rosalind Russell.

"You do, of course, realize the movie contains the racial slur 'pickaninny,' " I said as we carried bowls of my father's hearty chili and a plate of obscenely buttered corn bread (with chopped jalapeños baked inside) to the coffee table in front of the TV.

"Yes," she said brightly. "I'm not naïve. Racism has always been America's biggest export. Still, it's Cary Grant."

"Still," I said, "it's Cary Grant."

Ten minutes into the movie, I got a call from Detective Captain Leo Cowling requesting my presence at the Jefferson Avenue water treatment plant's third clarifying tank near Brennan Street.

Actually, his request was of the fire-breathing persuasion.

"Shall I go with you?" Tatina said.

"No," I said, giving her a light kiss. "Enjoy

163

the movie and the chili. I'll be back as soon as I can."

"Is it going to be like this with us?"

"I'd like it not to be," I said. "Why?"

"Because I'd like to think you trust me enough for me to be at your side when need be."

"Not quite the answer I expected," I said. "Thank you."

The weather the day before had been a shock to the system: subzero and colorless with mounds of snow that had had that Styrofoam crunch when you stepped on it. Now it was forty-four with sunshine and rivers of cold water rushing against the curbs. Welcome to another bipolar-vortex Michigan winter. Appropriately enough, I was wearing well-worn Peter Millar jeans, tan Cole Haan chukka boots, a pilling navy-blue wool crewneck sweater that was about twenty years old and my father's beat-to-hell grey motorcycle jacket.

Three DPD cruisers with flashers spinning, one dirty navy-blue undercover Ford and the Wayne County Coroner's tech van were already there when I rolled to a stop at the huge municipal clarifying tank complex.

A tall, slim, fresh-faced DPD patrolman stopped me.

"I'm Detective Captain Leo Cowling's

prom date," I said, holding out my driver's license for the young cop to see. The cop — a stoic Black kid with high cheekbones and alert eyes — spoke into his shoulder-mounted walkie-talkie.

"Send that mothafucka up here," Cowling's voice said, crackling through the walkie-talkie.

The young cop pointed the way.

There were a number of huge circular clarifiers, each holding several hundred thousand gallons of brackish wastewater, all in the convoluted process of being sanitized and fortified, then sent to faucets all across southeastern Michigan. The Brennan Street facility was one of ten such facilities, making the system the single largest wastewater treatment plant complex in the nation, pumping out eighty to a hundred million gallons of drinkable water a day.

The smell — mitigated somewhat by the air's chill — was an abomination.

Cowling, a couple uniforms and someone I assumed was a plant manager were standing over a body that had been fished out of one of the clarifiers. Kneeling by the body in a white moon suit with blue latex gloves on was my friend Dr. Bobby Falconi, Wayne County Coroner. Cowling saw me and sent the uniforms and plant manager packing.

"Roll him," Cowling said to Bobby without greeting me.

Bobby turned the body over; even though it looked as if it had been dipped in a sluice of motor oil, wastewater and fecal decay, it was easy to see it was a white male, between forty and fifty, maybe five-eleven, a gaunt one forty, expensive suit and shoes. He'd been shot once in the forehead. Small caliber, I assumed. Bullet probably bounced around his skull turning his brain into pinkish-grey slush.

"You know him?" Cowling said.

"No," I said. "Should I?"

"You sure 'bout that?" Cowling held up an evidence bag.

Inside the bag was a dirty, wet business card: On one side it said, "Sloane & Partners — Real Estate Negotiators & Facilitators." On the flip side was my name and cell phone number in what I assumed was the dead man's handwriting.

"Never met him," I said. "Can I go now? My girlfriend is —"

"Fuck yo girlfriend!" Cowling said.

"Try, and I'll kill ya."

"Where were you between eight and ten-thirty last night?" Cowling asked.

"With my lady friend, eating popcorn and

watching some British rom-com on Netflix," I lied.

"So, you don't know nothing about this dude, huh?"

"Not a damn."

"How about Eastern Market?"

"Something happen at Eastern Market?" I said.

After recapturing what calm he may have had, Cowling said, "If I find out you and this dead cracka was in on any shit — including that Eastern Market Shed Three mess! — you just might be workin' laundry in Jacktown for twenty to life. You feel me, Tex-Mex?"

"I feel you," I said. Then I said to Bobby, "How's it goin'?"

"Different day, different dead," Bobby said, giving me a salute. "I hear Tatina's in town. We should grab dinner sometime while she's —"

"You think this is a social call, mothafucka?" Cowling snapped. Glaring at me, he pointed to the dead man and said, "This dude had *you* in his pocket, and don't nobody wanna know yo ass unless they *got* trouble or mean to *cause* it. Either way, it means a fuck-up I gotta suck up and clean up. A head-shot body dumped with your name and number in his pocket? It's a

167

straight line with you at the other end. I'm getting a warrant to search your house, and that includes every weapon you got. So, get used to me bein' way up in yo narrow ass till I know which is what, understand me?"

I nodded that I did.

"Okay, get the fuck outta here," Cowling said. I turned and walked away. He called out after me, "And you'd *better* stay yo ass in town, Snow! Ain't no slippin' and tippin' out no back door to Sweden or Denmark or wherever you getcho transmission flushed!"

"See ya round, Bobby," I said.

"Dinner," Bobby said. "Think about it."

"You do, of course, know what I'm risking by talking to you about this," Bobby Falconi said when I called.

"A two point seven percent raise that won't even match COLA?"

"So, what's your impression of this Mr. Sloane guy?"

"Not really much to go on," I said. "He was more of an apparition than anything else. The folks who actually dealt with him described him as an instantly forgettable white guy, five-ten, maybe midforties, thin, male-pattern baldness, glasses, expensive but plain black suit and shoes. Talked like he went through life with a nosegay."

168

"Yeah, well, he's still talking but in my language now," Bobby said. "Did anybody say he looked particularly healthy?"

"Where you going with this, Bobby?" I said.

"The guy I'm looking at on the slab?" Bobby said. "If a bullet hadn't killed him, malnutrition and cirrhosis of the liver eventually would've; his organs and tissue show definite indications of premature senility and alcohol abuse. Muscles reveal signs of midstage atrophy. What hair he had had been recently shampooed and conditioned, but I found one larval parasitic infestation in his pubis region."

"Lice?"

"Lice," Bobby confirmed. "Considering the bacterial stew we fished him out of, anything's possible. But my guess is the nit attached itself prior to him being shot and dumped."

"Meaning?"

"If I were a betting man, I'd say the guy on my slab was homeless," Bobby said. "Has what looks like a rash on the deltoid of his right arm. Turns out it wasn't a rash; it was a recent laser burn. Tattoo removal. Whoever treated him to this did it postmortem and in a hurry. They didn't get all of

169

the ink. Looks like an army battalion insignia."

"What about his clothes?" I finally said.

"What about 'em?" Bobby said. "High-end, personally tailored, no labels. The shoes were high-end custom with some sort of embossed logo. Can't quite make it out but I'll take a deeper dive. Don't hold me to this, August, but I think you may have the right circus —"

"But the wrong clown."

While I let Bobby's download find various crevasses of my mind in which to settle, he said, "Since I've got you on the horn, tell me this: Is Leo Cowling really that much of a *magna pilosis* asshole or what?"

17

Looking like a million bucks doesn't really account for much when you're approaching the receptionist desk of Hunter Enterprises headquarters on the fourteenth floor of the Guardian Building; *everybody* looks like a million bucks on this floor.

Nevertheless, I was dressed to kill in a black two-button Altea cashmere topcoat, Tom Ford grey Prince of Wales Shelton suit, Proper Cloth 120s grey small check shirt, serious black silk tie and Ferragamo double-buckle shoes. Seated behind the blond-mahogany desk was a young man who looked like he'd just stepped off the cover of *GQ* magazine.

"Well, hello-ke-dokey!" I said, flashing the thousand-watt grin of a Mormon missionary.

"Hi," the receptionist said, gleefully exposing at least ten grand in cosmetic dentistry. "Welcome to Hunter Enterprises. How may

I assist you, sir?"

If you ever need a new alias for what my cop father used to call the "Rockford Fly-over," it's likely your local restaurant is unwittingly able to help; there's a fishbowl near the cash register with thirty or forty business cards swimming in it, each one hoping to be hooked so its owner can win a free lunch. For a great number of people, a business card is sufficient proof of identity.

The free-lunch business card fishbowl at Schmear's Deli had provided me with a new temporary persona. "Elwood," I said, handing the receptionist a business card. "Elwood Singer. Friends call me Woody. Or Lockjaw. Purple Elite Pool Systems, Keego Harbor. Got a twelve-thirty-five appointment to see the big man himself, Mr. Vic Bronson."

"Mr. —"

"Singer," I said. "With an *S.* Capital *S.*"

"Yes, I think I can spell 'Singer,' Mr. Singer," he said, typing my name into his computer. "With a capital *S.*"

"Purple Elite Pool Systems, Keego Harbor," I repeated. "Institutional pools. Competitive pools. Medical therapeutic pools. High-end residential pools. You got a pool? You really should have a pool. *Everybody* should have a pool. It's the number-one

172

full-body cardio workout, bar none. I mean, it *looks* like you swim, 'cause, I mean, everything's — you know — in the right place."

I watched his movie marquee blue eyes dance over his monitor for a few seconds.

"I'm sorry, Mr. Singer," he said. "I'm afraid I'm not finding you on Mr. Bronson's schedule."

"Oh, you are just *poopy scooping* me, right?" I said with mock disappointment. "I made the appointment, what — a month ago? I talked to a — oh, what was her name? Not you —"

"Monique?"

"*That's* her!" I said. "Yeah! Monique! Dog*gone it*! Would you mind trying again, mister —"

"Tanner. Just Tanner."

"Mr. Tanner." I leaned over his desk and twisted to get a glimpse of his monitor. "It's Elwood . . . Singer —"

"Capital *S*," he said. "Right. I got it."

"Purple Elite Pool Systems," I said. "We're bidding on any and all water-based entertainment and health systems Mr. Bronson's thinking about putting in his new downtown residential high-rise. We're the best, you know. We did Eminem's pool. *And* Bob Seger's."

"Tremendous," Tanner said with all the conviction of an Irish Protestant at a Catholic mass.

Once again, he typed my name into the system, and we waited.

"Boy oh boy," I said. "I'd have a talk with that darned — what's her name?"

"Monique." Then, shaking his head, Tanner said, "I'm sorry, Mr. Singer. I'm still not finding you at all on his schedule. I do apologize."

"Gosh *dang* it!" I said. "Sorry. Don't mean to cuss. I mean, I made the drive all the way from Keego Harbor this morning." I issued a sigh of Shakespearean proportions. "Well, I mean — can you just *call* him? Let him know I'm here? He'll know who I am. I can unpack my presentation in three minutes. Tops! And" — I lowered my voice to a conspiratorial whisper — "there's a fifty-dollar Godiva chocolate gift card in it for you, Mr. Tanner."

"I prefer the chocolates from Bon Bon Bon," Tanner said dismissively.

A large set of frosted glass doors behind the receptionist desk slid open, and Vic Bronson — real estate billionaire, part owner of a mediocre southern NHL team, legendary Lothario and America's Cup racing enthusiast — emerged looking like, well, a billion land-baron dollars. On point were two tall, beefy private security guards, followed by a stocky, overly developed security cleanup man.

You can never have too much security when you're a billionaire in a platinum bubble rolling through the muck, mire and menudo of everyday wage slaves.

"Mr. Bronson!" I said, quickly following his security detail. "A minute of your time, sir!"

Bronson and his team stopped and looked back at me. The last man standing advanced to meet me. The receptionist — panicked and in full cover-his-admirable-ass mode — stood. "Sir, I *told* Mr. Singer he didn't have an appointment with you. *Twice!* Should I call security?"

"What is it you'd like, Mr. Singer?" Bronson said.

Last Man Standing put a hand on my chest to stop my advance.

"I just want to ask what your property interests are in Mexicantown," I said.

"That is *not* what he told me, Mr. Bronson," Tanner said. "He said he was a pool company representative."

Bronson stared at me hard for a few seconds before he said, "I have no interests in southwest Detroit."

"You sure about that?" I asked.

Bronson and his team turned and began walking away.

"Then you have no idea who a Mr. Sloane is?" I said. "He doesn't represent you, Hunter Enterprises or Sextant Properties in any way, shape or form?"

Bronson stopped abruptly. The pulse in his carotid artery visibly increased.

His security team brought their crosshairs back to me.

"I'm calling security —" the receptionist said.

"Tanner. No," Bronson said without facing either of us. "As I said, I have no real estate interests in southwest Detroit through Hunter Enterprises, Sextant Properties or any other Hunter entity. I'd suggest you talk to your Mr. Sloane, whoever he is. And next time, might I recommend you make an actual appointment? I would be glad to speak with you then."

With that, he rounded a corner to a private hallway with two of his security detail.

Last Man Standing, who even at a modest five-nine looked as if he could bench three hundred pounds, sneered, "Like Mr. Bronson said, next time, make an appointment."

A hard second or two passed between us.

Then I said, "Oh, you are just *adorable*! You in your big-boy-going-to-church suit! Would you like a cookie? You wanna cookie, little big man?"

He briefly opened his suit jacket to give me a glimpse of the handle and magazine of his semi-auto weapon, discreetly flipped me the finger, then said, "Tanner? Why don't you make that call to security? Now. *And* the local PD."

"No need," I said, heading to the bank of elevators.

By the time I got home, there was a navy-blue Ford DPD undercover sedan parked at the curb in front of my house.

I found a young olive-skinned man in a dark suit sitting at my kitchen island finishing a bowl of my chili and a square of corn bread. Tatina was refreshing his cup of coffee.

"Patrolman Aswan?" I said, recognizing the Chaldean DPD officer.

"Not a patrolman anymore, Mr. Snow," Aswan said standing and offering a hand. "Detective. Newly minted."

We shook. "Holy shit!" I said. "*Detective* Aswan! Congratulations, man!"

"Thank you, sir."

"Detective Aswan says he arrested you

several years ago," Tatina said brightly.

"Yeah, but he's one of the good guys for sure," Detective Aswan said. "I looked into him. His record. All the news stuff. If it weren't for guys like him, guys like me wouldn't have much of a shot on the force. Yeah, I'd put in with him any day of the week."

"What brings you to the hood, Detective?" I asked.

"You, Mr. Snow."

I sat at the kitchen island next to him. Tatina asked if I wanted some chili. I didn't.

She gave me a light kiss, handed me a cup of coffee and said, "Is this privileged police talk?"

I said to Aswan, "Anything you can say to me, you can say in front of my bouncer."

"We got a 911 call from Hunter Enterprises in the Guardian Building," Aswan said. "Somebody fitting your description going by the name of Elwood 'Lockjaw' Singer was intimidating Mr. Bronson."

"Tha'd be me." I took a sip of coffee. "Though I'd hardly call it 'intimidating.' Exactly how do you intimidate a billionaire with a three-man security detail equipped to meet the zombie apocalypse head-on?"

"Lockjaw?" Aswan was unable to conceal his amusement. "Really?"

"The only known Black associate of the Purple Gang," I said. "Cops tried to drown him in a toilet. Didn't know he was a marathon swimmer who could hold his breath for three minutes."

"I was asked — *commanded* by my boss to pay you a visit," Aswan said.

"And your boss is?"

"Captain Leo Cowling."

"What exactly did *Captain* Cowling say, Detective?"

"You sure you wanna hear, sir?" His cheeks flushed as he glanced at Tatina. "I'm not sure this is language fit for your, uh, 'bouncer'. Bottom line is I'm here because he's afraid if he were here, he'd hurt you."

"Unlikely," I said. "Have you seen his hands? Like creepy little doll hands!"

"Those are the hands that fork over my check, Mr. Snow," the newly minted detective said, presenting me with a warrant.

I escorted Detective Aswan upstairs to my small gun safe, spun the combination dial and gave him my *other* Glock 17 and my father's service weapon, which I'd cleaned but never fired. He put both into an evidence bag and apologized profusely.

"Thank you very much, ma'am, for the chili, corn bread and coffee," Detective Aswan said to Tatina. "I hope you enjoy your stay." Then he pointed to the painting of Octavio Paz. "Mind if I ask who did that painting? It's beautiful."

"You have good taste, Detective," I said. "My mother painted that."

"She's very good."

"She's gone now."

"I'm sorry," he said, instantly making me believe he was sincerely sorry. "My mother's a fabric artist. Mostly pieces based on Persian myths, music and folklore. She's good. Shows in a couple local galleries."

" 'She makes linen garments and sells them, and supplies the merchants with sashes,' " I quoted. " 'She is clothed with strength and dignity; she can laugh at the days to come.' "

"Proverbs 31," Aswan said.

"Does *every*one in this city know *every* verse from the Bible, Buddhavacana, Koran and Torah?" Tatina said.

"If we didn't," I said, "we'd probably be in deeper shit than we already are."

"Maybe you could add your constitution to the reading list?" she said.

Detective Aswan took out one of his cards and handed it to me. He told me it might be a couple weeks before my weapons were tested and possibly returned. I told him I didn't care about the Glock. But my father's

180

service weapon was important to me. Then, donning a ridiculous noir-along-the-Seine trench coat, he started for the door. He stopped, turned back to me and said, "Why would you do that, Mr. Snow? Why would you 'intimidate' Vic Bronson at his office?"

"Because I believe he is taking a less-than-legal approach to buying property on the cheap in Mexicantown," I said. "That or he's being used. People are getting hurt. Even killed. And I'd like to know why."

Detective Aswan nodded. "So, do I have your word you will not bother Mr. Bronson at his office again?"

"You have my word I will not bother Mr. Bronson at his office again, Detective."

He smiled. "Why doesn't that fill me with confidence?"

I lifted my cup of coffee to him. "I think you're going to be an outstanding detective, Detective."

He left.

"Everyone seems to either love you or want you dead," Tatina said.

"Which side are you coming down on?" I said.

"Let's take it day by day," she said, pouring two freezing cold tumblers of Long Road Distillers' aquavit, which I had turned her on to the year before.

181

"I could have sworn you tossed all my booze, lady," I said.

"I did," she said. "I bought this today because I know you can handle your drink. *If* you moderate it. And I knew there would be a reason to celebrate."

"And that reason is?"

"I'm young, pretty, smart and have a doctorate degree in cultural anthropology," she said.

"Nothing involving me?"

"And you have good taste in women." She lifted her glass. "Cheers!"

I suggested, since I was still dressed to the nines from my visit to Hunter Enterprises, that we have a swanky dinner. Maybe Republic. Or Vertical. She said she didn't have anything swanky to wear. I said she'd look like royalty in a burlap sack. She said I looked fabulous in my suit. I said I knew that. She said she wanted to see me without a stitch on.

We ordered a pizza a couple hours later.

At 3:30 A.M. I gave her a light kiss on the forehead and dressed in tactical black for an early morning's work.

182

18

Like most multimillionaires and billionaires
— save for me and Warren Buffett — Vic
Bronson felt compelled by virtue of his
wealth to build a home that required its own
access road and zip code. To that end,
Bronson had cleared four acres of pristine
woodland in the affluent northwest Detroit
village of Franklin to accommodate a
twelve-thousand-square-foot reinforced-
concrete-and-steel monstrosity that included ten bedrooms, an indoor Olympic-
sized swimming pool, game and video
entertainment suite, indoor basketball
court, two professional kitchens, conference
room, security suite and a hermetically
sealed, environmentally regulated computer
server network.

The helipad on top of the house was still
under construction.

In fact, much of the house was still under
construction, including the modest twenty-

eight-hundred-square-foot guest-house, which, one might assume, would be used for visits from any of his five adult and two teenage children (by three ex-wives), who were, not unlike his semen, spread across the US, Canada, Mexico and Europe.

My original intent was recon — to observe who came and went over several evenings, take pictures, have Lucy run them through her facial recognition software and see if any winners popped up.

Itching at the back of my mind was the thought that Bronson was being used as a cutout. Unwittingly participating in the execution of someone else's agenda.

Francine Evers, Authentico's accountant, hadn't been able to positively ID the remains of the man fished out of the water treatment tank.

"She said he looked like the guy who came into their office," Bobby Falconi had told me earlier. "But she said something was off about the man on the slab. Honestly, August, she's got these thick trifocal glasses, so —"

"And Jackie?"

"Oh, she was damned sure the body was this guy Sloane," Bobby said. "But after a two-second viewing, she and her lawyer shot outta here like they were late for tea with

184

the queen. Nice gastrocnemii, though."

"Is that, like, coronerspeak for 'legs,' Bobby?"

I was fairly sure Sloane — the *real* Sloane — was either waiting in smoke and fog calculating a new approach vector or, worst-case scenario, in the wind with probably close to $10 million culled from some very bad people. In the latter case, whoever he really worked for was likely to whirl up a shitstorm looking for Sloane, their money and anybody who had even slightly brushed up against his shadow.

That would include me.

Once I was on the perimeter of Bronson's property, though, the prospect of lying prone in snow, felled trees and construction equipment held very little appeal for me. I'd had enough of lying prone in either bug-infested heat or bone-chilling cold as a marine sniper. Plus someone somewhere had put a target on my back. My planned recon evolved into my sitting on a long, curving white leather sofa in Vic Bronson's master bedroom, sipping an impossibly delicious malt whiskey and waiting for old Vic himself to get out of the shower.

I got a bit of a surprise when Vic Bronson exited the bathroom accompanied by the shortest member of his three-man security detail. The little man with the big gun. They were holding hands and laughing in their white terry cloth bathrobes as they trod across an expanse of thick carpet toward the bed.

I said, "Y'all moisturize?"

Bronson jumped at least a foot in the air.

His partner suddenly struck a martial arts stance. I think it was "crouching dickweed, hidden asswipe."

I shot him with a Taser. He did a twelve-hundred-volt jitterbug/krump for maybe three seconds before collapsing unconscious to the floor.

After Bronson recovered from his initial shock, he managed to fumble a phone from the pocket of his plush white robe. "Security alert," he said. "Master bedroom. Security alert."

"Yeah, about that," I said, standing. From my black tactical bag, I proceeded to pour out an arsenal of Tasers, semi-auto pistols, four retractable composite batons and two MAC-10s I'd taken from his now mostly unconscious perimeter security team. "If I were you, I'd start interviewing other personal security firms. In the meantime, why don't you have a seat and we'll have a chat?" I gestured to a corner of his high-tech king-sized bed. "Do I smell lavender with a hint of patchouli?"

"My — bodywash," Bronson said distractedly.

"Seriously, Vic — you need to try African shea butter," I said. "Best moisturizer on the planet."

"I don't keep cash here. Anything else, you can have."

"Wow," I said. "Generous. But let's start with you handing over the truth."

"The — truth?"

"Yeah, I know that's a hard concept for your billion-dollar brain to wrap itself around." He started to say something, but I stopped him. "Before we begin, I should probably warn you: I'm having a really shitty winter so far. My best friend — my godfather — was shot. An old man who owned a building I think you were trying to acquire through less-than-legal means was murdered. Three freshman assassins came after me, and I killed one of them. And a little man called Mr. Sloane made a lot of trouble for me before staging his own death and disappearing with ten million dirty dollars. And that's put me in somebody's crosshairs as the thief —"

"Sloane is — he's dead?" Bronson said.

"He'd like everyone to think so."

"But you . . ."

187

"I'm not buying it," I said, pacing in front of a clearly distraught Bronson. "I think he's probably been looking for a way out of whatever this is for a long time. The planets aligned in Detroit, and *poof* — he's a ghost."

"Oh, Jesus," Bronson said, his eyes wide with disbelief. "Jesus."

I gestured with the barrel of my Glock for Bronson to sit on his bed. He did with a slouched, defeated posture. "Which brings me to you, Vic. You're up to your neck in whatever this is, and since bad people are making runs at me, I want to know why. And trust me, Vic — I will tag your lavender-and-hint-of-patchouli balls with every Taser I just poured on the floor. *Then* I will start to hurt you."

"Are you going to kill me?" Bronson said.

"As a socially progressive political independent, the temptation is there, but no," I said. "I'm not going to kill you. Truth of the matter is I've got enough on my mind without worrying about which parts of you to bury where and how deep. Now spill."

Bronson nodded once.

"Who the hell is slash was Mr. Sloane?"

"The financial tip of a very dangerous sword," Bronson said. "One that threatens to impale me, my company, you — anybody or anything that gets in its way."

"Who's wielding the sword?"

"I — I don't know," Bronson said. "At this point in time, I don't really care."

"And why's that, Vic?"

Bronson stood and walked to a bedside table. I warned him that a Taser dart in the ass was just as painful as a dart in the nuts. Slowly, he pulled a drawer out and extracted a nicely framed photo. He handed it to me: a young girl — maybe twelve or thirteen — in a school uniform, smiling.

"My youngest daughter, Emmaline," Bronson said, sitting back down on his bed. "Ever hear of a private school just outside of Geneva called l'École de Brève?"

"No."

"Very few have," Bronson said. "Which is why she's there. More than her education — with my financial stature — her safety is paramount." He looked down at his bare feet for a moment. Then he looked up at me with wet eyes. "I'm a billionaire fifteen, twenty times over. And that means I'm either everybody's appointed savior or everybody's favorite villain." Tears began to trail down his cheeks. "I'm — you know — bisexual. I've got seven kids by three ex-wives. Emmaline is the only one that — likes me. Loves me. Of all the chinless worms and brainless slags I've bedded or bred,

Emmaline is the only one I truly love." People can fake a lot of emotions, but Vic wasn't faking. He was truly distraught. Sick to his heart.

He got some other photos and handed them to me: Emmaline with friends, laughing. Emmaline in her dorm room studying.

"They're watching her — and they said that's all they'd do until the deal is done," he said.

"What deal?"

"Upscale, off-book, off-the-grid apartments, condos and houses." He resumed his seat on the bed. Staring at the pictures of his daughter, he continued, "From New York to LA and all viable points in between. 'Ghost towns' is what they call them. Places without addresses expressly for people without names, countries or allegiances."

"Safe houses —"

"Even safe houses have a discernable business architecture," Bronson said. "I know because I've set up safe houses — black sites — for the government. I'm good development cover. But *these* places, these 'ghost towns' — they're different. They're *completely* off the grid. No mail. No utility bills. Nothing. You'd have to buy, well, *everybody:* local politicos, city planners, tax officials, police — *everybody*! Mr. Snow — even *I* don't have that kind of juice."

"Who's the running the operation?"

"I don't exactly know," he said. "I — I've only ever heard stories. In real estate, there's always some convoluted, switchback deals designed to hide off-shore or silent third-, fourth- or fifth-party finances. Panama wasn't the only Central or South American country providing safe haven for mountains of tax-free cash, for drug cartels and politicians. Services to facilitate real estate holdings by North Korea in France and Italy or Russian-fronted land deals in the UK. Chinese back-channel acquisitions in New York City, Chicago and LA." He fell silent for a moment, weighing what he had said and was about to say. "There's a man named Xiang. Young Australian-Chinese man. Very dangerous. Very — convincing. But there's power behind him."

"What power?"

"I don't know," he said. "But I know what power — *real* power — looks like. Feels like. And Xiang's not it."

I stood to leave. A lump was forming in my throat. An extension of the Gordian knot in my stomach. "Do you want someone to assure your daughter's safety?"

"What are you saying?"

"I may know how to keep your daughter

191

safe," I said.

"Cost is no object —"

"This one's on the house."

"Why would you do this?" Bronson said. "It's rather obvious you don't like me."

"The sins of the father should not be visited upon their children," I said. "I don't give a shit about you, Vic. Your hockey team sucks, and your adjustable-rate mortgages are stabbing at the heart of the American Dream. But no kid should have to suffer for their parent's shittiness. I need to hear you give me permission to help your kid."

"They — might hurt her, kill her, if you do something."

"And they might kill her if nobody does anything," I said. "Your choice."

After a moment, he said, "Yes. Help her. Please." He cocked his head like a confused beagle. "How — how would you —"

"Trust me," I said. "You don't want to know." Then I said, "It would pay for you to remember that if you're fucking with me on this or anything else, I will come after you with a vengeance that will make God weep and the devil blush. And neither you with your billions nor men with guns nor nations with bombs will be able to stop me."

"And — this?" he said, nodding to his unconscious lover.

"Sweet dreams, Vic." I gave his hair a playful tousle. "Jesus," I said wiping my hairproduct-slicked hand on my tactical vest. "Lay off the Brylcreem."

Walking past three unconscious, unarmed security personnel and two in a futile, halfconscious struggle against gags and zip ties, I thought about a man I'd met several years back. Less a man than a malevolent being who found perverse reason to consider me a kindred spirit.

An assassin.

I knew him as the Cleaner.

19

I had a little banking trouble a while back.

Not the kind that's easily resolved by a twenty-five-year-old assistant bank manager still wearing a fresh MBA diaper from the University of Michigan.

No, this was the kind of banking trouble that involved a dead businesswoman, highly trained killers, briefcases full of dirty off-shore money, a rogue CIA agent, the FBI and a phalanx of Detroit cops ready to douse my testicles with lighter fluid and strike a match. Trouble I hadn't asked for and could have easily lived without.

And there was a very erudite professional killer.

More correctly, there was the silhouette of a very erudite assassin who, for whatever unnerving reason, took a liking to me before slithering back into the borderless ether of night.

At the end of it all, I was interviewed for

several long, tedious hours by the FBI, then released.

That early morning when I arrived back at my rental Cadillac, ready to go home and sleep for a good five hours (an eternity for me considering the Afghanistan dreams that occasionally invade my mind), there was a business card tucked beneath one of the car's windshield wiper blades: a card for a pastry shop in the old town of Geneva, Switzerland — La Corsican — with two phone numbers and a tagline: *You deserve a sweet today!*

For several years, I had kept the card in its own security lockbox in a drywall cutout at the back of my guest bedroom closet. I don't know why I kept it. Maybe on my darkest days and cold-sweat nights, I did somehow feel a kinship with this assassin. Maybe I thought he could help me reconcile myself with the dark mirror reflection.

I had a pretty good idea how Pandora must have felt as I thought about opening the box at the back of the closet for the sake of Vic Bronson's daughter.

I called Lucy Three Rivers as I made a pot of coffee, mixed up a batch of huevos rancheros and got some bacon going. Aromas that would certainly coax Tatina out of her sleep and bring her downstairs.

"You in the middle of anything?" I asked.

"Just watching a romantic comedy," Lucy said, "and eating a quart of Ben & Jerry's Lonely Girl Strawberry and Tears ice cream."

"Really?"

"No, jerk wad!" she snapped. "When have I ever — seriously, ever! — given you *any* clue that I was a romantic comedy kinda girl?"

"Well, I don't know," I said, feeling oddly embarrassed that I didn't know what types of movies Lucy liked.

"I *hate* strawberry ice cream!" she bellowed. "Some things don't belong together. Ever. *Never!* Like cow's milk and fruit. Cow's milk is a fat-bloated growth hormone meant for three-hundred-pound calves, *not* humans. And any fruit that carries its seeds on the *outside* —"

"Can you rein in the crazy for a minute, Lucy?" I said.

Lucy stopped talking and tried regulating her breathing. In . . . out . . . and in . . . and out . . .

I took a sip of my coffee, let the eggs cook on low and sat on one of the two stools at my kitchen island.

"Okay," Lucy said, having stowed away her youthful righteous rage. "So what's up,

Sherlock?"

"I need you to trace a phone number for me while I'm on the call," I said. "Simultaneously, I need you to monitor the number to make sure nobody's back tracing it."

"You into some superspy-ninja shit?"

"Can you do that?"

"Well, that's a dumb question," she said before abruptly disconnecting.

Three minutes later Lucy was setting up two laptop computers on my coffee table. Next to the laptops was a large key ring loaded with thumb drives.

"Oh, my God, that smells good!" she said, grabbing one of my burner phones and linking it to a laptop with a USB cable. "I just had Froot Loops with almond milk. Can I have some of that?"

"Yes," I said. "And it's *'May'* I have some?' "

"What*ever.*"

"It does smell good down here." Tatina, descending the staircase wearing my beat-up Wayne State football jersey. "*God morgen,* Lucy."

"Hey, Tats," Lucy said, quickly followed by, "Holy shit! You make Sherlock's funky old jersey look like a Victoria's Secret catalog cover! How do you *do* it?"

"I try to maintain a healthy diet — until I

get here, of course." She and Lucy shared a quick embrace. Seeing all of Lucy's equipment spread out on the coffee table, Tatina said, "What are you doing?"

"Sherlock's gotta make some supersecret, supersecure call," Lucy said, typing at lightning speed.

"Oh, really?" Tatina shot me a look.

I gave Tatina a brief yet concise download of my early-morning activities at Vic Bronson's compound. As I spoke, I watched her eyes, her face, assessed her body language, listened to her breathing.

I came to the conclusion she would make a top-level professional poker player.

"How about I finish breakfast and you do what you have to do?" she said, adding, "And remember, I speak Romandy — Swiss French — German and Italian if you need an interpreter."

"Show-off," I said.

"Not really," she said. "Just goes to show what people can achieve in a country that has an *actual* education system."

"God," Lucy said, squinting at a laptop screen, her fingers flying over the keyboard. "I want to be you when I'm in my thirties, Tats."

"*Barely* in my thirties, young lady." Tatina laughed.

"Okay, Sherlock," Lucy said, flopping back on my sofa. "Cross your fingers and clench your butt cheeks. Ready when you are."

It's always best to enjoy a hearty breakfast with loved ones before talking to a contract killer.

"Next time August comes to Oslo, you should come, too, Lucy," Tatina said.

The thought of chaperoning Lucy had me grinding my teeth for a moment.

"They got natives there?" Lucy said with a mouthful of huevos rancheros.

"The Sami," Tatina said. "Very beautiful and proud people."

Breakfast gave me time to think through what exactly to say to an assassin. It was quite possible he was dead, a victim of his own profession. If that was the case, I'd find another way to protect Bronson's daughter. Of course, if he *did* answer, I doubted any conversation I might have with him would begin with "Hey, you got a minute, old pal? Yeah, hey, let me run something past you . . ."

After an hour or so, I said it was time to make the call.

"What exactly do you know about this man?" Tatina said.

"He's a hit man, maybe in his late fifties, early sixties." I felt my mouth go dry, and I may have audibly gulped. "Smart. Erudite. Efficient. And for some reason he took a shine to me."

"Maybe he recognizes the good in you that he once saw in himself," Tatina said.

"And maybe he sees a talented killer who can talk shop."

"Either way," Tatina said, giving me a light kiss on my lips, "think only of the girl you're trying to help."

In for a penny, in for a pound.

I called the number on the card.

"Clock's running," Lucy whispered, her eyes fluttering over her two laptop screens.

After a few seconds, a woman's voice came through: *"La Corsican. Comment puis-je vous aider?"*

"Hi. Hello," I said. "Do you speak English?"

"Oui," the woman said brightly. "Yes."

"Oh, good," I said. "Great. Thank you. I met a man in Detroit, Michigan, a couple years ago. He gave me your card. Said if I ever needed any cleaning done —"

"Back trace started," Lucy whispered.

"I'm sorry, sir," the woman said. "This is a — how do you call it? — shop for sweets."

"Ten seconds," Lucy whispered.

"I apologize," I said. "That was his occupation. Cleaning."

"Six —"

"I actually met him in Traverse City, Michigan," I said.

"Even so, monsieur," the woman said apologetically.

"Hang up!" Lucy shouted.

"Well," I said to the woman, "thanks anyway —"

"Hang up now!"

I disconnected.

"We clean?" I said to Lucy.

"We are clean," she said. "But whoever was tracing the call was next-level good."

After waiting for thirty minutes, I was ready to pull the plug.

The burner phone rang.

"Hello," I said tentatively.

"Mr. Snow?" A man with a not-quite-German accent. "How nice to hear from you. It has certainly been a while."

"The trace has started again!" Lucy whispered.

"Are you tracing this call?" I said to the man I knew only as the Cleaner. "Or do we have a listener?"

"Jesus!" Lucy said. "They're almost on top of us!"

"Oh," the assassin said. "That would be

201

me. Here . . ."

"Three seconds!" Lucy said. Then she said, "Wait a minute — what?"

"Is that better?" the Cleaner said.

"Trace is gone," Lucy said, flopping back on my sofa and sighing with relief.

"That's better," I said. Suddenly, it hit me: I was talking to an internationally wanted criminal who made a living shooting people in the head with custom weaponry. I faltered, cleared my throat and said, "So — uh, yeah — how've *you* been, big guy?"

The looks from Lucy and Tatina were incredulous.

"Do you have people with you, Mr. Snow?"

"No."

"Mr. Snow . . ."

"Yes," I conceded, feeling a lump form in my throat. "No one you need know about — and no one who presents a threat to you now or in the future."

"Good," the Cleaner said. "You struck me as one who could be trusted. Skilled and personable. Which is, of course, why I left you my card."

I told him the reason for my call: I seemed to have made myself the fully dilated pupil in the bull's-eye of a high-end international real estate scheme. A scheme that threatened to populate areas of the city with — well — folks like him. All at a time when regular folks were being bulldozed and buried under the rubble of "progress." And if I was right, he was much closer to the boarding school near Geneva, Switzerland, than I was, and that a young girl needed protection.

"Did you take these people's money, Mr. Snow?" he asked.

"No," I said. "I have no need for it."

There was silence on the line for a moment. Then he said, "I've heard of these people. Hundreds of millions funneled through Hong Kong, Germany, Belgium, Argentina and France. Estate specialists for terrorist cells, weapons and drug dealers, black-market art and antiquities dealers and freelance intelligence. They've grown fast, but like most fast-growth businesses, their layers of management are unstable."

"Have they ever offered *you* work?"

"Yes," he said. "Nothing of interest."

I asked him if he had any interest in providing cover for a schoolgirl in Switzerland.

"I can pay," I added.

"This organization," he said, "they're threatening a child?"

"Yes."

"There are lines one simply does not cross," he said. "That is one of them."

"I'm not asking you to put anyone down," I said for clarification. "Just nonlethal protection."

"I understand," he said. "However, you must agree — there are those in this world who should be culled from the herd."

"I'd rather leave the culling to God."

"My friend," he said, "God is on holiday, and He has left the likes of you and me in charge of pruning His garden."

"I don't even know your name," I heard myself say.

"Try Dieter — August."

"I'll text you the details," I said.

He disconnected.

I doubted very much his name was Dieter.

20

It's rare that I have cause to visit District Six Council Member Nadine Rosado's two-story Colonial in Mexicantown. Jimmy and Carlos had done some work on her house maybe six weeks before, installing a state-of-the-art security system. A job that came from a request through Elena, not me. The last time I was there personally was eight months ago, when I accompanied Elena to a meeting on "energizing community policing and cultural engagement." During that visit, I simply sat by Council Member Rosado's eighty-year-old family heirloom: a Detroit-made Grinnell spinet piano crowned with silver-and-glass-framed family photos going back a hundred years on this side of the southern border.

After that meeting I asked Elena why exactly I had been invited, since I had contributed close to nothing.

"Eye candy," she said, issuing a hearty

laugh. Elena told me that the women —
prominent business owners and community
influencers — had heard about me: My
family roots in the community. The fact that
I was a decorated marine (perhaps a bit
more decorated in Elena's telling). What I'd
done to revitalize Markham Street and the
personal and professional cost this revital-
ization had had for me. And even though I
was no longer a cop, it was thought in this
group that I still had a modicum of "influ-
ence" with the DPD.

Then there were the robusto blends of
truth and fiction that also made the rounds,
whispered legends fluttering on Spanish-
speaking tongues: I was both Batman and
Chupacabra. Superman and Satan. A half-
breed angel with blood-soaked wings in
search of cultural and holy redemption.

Today my intentions were to ask Rosado
if she'd heard any subsonic Detroit City
Council rumblings concerning property
developments or land acquisitions that
weren't exactly kosher.

A shiny black Ford Expedition SUV with
blacked-out windows was parked in front of
Rosado's house on Vinewood. As I was
about to park behind it, her front door
opened, and a tall, lean Black man wearing
a navy-blue wool car coat and matching

fedora exited. Rosado, who had seen him to the door, looked pale, as if she'd just been visited by the ghost of a long-dead deviant uncle.

I rolled past the house and rounded the block.

By the time I came back around, the black SUV was gone.

I parked, bounded up the steps and knocked on the door.

It opened a sliver, a steel chain between Councilwoman Rosado and me.

"Yes?" Rosado said in a mousey voice. Her eyes were red and swollen.

"Remember me, Councilwoman Rosado?" I said.

"Mr. Snow?"

"Yes, ma'am," I said. "August. May I come in?"

"I, uh — maybe tomorrow?" she said, unsure of herself. "Right now — it's — not a good time."

"Maybe it's the perfect time," I said. "Was that City Council President Lincoln Quinn who just left?"

Her eyes widened. "What is it that you want, Mr. Snow?"

"Seems parts of Mexicantown are on someone's secret auction block," I said. "A man has died because of this auction —"

207

"Mr. Ochoa, yes," she said.

"So, you *do* know what I'm talking about."

"No, I — I just assumed —"

"Ms. Rosado," I said. "It's cold. I'm tired. And it's pretty easy to see you're scared. Maybe Lincoln Quinn said something to upset you. How 'bout five minutes and a cup of coffee? Five minutes, then I'll leave. No harm, no foul."

She finally unchained the door and opened it enough for me to enter her house, but not before she checked the street for watchers.

"I — I think I'd like a drink," she said. "May I get you a mescal?"

"I would love a mescal. Gracias."

I actually hated mescal, but in the pursuit of information I thought it best to appear amenable to the foul stuff.

Rosado packed two tumblers with ice and gave each a healthy pour of Mezcal Mano-Negra Tobalá. I suspected she needed it more than I did. By the time I'd lifted my glass to hers and said, "Cheers," she'd downed most of her drink.

I sat in the same seat as the last time, a high-back brown leather recliner near her spinet piano. She sat on her wine-red Jacquard fabric sofa. In an effort to control our conversation, she declared, "The barrio story is you're both benefactor and boogey-man. Which one is sitting in my house, drinking my mescal?"

"Depends on which wire gets tripped."

She slipped a hand between the sofa cushions, extracted a Smith & Wesson S&W500 HI VIZ revolver and pointed it at me.

"Did that come with the sofa?" I said.

"What do you want, Mr. Snow?"

"Well, for starters, I'd like a pen and piece of paper, please."

"Why?"

"Because I need to give you the name of a cleaning service I use on occasion," I said. "You'll need them if you shoot me with that blunderbuss at this range. Otherwise you'll be finding bits of my intestines, spleen, stomach and maybe a kidney in your living room until next June. Not to mention the way you're holding that gun the recoil could break your thumb and sprain your wrist."

"Are you suggesting I can't handle such power?"

"I'm suggesting nobody can handle such power in close quarters," I said. "Do you really want to ruin this comfy recliner?"

"It *is* nice," she said. "My father's. Like this gun. My sister and I gave him the recliner when he retired. He passed away in it ten years later, taking his usual noontime nap in front of *The Price Is Right . . .*" After a second or two, Rosado toggled the safety on her gun and stuffed it back between the sofa cushions.

"Tell me about your visit from Lincoln Quinn."

She was reluctant. So much so that she drained her glass of mescal and took the time to pour herself another.

"What business would that be of yours?" she said.

"I know the bastard," I said. "During my trial he accused me of things that made my dying mother even sicker. I need answers from him on his involvement in a dicey real estate deal in Mexicantown. Maybe you know something. Maybe you don't. Either way, I'd hate to think he was intimidating my district rep."

Rosado searched my eyes for a moment. "She was a good woman, your mother. Your father was a good man, too. He — Lincoln — met with a man named Sloane two or three times in his council office. I'm sure you already know Lincoln is as dirty as they come: building-contract and city-real-estate-inspection kickbacks, velvet-glove treasury department employee extortion. Rumor is he even gets kickbacks from custodial crews at Metro Airport. He was the *real* power behind the old mayor. The kind of power that still keeps the old mayor quiet after sitting in a prison cell for five years." She took a long pull of her drink and stared at the ice cubes. "But this — this is something different. I've been lobbying for a police substation near Clark Park. It made me sick to think I needed his support, but — well, politics." She took a deep, ragged breath, then downed the rest of her mescal before saying, "It was going to be a tablet-to-tablet video chat since I can't stand to be alone in the same room with him. He — he kind of — touches his crotch when we're —"

"Jesus," I said.

She rose from the sofa to pour herself another mescal.

"Did you know there's a glitch in some video-call software, Mr. Snow?" she said, packing her glass with fresh ice. "Apparently, most tech companies offering video-conferencing software have fixed the glitch. The software vendor city council uses hasn't. The problem is this: if I call you on video, your laptop or tablet may ring — if your ringer setting is on — but if you don't pick up, my call still opens a listening line."

For a moment, she disappeared into a side room.

I was kind of hoping she wouldn't return with a shotgun.

Instead, she returned with a tablet computer.

Handing me the tablet, she flopped back onto the sofa. The mescal added a sloppy weight to her body.

"I heard his conversation with Sloane," she said. "And he must have seen me in his call log. I'm sure that's what his visit was all about, trying to find out if I'd listened in through his tablet. I played dumb." She paused, took an audible gulp of mescal, then in a quivering voice said, "I — I think they — this Sloane — he may have had Lincoln's ex-wife killed."

21

The women who ran Café Consuela's in Mexicantown had decided to escape the early onset of another Michigan ice age by jetting off to Mexico for a month's visit with family and friends, which meant my favorite restaurant haunt was closed. Since their homemade pulled pork stew was out of the question, my stomach led me to the change of pace offered by Flowers of Vietnam, a trendy yet intimate Southeast Asian restaurant that stood shoulder to shoulder with small Mexicantown businesses along Vernor Highway.

After a moment of letting the intoxicating warm and spicy aromas play merry hob with my senses, I ordered *bò nướng lá lốt* (sakura pork, prime beef, lemongrass and betel leaves), *cơm chiên Sài Gòn* (Saigon southern fried rice with Chinese sausage, shrimp and garlic lemongrass butter) and *phở chay* (soup with oyster mushrooms, purple yams,

213

beachwood mushrooms and fresh bamboo).

Seated near me, a statuesque blonde woman, unafraid to show an impressive length of her well-toned, shiny legs, smiled. "Could you pass the chili oil?"

I pointed. "Looks like you've got some of your own already."

Her smile faded.

Her legs didn't.

Easing my gluttonous order down to my overjoyed tummy was a *nước sâm* herbal iced tea.

Accompanying me at my feast of Vietnamese delicacies were Council Member Nadine Rosado's tablet and a pair of in-ear headphones.

[*Door closing. Unintelligible voices.*]

QUINN. I thought we agreed not to meet at my office. I don't need mothafuckas nosin' around.

SLOANE. I thought — [*Clears throat.*] Excuse me. I thought the urgency of the matter dictated a brief meeting.

QUINN. What the fuck's so urgent? I told you I was in and so I'm in. Didn't we set protocols for —

SLOANE. We need assurances — further assurances — that — [*Clears throat.*] I'm sorry — would you have a tissue and a bottle of water?

214

QUINN. The fuck's wrong with you, man? I don't need no flu up in —

SLOANE. Cigarette smoke. I walked through a cloud of it coming into this building. Isn't smoking illegal within twenty-five feet of a building? A municipal building, no less? [*Succession of coughs.*]

[*Indeterminate sound. Nose being blown.*]

SLOANE. Thank you.

QUINN. Better?

SLOANE. Yes. Much. Thank you. [*Unintelligible*] just for you.

QUINN. I know. You don't think I know? The right people are getting their cut. Course I might need a bit more cheddar in the short term to guarantee success in the long —

SLOANE. Is that perhaps because of your ex-wife? Alimony demands?

QUINN. The fuck you talkin' about?

SLOANE. You no longer have to worry about that, Councilman Quinn —

[*Unintelligible sounds. Paper rustling.*]

QUINN. Jesus — oh, God — what the — what the fuck did —

SLOANE. You'll be getting a call from the Dallas police. Probably within the next six to twelve hours. Nothing more than a courtesy, since you, of course, are here and she was, of course, there.

QUINN. You —

SLOANE. Unfortunately, the word of a man — any man — is no longer the coin of the realm, wouldn't you agree? Certain . . . precautions . . . must be taken. Guarantees of timely, precise performance —

QUINN. This ain't mine, man. It ain't on me! You can't — I didn't —

SLOANE. Oh, of course you didn't. How could you have? Unless — Well, the talents of a third-rate hit man can always be acquired via the dark net. You don't even have to be in the same city! Isn't that amazing? And like the proverbial elephant, the Internet never forgets. Do you understand what I'm saying, Councilman Quinn? I'd like to make quite sure I'm understood.

[*Long pause. Mumbling.*]

QUINN. You mothafuckas.

SLOANE. What are we asking of you? Barely anything! The deletion of certain building permits and records, vendor applications, tax-roll exclusions. Essentially, we're simply asking you — paying you — to do something you've already proven to be quite skilled at! And at the end of your service, you'll be a very wealthy man.

QUINN. Did — did she —

SLOANE. What? Suffer? I assume her only suffering was being married to you,

216

Councilman. No, we're not in the business of making people needlessly suffer. We're in the business of solving elite-level locational problems and providing safe, reliable, luxury residential solutions. [*Phone rings.*] Excuse me, Councilman. Hello? [*Pause.*] Yes, I will meet you there. Yes. Yes, everything's taken care of. Of course. [*Pause.*] I really must be going. Shall I leave the picture of —

QUINN. No! Get that shit outta here!

SLOANE: Well — thank you for the tissues and water. And you really must stop people from smoking so close to this building. It's a danger to people who actually value their health.

QUINN. I — I don't know if I want to be a part of this anymore.

SLOANE. I don't know if you have much of a choice in the matter.

[*Indeterminate sounds. Footsteps. Sound of a door opening and closing. End of recording.*]

I took my earphones out just as my waiter, a young server with a ginger hipster beard and a variety of earrings, came over to my table.

"Need anything else, Mr. Snow?" the waiter said.

"Yeah," I said. "Hemlock with a splash of tonic."

"How 'bout another iced tea instead?"

"Yeah, let's go with that."

22

It wasn't quite whiteout conditions, but the downfall of snow turned my usually quick drive from Mexicantown to downtown into a white-knuckle, slip-and-slide adventure.

While I was making every effort to avoid fishtailing into road embankments, other vehicles and pedestrians staring at their phones, a call came through the dashboard's entertainment system. It was from the Wayne County Coroner's Office.

"Bobby," I said, accepting the call. "What's up?"

"Did you know there are shoes that cost as much as a new car?" Bobby said, his voice filling the cavernous cabin of the GMC Yukon. "Who the hell buys shoes that cost what a car does?"

Bobby's ongoing analysis of the dead man pulled from the water processing plant had introduced him to the rarified world of custom footwear.

"Figure out that embossed logo yet?" I said.

"Two letters," Bobby said. "Looks like *FM* or *EM*. Second letter could be an *N*. I'll keep trying to raise the embossing."

"Thanks, Bobby."

"One more thing. My fabric-forensics friend? The one who's at the Louvre? I sent her my analysis of the shoe leather. A lot of wastewater had soaked in, but she was still able to make an eighty-five percent determination. She said the tanning methodology and chemical signatures point to a Central or South American manufacture."

"I owe you a single malt, Bobby."

"No, August," he said. "You owe the City of Detroit and the Wayne County Coroner's Office six thousand four hundred thirty-eight dollars and seventeen cents for putting a shoe under a microscope."

"Ouch."

Lincoln Quinn's office at 2 Woodward Avenue, City Hall, would make a *Fortune* 500 CEO envious. It had the overall vibe of an English gentleman's club reading room, complete with varnished dark-wood floor-to-ceiling bookcases, a large Persian rug of indeterminate age, overstuffed leather wingback chairs and an expansive desk that might very well have been an ornate cherry-wood heirloom from John R. Williams, Detroit's first mayor. The office included an impressive lord-of-the-village corner view of Jefferson Avenue and Woodward.

At last estimate, the office had come at a cost of two blackmailed former council members, a couple of black-budget cops taking sizable backhanders, three city Parks and Recreation officials, a senior programmer in the Department of Management and Budget and a tax-roll auditor who was addicted to cocaine and high-end hookers.

But of course, nobody knew nothing about anything, "swear to God."

Being more familiar than most with the visceral seduction of violence, I let myself follow my muse: a focused desire for vengeance in the pursuit of information. A heady mixture — musky, with aromatic notes of blood, bruised flesh and the nickel smell of newly exposed broken bone; it swirled in my nostrils as I, in a state of focused fury bounded up the cracked and crumbling City Hall steps. A weightless, dark energy expanded in me, spreading across my chest.

I was without my Glock — security at City Hall was tight. Most of the guards looked like they'd shoot somebody just to break the boredom.

As the devil's good graces would have it, Quinn was preparing to leave for the day. In tow were his two muscle-bound bodyguards, making their expensive suits look cheap. They seemed more interested in assessing the assets of an attractive middle-aged Black lady passing through the cavernous main floor hallway than in the security of their boss.

Without hesitation or greeting, I walked up to Quinn and gifted him with a solid right cross to the jaw, which instantly laid him out on the cold marble floor.

The first of his security detail to pry his eyes from the woman instinctively reached inside his suit jacket to grab a 9mm, .45 or maybe a Scottish basket hilt broadsword. Who knows? All I knew was by the time he had the handle of his weapon in his hand, I'd jackhammered his solar plexus with my fists and brought an elbow up to his chin. A foot to his chest sent him crashing into his partner, and the two men tumbled ass over elbows down the marble hallway.

"Nothing personal, guys," I said.

I lifted Quinn from the floor by the lapels of his expensive car coat, popped him in his left eye and pushed him hard against a wall.

By this time, we had a wide-eyed, slack-jawed audience, including several cops and security guards who'd suddenly tuned in.

"Remember me, fuck face?" I whispered into Quinn's ear.

"Jesus," Quinn said, blood running from his nose and mouth. "Detective Snow?"

"Freeze, goddammit!" an elderly Black building security guard shouted. He was pointing a revolver at me. Two DPD officers joined the old man, their Glocks leveled at me.

"It's all right, Billy!" Quinn said to the security guard. "Everybody just cool down. It's just a little — haha — dispute over last night's poker game is all. Everything's *cool*! We *cool*!"

I felt the barrel of a gun press into the back of my ribs. One of Quinn's private security guards was leaning hard against me his breath condensating on my neck when he said, "Mothafucka, you'd best be easing up."

I clamped the four fingertips and thumb of my right hand on Quinn's trachea and said, "You're gonna tell this slab of beef to stop humping my ass right now, or swear to God — I will rip out your throat."

Quinn managed to squeak, "Do what he says."

"You sure, boss?"

"Does it look like he's fuckin' around, asshole?" I bellowed.

The barrel of the bodyguard's gun eased out of my ribs, and he took two steps back. I loosened my grip from around Quinn's throat.

One of the cops spoke into his walkie: "City Hall detail eight one eight. We have a situation —"

"We *do not* have a situation!" Quinn shouted. "Now everybody go about your damned business!" He pointed to his bleeding bodyguard. "You're fired. You *and* your partner. I'll leave a jar of pennies on the steps for you."

"Boss —"

"Get the fuck gone!" Quinn said. "Billy, escort these two cooning-and-baffooning jagoffs outta here. They're the real problem!"

"Yessir!" Billy gestured for the two very confused DPD blues to help.

"So, what now, Detective Snow?" Quinn was trembling.

"I'm thinking we move this party to your office, where I can beat the bloody shit outta you and *still* be well within reach of a good scotch."

"How 'bout that scotch first," Quinn said quietly. "Then we can discuss your daily rate for personal protection services."

"Well, I did not see *that* coming."

Behind the closed doors of his opulent office, Quinn was about to offer me what I was sure would have been an exceptional scotch whisky. I gave his left popliteal fossa a good kick. He dropped to his Persian rug.

"You said I was 'screwing' the people of Detroit," I said as he tried to scramble away from any more damage. "You called me a 'con artist' and an 'opportunist.' "

"Hey, man, that's what the *people* was saying about you! If I wanna keep this job, I say what *they* say. It wasn't nothin' personal, man! That's *all* it was, brotha! Politics!"

"My mom lost fifteen pounds during the trial," I said, following him as he crawled away from me. "Couldn't eat. She got sicker and sicker. Down to ninety pounds. Cops my dad knew his whole career — guys he'd partnered with! — blue-walled him. Blood pressure through the roof. Blood sugar spiked. That sound like 'politics' to you, you sonuvabitch?"

"Snow, please — come on, man," Quinn pleaded. "I need *help,* man! Word around town is you somebody who knows how to handle a ruckus. *Any* ruckus! I'll — I can pay you!"

I gave him a light kick in his right knee and said, "I've got enough money to last me ten lifetimes. Why do I need dirty money from you?"

" 'Cause if you don't help me, you gonna regret what you could have done to help Mexicantown — *all of it!* — from turning into a 'ghost town'!"

I gestured for him to get up.

Favoring his left leg, he did.

"Sit at your desk," I said. "Pour us a couple scotches — the *good* stuff — then start talking. And don't even think about reaching for that gun in your desk drawer. You do and that'll be the last ineffectual thing you do on God's green earth."

"How'd you know —"

"About the gun?" I sat in one of the leather wingback chairs in front of his desk. "If I was on the Detroit City Council, I'd sure as hell have one in my desk drawer. *Especially* with a council president like you and constituents like me."

Quinn trembled as he poured two crystal tumblers of whisky, managing to spill only a drop or two from the one he handed me.

I wasn't the one he was scared of anymore.

I could beat his flesh purple and snap his bones one by one, and he'd take it and ask for more — just as long as it meant keeping the *real* boogeyman at bay.

I knocked back my whisky, tossed my

empty crystal tumbler on his Persian rug and said, "So what's got you wanting your worst enemy as your best friend, Councilman?"

"I, uh — I may have gotten myself in a — a seemingly inextricable situation."

"Such as?"

For the next ten minutes, he breathlessly told me about his involvement in a complicated real estate scheme fronted by someone he knew only as "Mr. Sloane." Quinn had taken close to half a million in cash personally and another two million for cash distributions to keep certain real estate purchases and developments off or opaque on the city's books: apartments, luxury condos and housing developments in Detroit's historic and upscale neighborhoods. Indian Village. Boston-Edison. Palmer Woods. And a variety of new condo and apartment developments catering to young nouveaux riches. Properties that would soon to be without street addresses, dots on maps or GPS coordinates.

Ghost towns.

"Electricity?" I said. "Water? Postal service?"

"False fronts and dead drops," Quinn said. "Paid-off city service employees. Cops in the pocket. Plus — these guys —"

"Meaning Sloane."

"Meaning Sloane and the other guy."

"Xiang?"

"No. Xiang's just the tactical delivery boy," Quinn said. "A killer, but mostly just delivers money, assignments, threats. But *his* boss? The Albino? That mothafucka's like middle management — the strategist. You need high-speed Internet? He's got you. Cell and sat-phone service? Done. Medical? Mail? Property management? Everything! Yo goddamn toilet backed up at two in the morning? The Albino's got your back. Until he sticks a knife in it."

"And you're this Albino's point man for 'services,' right?"

"Yeah," Quinn said, his trembling hand pouring another whisky. "Sloane gives this Albino dude a spreadsheet outlining expenses, cash distributions, contacts and contracts, then the Albino gets Sloane more cash to make the connections."

"And you're one of the 'connections.'"

Quinn fell silent for a moment, staring into the small, glimmering amber pool of his whisky. His red eyes began to flood, and his breathing became uneven. I suspected even the devil felt the occasional crushing remorse and loneliness at having been the only angel his father never loved.

"Why me? Why now?" I said, though I already knew.

"I, uh —" he began, still staring at his drink. He inhaled a ragged breath. "I think — my ex-wife — They may have —"

A knock on his office door.

"Councilman Quinn?" a voice said.

Quinn quickly settled, wiping his wet eyes on a sleeve and reacquiring an easygoing smile. He sat back in his chair and began casually swiveling from side to side. The consummate political showman.

"Yeah?" Quinn called out.

"Detective Captain Leo Cowling, DPD. Are you all right, sir?"

"Leo! Get on in here, my brother!"

He did.

With two patrolmen in tow.

I turned in my chair and gave him a fetching smile and a dashingly nonchalant salute. He returned neither.

"I understand there was a dustup earlier, sir?" Cowling said. "One maybe even involving this man?" He nodded to me.

"You don't come around much anymore, Leo," Quinn said brightly. "I miss our chats. You good, son?"

Cowling suddenly looked unnerved. "Uh — yeah — yessir — I'm good."

"A 'dustup.'" Quinn laughed. "Naw, ma

229

man. Ain't no dustup round here. Just a couple brothas in the middle of burying the hatchet is all!"

"Kinda looks like one of them hatchets got buried in your eye, Councilman," Cowling said.

Quinn's left eye was puffy, about to close from swelling.

"Club Brutus," Quinn lied with the quick believability of a seasoned politician. "Noon-time boxing workout. You belong to Club Brutus, Leo?"

"No, sir."

"Well, we'll have to get you a member-ship, won't we?" Quinn said. "You belong, right, Snow?"

"I do," I said, giving Cowling a scrutiniz-ing look. "They are, however, fairly selective in their membership criteria."

"Can't be that selective if you there," Cowling grumbled.

"Is there anything else, Leo?" Quinn said.

When someone like Lincoln Quinn says, "Is there anything else?" that usually means your audience is at an end.

Cowling said, "No, sir," then turned to the door. "Yo, Snow — I'd love to catch up with you later this evening, tomorrow morn-ing latest."

"Sure, Leo," I said. "Maybe over a nice

breakfast at Schmear's? Or maybe cocktails at Republic?"

He left without a word.

I stood.

"Where you going?" Quinn said, panicked.

"Home."

"But —"

"As soon as Councilwoman Rosado gets your approval on a DPD substation in Mexicantown, we can resume our conversation," I said. "Until then, you might want to sleep with a .50 caliber rifle under your pillow."

"My ass is hangin' out on this one, Snow!"

"And I couldn't care less," I said. "Your paymaster? Sloane? He's disappeared with ten million cash. Maybe more. I'm betting somebody wants to know where their money is. How much you want to bet that 'somebody' will try to sweat both of us, starting with you?"

"Snow!"

While descending the steps of City Hall, I made a call to Lucy Three Rivers.

"Tell me you got everything," I said.

"From first punch to macho luchadore exit line," Lucy said.

"Good," I said. "And you know what to do."

"I get raw copies out to your FBI friends

231

and to this Leo Cowling dude," she said. "You *do* know you're not gonna come out of this smelling like extra-virgin olive oil?"

"Yeah, I know. But aggravated assault is way less time than racketeering, conspiracy to commit grand larceny and accomplice to murder." There was a long pause, and not knowing if I'd lost my connection, I said, "Lucy?"

"Yeah, I'm still here," she said. She drew in a long, slow breath, then said, "If you don't mind my saying, Sherlock, that beat-down of this Quinn dude and his body-guards? Pretty savage. You're starting to worry me. And I don't really worry about nobody. But *you*? I kinda look to you when it comes to doing the *right* thing, ya know? And that was seriously fucked up, dude."

"My mother died from ovarian cancer during my wrongful dismissal lawsuit," I said. "She heard and read what that bastard said about me, and it made her sicker. Quinn got off light today, Lucy."

"Somehow, I don't think your mom is looking down on her baby boy from a Christian heaven and saying, 'Yeah! Kick the bloody fuck out of that guy!' " Lucy said. "Just my two cents, Sherlock. Adjusted for inflation."

23

Every fiber of my being wanted Tatina to go.

To run as far away from me as possible.

I could feel what I was becoming and, perhaps, had always been — a perpetually evolving Möbius strip capable of attracting only dark materials while repelling the healing properties of light. One for whom the answer to every problem was the strike of a fist or the squeeze of a trigger. One for whom collateral damage was easily forgiven through a fleeting sanctimonious thought and well-rehearsed Catholic prayer.

I was looking at my hands; they were trembling.

Not from fear but from dark and violent energy yet to be released.

A prince in the kingdom of spilled blood.

I was sitting on my sofa, Tatina kneeling at my side, gently icing my bruised and swollen knuckles. She said nothing. I joined her in her silence. After a time, she stood and walked to the kitchen, where she gave a fresh bottle of Iron Fish Maple Bourbon a healthy pour into a tumbler and brought it to me.

"When did you get this?" I said, taking the glass from her.

"Elena and I went shopping today," she said. "She wanted to get Tomás some new clothes since he lost weight in the hospital."

"You get anything?"

"The whiskey," she said. "For you."

"I thought you were cutting me back on the booze."

"I brought you a glass," she said, "not the bottle. Appreciate the glass."

Then I felt it. A teardrop on my hand. I went to wipe away her tears. She brushed my hand away.

"No," she said, abruptly turning and walking to the kitchen.

I followed.

Without looking at me, she said, "I hate crying. It's a waste of time and effort and it's selfish." She sucked in a ragged breath of air. "That's what my mother said to me once. I was nine. A couple of teenaged boys tried to catch me — rape me — by the docks in Mogadishu. I outran them. I knew places to hide no one else knew. When I got home, I told my mother. I was crying when I told her. She let me cry for a little, then she said, 'Stop,' and I did. 'Crying is good for the soul when you have the time and luxury,' she said. 'Here, in this place, there is neither the time nor the luxury. In this place, tears are a waste of water and salt. It is your mind, skills and Allah that kept you safe and brought you home to me. Focus on and be grateful for these things.' " After a breath, she brought her wet eyes to mine and said, "You make me cry, August. Your chosen distances. Your hard silences. Choosing to be alone with your burdens. You make me cry for *these* things — and I don't know if it's a waste of water and salt. If it is, I'll go home and remember you always."

Two hours later we were standing at the main altar of St. Al's on Washington Boulevard facing Father Grabowski.

"Let me see if I'm hearing you on this," Grabowski said. "You're not engaged. And you're not asking me to marry you. But you want your commitment to each other consecrated before each other and God?"

"Yep," I said. "That's about right."

"*About* right ain't good enough, son," he said sternly. "It either is or it ain't. God don't do just 'about right.' "

"Yes," I said. "We want to do this."

235

"Tatina?" Father Grabowski said. "Are you a Catholic?"

"Muslim," she said, "with a bit of my father's German Protestantism in the mix. Mostly these days I must confess to being more of a pantheist."

"You ain't alone, sister," Grabowski said. "Still, you want this of your own free will?"

"Yes, Father," she said. "With only one condition."

I felt my heart skip a beat.

She told the old man her condition. Grabowski let loose with a belly laugh that bounced off the marble walls of the cavern of the church.

"Darlin'," Grabowski finally said while pointing an arthritically bent finger at me, "I've been pushing that agenda for the past ten years with this guy. Hope you got more pull than me. Does she, August?"

I swallowed hard and said, "Yes."

After a moment of staring at us, the old man laughed, gave his hands a clap and said, "Well, *all right*! What are we waiting for? Let's *do* this thing, people!"

After blessing the two Pomellato eighteen-karat bands we'd quickly bought and had sized, Father Grabowski performed a brilliantly improvised "commitment" ceremony including scripture from Proverbs 16:3,

Philippians 3:13–14 and Corinthians 13:7. He told Tatina stories about me as a boy that had my cheeks flushed and brought her to both laughter and tears. And after Tatina and I exchanged rings, Grabowski said, "I now declare you committed in the eyes of the Lord to each other. No secrets or jealousies, fears or challenges of heart, mind, body and soul shall break this bond. And if you do decide to close the deal with *actual* marriage later on, tell whoever performs the ceremony I've already cut about thirty minutes from whatever they would do, so you get a thirty percent discount."

Tatina wanted a few minutes alone to pray at the altar, so Father Grabowski and I sat in a pew at the back of the church.

"Well, son," the old man began, "ya done gone and almost did it. Just remember what Saint Francis said."

"That being?"

"A man doesn't know what happiness is until he's married. By then, it's too late."

"Ah," I said. "The Gospel according to Saint Francis Sinatra."

After a quiet moment, Father Grabowski said, "Thanks for this, August."

"For what, old man?"

"This," he said. "My last service here. The diocese is making some — changes. Old

237

sandal-and-frock-wearing hippie Francis-
cans like me are out. Bringing in some
youngblood who's never held a chalice in
his life. Figure he'll appeal more to the new
monied kids that have moved back to the
city."

"That's bullshit," I said.

"This is still a House of God, August, so
watch your freakin' mouth," the old priest
said. "I guess I've been ready to go for a
while. And I think God's had a pasture
ready for me for the past ten, twelve years."

"You baptized me," I heard myself say
quietly.

"That I did," he said. Lifting one of my
hands and examining my swollen and
bruised knuckles, he said, "In the service of
a good choice gone bad?"

"Bad choice that felt really good."

"I'll pray for you."

"Since you've been fired, your prayers got
any juice in 'em?"

Tatina stood, bowed to the altar, then
turned and began walking our way.

"And no," the old man scowled at me. "A
big, fat donation from you while you're
smoking Cohiba cigars and bending the ear
of the archbishop is not something I want
you to do for me, August."

"I didn't say anything."

238

"Like you said — I baptized you. I *know* you, son."

Before leaving St. Al's, Tatina gave the old man a hug and a kiss on his furry cheek.

I hugged him, too, whispering, "I love you, old man."

He whispered back, "I love you, too, August Octavio Snow. And remember the promise you made to me *and* Tatina in front of God the Father."

Then Tatina and I left to celebrate our commitment.

It was a cold Tuesday evening and we were in luck: to celebrate our neo-nonnuptials, Tatina and I went to the Northern Lights Lounge on West Baltimore.

Northern Lights has the look of a large sixties basement recreation room where neighbors collect to drink Falstaff beer, throw darts, play air hockey and bullshit while surrounded by knotty pine walls decorated with posters and memorabilia of Marvin Gaye or maybe the great Alex Karras, Lions number 71, 1958–70.

The food at Northern Lights is simple, nicely portioned and damned good. The drinks are never shorted and they're reasonably priced. The service is quick and often quite attractive.

And it was the one night of the week that one of the last living Motown Funk Brothers — Mr. Dennis Coffey — demonstrated his still-enviable mastery of the jazz-funk-soul guitar.

Tatina, needless to say, was beside herself. I had taken her to the Motown Museum on one of her previous visits.

"Oh, my *God*!" she said as she watched Coffey and his band set up. "My father *loved* him. Absolutely *adored* him! Remember 'Scorpio'? My father played that *all* the time! He'd do that stupid white man dance and play air guitar until the family couldn't breathe from laughing."

She went on to regale me once again with her knowledge of Motown by listing some of the songs Coffey and his Funk Brothers had played on: "War," "Just My Imagination," "Bernadette," "Someday We'll Be Together" and more. During the band's break, Tatina even got to shake Coffey's hand and tell him what a lifesaver his music had been for her family.

We closed the place.

I dropped Tatina at the front door of my — *our* house and maneuvered the lumbering tonnage of the GMC Yukon up the narrow drive, into the shed/garage, which barely accommodated the beast.

Once I'd dropped the shed door and locked it with my code, I started through the accumulation of snow to the back door of the house.

I didn't make it.

Once I'd dropped the shed door and locked it with my code, I started through the accumulation of snow to the back door of the house.

I didn't make it.

24

Slowly, I regained consciousness.

As I did, I found myself simultaneously shivering from excessive cold and baking from a stinging heat.

It didn't take my recovering consciousness long to find I was naked and tied to a wooden chair, its legs reinforced with rough-hewn wooden wedges nailed to the floor. My ankles and wrists were double zip-tied to the chair's legs and arms.

There was no bottom to the chair, and I sat suspended by my thighs on the seat frame.

As the fog swirling behind my eyes cleared, I discovered why I was simultaneously freezing and baking: while two high-powered halogen work lights on tripods, powered by a portable generator, slow roasted the front of my body, I was exposed to a broken window behind me and to the left. Michigan's icy and unrelenting winter winds rippled across my back.

"Good," a silhouetted figure said, standing between the blinding work lamps. "You're awake. 'Bout damned time."

"Who — who are you?"

"I, my friend, am the ugly aftermath of a self-proclaimed honorable man," the figure said, slowly approaching me. "The cold, grey ash blown away after a long-forgotten fire."

The smell of this place — crumbling red brick, waterlogged concrete, rusted steel and rotting wood — was familiar . . .

I squinted at the silhouette as it approached. "You might want to be a little more specific?"

The man stopped a couple feet in front of me and leaned forward: a rugged Black man, maybe in his late forties, with chiseled features and dark, fathomless eyes. He grinned, exposing perfect white teeth.

"How's this for 'specific,' Detective Snow?" he said.

I may have still been in a pharmaceutically induced fog, but I knew that face.

"Lieutenant Hayes?" I heard myself say.

"Bingo!" he said. "Detective Lieutenant Valentino Hayes, Fourteenth Precinct, mayor's DPD protective detail, *sir!*" He suddenly came to attention and snapped a crisp salute. As he eased out of his salute, his steady dark eyes met mine. "Of course, you changed all of that, didn't you? You changed *every*thing."

"I did what I had to do —"

A quick, jagged-knuckled right cross to my left cheek.

"You blew up the worlds of fifteen good men!" he growled. "You dug a trench, and one by one you threw their bodies in. *Including* me! Seven years! Seven fucking years in Jackson because of you and your smug, sanctimonious arrogance. You have any idea what a special hell prison is for somebody who gave blood, muscle and bone for a city he served and protected?"

"You were bought-and-paid-for muscle," I said. "An extortionist who collected and distributed bribes, then licked his chops at the dirty money he pocketed." I spat out some blood. Even in a rage, he delivered a punch I could take. For a while. "You and Marco Jennings and Sal Lanzotti and that nut-sack mouth breather Neil Bayman broke legs, kneecapped and honey trapped on behalf of the old mayor."

Another right cross to my jaw.

Blood pressure: 160 over 70.

Bruised but not broken.

"Cheap thugs in polyester pimp suits hiding behind shit-stained badges," I continued. "Wha'd the newspapers call you and your crew? The Four Horsemen of the Apocalypse? Of course, the news never gets it right. They should have called you guys the Four Fuckin' Stooges."

Hayes unleashed a right cross, a left cross and another right before landing a solid, lingering punch to my midsection, forcing every bit of air out of me. I figured even with his current level of brutality, I could last maybe twenty minutes, a half hour. After that, it was anybody's guess.

With a gloved hand, Hayes grabbed my throat, and bringing his face within inches of mine, he hissed, "Jennings got out a year before me. Spent a grand at a strip club, then went to the restroom and ate a bullet. Lanzotti? Opioid overdose, probably from his back troubles. See, he got the shit kicked out of him in Jackson before he was released. Good men who just needed a little more cash for their wives. Their kids. So please, Detective Snow. If you would. Spare me your self-righteous, holier-than-fucking-thou assessment."

He released his choke hold on my throat.

As thanks, I slammed my forehead hard against the bridge of his nose.

A Scottish Kiss.

Hayes stumbled back, his nose bloodied. He laughed. Then he said, "I could use some coffee. You want some coffee?"

"Cut me free and I forget about this whole thing," I said. I could feel the zip ties biting into my wrists, my ankles. "I'll even pay you. What's your asking price these days?"

At a small table behind the work lights, Hayes poured steaming black coffee from a thermos into two white Styrofoam cups.

"Oh, no, see, I'm already spoken for, sweet cheeks," he said, blowing the steam away from one cup and taking a cautious sip. "Imagine my surprise when I find an envelope with twenty-five crisp C-notes slipped under the door of my one-bedroom apartment in Redford and a note kindly requesting me to give former detective lieutenant and gold-plated snitch August Octavio Snow a nice little tune-up. You know, it felt just like Christmas! Apparently, you've been a naughty boy, Detective Snow, making off with somebody's five mil, for which I get a ten percent recovery fee —"

"It's *ten* mil, you fucking moron," I said. "And I don't have their money. But listen: I'll hand deliver two mil of my money. Cash. All you have to do is —"

"No, see, you don't understand," Hayes said, walking toward me with a cup of coffee in each hand. "I would do this for *free*! Here's the thing: life on the inside was hard, but it was made just a touch harder when I got served divorce papers. My kids — two sons and a daughter — they wouldn't visit me or take my calls. My letters went unanswered. Next thing I know, my wife's granted sole custody of the kids, and the nice brick Tudor with leaded glass windows in Palmer Park? Poof! Sold! Ah, well — here's your coffee."

He pitched the scalding hot liquid at my exposed genitals.

I screamed, bright shards of light corkscrewing into my optic nerves.

Hayes knelt and said, "So, see — I have no interest in your blood money. I'd be *right* here, *right* now, doing this for a Popeyes two-piece chicken dinner with red beans and rice."

"I need . . ." I heard myself say with a wheeze

"What?" Hayes said, bending closer to me. "What do you need, Detective Snow? An intermission from our feature presentation? A go-potty break?"

"I . . . need . . ."

"Go ahead, sunshine!" He laughed. "Spit it out!"

"An eleven-letter word for the study of

247

letters and spelling."

Slowly, Hayes stood.

He took a sip of his coffee, then threw the rest at my chest.

"Oh, you a funny mothafucka, huh?" he said. "Let's see you laugh this off."

Right cross to my jaw.

Left cross.

Foot to the stomach.

Another right cross.

Barely conscious.

Spit out a piece of a molar.

"Orthography," I heard myself say. "*That's* the word! Now I need a five-letter word for asshole. Wait a minute. Is it — 'Hayes'?"

Hayes walked back to the small table behind the work lights. He unzipped a small nylon backpack, fished around inside for a moment or two, then walked back to me. My body begun convulsing from the cold on my back.

"You know," Hayes began, "I've always wondered about you, Detective Snow. Half-Mexican, half-Black. Myself? Somewhere in the way-back woodpile, there's an Irishman who couldn't keep his pudgy shillelagh out of the molasses. But, well, like they say — an Irishman ain't nothin' but a niggah turned inside out, right? But *you*? Black *and* Mexican? How's *that* work? Can you tell

248

which side is which?" He held up a carpenter's knife for me to see and slid the blade out a quarter inch. "Maybe I can help with that. I think maybe your Black side is — on the right."

Slowly, he began carving.

Arcs of white electricity throughout my body.

I screamed and felt myself losing the battle to remain conscious. I *wanted* to lose the battle.

I must have mumbled something.

"Oh, wow," Hayes said, standing erect with the blade covered in my blood. " *'Pater, in manus tuas commendo spiritum meum'*? Father, into thy hands I commit my spirit? You know, *I* was a Catholic once, Detective Snow." He made the Sign of the Cross, then gave a dismissive shrug. "Maybe I'll look into it again when they anoint one of them purple niggahs from Nigeria pope. But you? You think you're all innocence and light being sacrificed on an altar of evil miscreants." He leaned into me and began carving an *M* into my left pectoral. "Let this be the weight of your cross, my son."

As I dissolved in the hydrochloric acid of pain-induced memory, I saw each of my sins. Clearly. Precisely. Horrifically. None worse than killing that boy in Afghanistan.

Perhaps this moment was my payment. My due.

"Still with me?" Hayes said. He was wiping his hands with a rag.

I may have been mumbling the Lord's Prayer in Latin.

"You know your greatest sin, Detective Snow?" Hayes began. He slapped my cheek several times. "Hey! Stay with me, sunshine! Your greatest sin is pride. You think you're better than everybody else. More — noble. As if sanctioned by God to be His example on earth to man. Don't shrinks call that a messiah complex?" He pulled a Ruger 9mm from a shoulder harness. "Let's see how much of a messiah you *truly* are. Tune-up be damned — I'm ready to empty a clip in you, wait around for three days and see if you come back for my ass." He chambered a bullet and pressed the cold barrel to my forehead. "Ready?"

"Stop!"

A voice behind me.

A woman's voice.

Tatina.

His eyes cut away from me for a split second. "Who the fuck are *you*?"

"I'm with him —" she said.

"And I'm his godmother."

Elena?

250

I tried to look over my shoulder to see them. To make sure my mind wasn't beginning to spiral into delusional wish fulfillment, searching for a moment's comfort before slipping weightless into the great black expanse.

"Ladies," Hayes said, spreading his arms out to his sides. "We were just having a little fun's all! Can't ya see? We're just having one *helluva* good time!"

The crack of a 9mm pistol unleashing a supersonic bullet.

The bullet hit his right shoulder, spinning him. He yelped and dropped to a knee.

"Not very sporting of you," he growled, blood pouring from his shoulder wound. He struggled to his feet. "Ah, well — fuck *all* y'all bitches!" He raised his weapon toward me. Before he could get a shot off, he was met with a volley of six shots from behind me.

He collapsed to the floor.

Dead.

A woman stood over me.

My head wobbled up to see her.

My angel.

Tatina.

"Hi, honey," I said, my words slurring. "I'm not — you know — feeling too good."

"It's all right," she said. "Jesus. What did

251

he do to you?"

I looked down. Elena was cutting the zip ties restraining me.

"Is — is it just me, or is it cold in here? I'm cold. *And* hot," I said as they lifted me out of the chair. "And where is here?"

"One of the buildings around Russell Street Industries," Elena said. She stripped Valentino Hayes of his long black coat and wrapped me in it. Then she pulled his unlaced boots onto my feet. A little small. Never trust a cop with small feet.

My arms were draped across their shoulders as we found our way out of the crumbling industrial wasteland.

On the street, Tatina shoved me into the back of Elena's Prius.

I laughed. "Holy shit. We — we're making a getaway in a — a *Prius*."

"Stay with me, August!" Tatina said. "Baby, please! Honey? Honey, stay with me! Aaau . . .

". . . gust . . .

". . . staaaay . . .

". . . with . . .

". . . *meeeee* . . ."

And then the lights went out.

25

Marine First Sergeant Michael "Doc" Thornhill took two Taliban bullets: one ripped through his intestines; the other ricocheted off the top left side of his skull, leaving a small portion of his brain exposed.

Nobody thought he was going to make it.

His first words upon awakening after surgery were: "I saw Him. I saw God." After that he wept.

My spotter, Corporal Maximillian "Maxie" Avadenka, took IED shrapnel that tore through his right lung. A shard measuring one-sixteenth of an inch by one-eighth of an inch stopped two centimeters from his beating heart.

Nobody thought he was going to make it.

When I called him two weeks later at the hospital in Wiesbaden, Germany, he said, "I didn't see God or Abraham, Jesus, Muhammad, Buddha, Shiva or the human maker. Sorry to be the one to tell you, altar boy, but after you check out there's just a whole lotta nothin'."

Then there was that cold winter's evening I died in Detroit.

No left or right, up or down, east or west. Just . . .

. . . the sensation of simultaneously expanding and contracting. Falling through invisible arteries where liquid electricity vibrates, spins and flows.

And silence.

The silence of long-past millennia, unheeding and crushing in its loneliness. Then, a whisper to whatever was left of me: "Goodbye . . ."

I am subatomic singularities, superheated and no longer in need of forgiveness in the shell of *Homo sapiens sapiens.*

A pinprick of light growing in the indeterminate distance.

The birth of a scent . . . a river or waterfall . . .

"What the hell you doin' here?"

In my formless, unbound state, I say, "Dad?"

I turn.

See him.

His form is that of a greyish-blue stingray shimmering with bioluminescent light; tendrils float from his belly, and at the tip

254

of his sinuous tail is a pulsing blue spike. Still, he is without question my father.

There's another.

"Octavio?" my mother says. "Does this mean —"

"Of *course* that's what it means, woman," my father says impatiently.

"Still — he looks good," my mother says reassuringly. "In spite of — you know —"

"I've missed you," I hear some incarnation of my voice say. "I've missed you so much. Is this — heaven?"

"It's one of the multinonlinear dimensions of pi-times-quadrillion-squared transitional incarnations of what some folk call 'the afterlife,' " my father says.

We are quiet for a moment. Then I say, "Jesus. You do math now?"

"Never mind that, boy!" my father says. "You ain't supposed to be here for another —"

"But I *want* to be here," I say. "I love you. I —"

"Oh, 'I, I, I,' " my stingray father says mockingly. "Dammit, boy, it ain't *never* been about you. Didn't you ever hear a word I told you? You got time enough for *you.* But right now, you got things to do. Your work ain't done, boy!"

"Have you been eating right?" my mother

says as she circles whatever form I may be in. "You know I worry about you eating right. I mean, if you don't have your health, you don't have anything, right, Octavio? Tell me about your breakfast. How you start your day —"

"He's losing time!" my father says sharply. Then he whispers something to her, and she nods what I think is her head.

"I made your chili," I say to my father. "And your salsa," I say to my mother.

"Mi hermoso chico," my mother says softly to me, "This — it may hurt just a bit. Un poco."

My father arches his spike-tipped tail, then strikes at the center of me. I feel the sharp spike cleave deep into me . . .

. . . whiplash of light . . .

. . . beeping . . .

. . . sudden gasp for air . . .

"Okay, he's back, people! I need twenty ccs of adrenaline! Don't make me wait for it!"

A man in a white mask stood over me, holding two defibrillator paddles in his hands. I tried to say something. It hurt to breathe.

"Don't say anything," the doctor said. "We got you back, and we're gonna take good care of you."

256

The man in the white mask became blurry . . .

. . . faded.

Again, darkness rose.

In a room surrounded by ticking, pulsing, beeping machines. Plastic tubes fed oxygen into my nose while clear liquids dripped into a vein. My chest and ribs were compressed with bandages. Standing over me was a doctor I know. He pressed two fingers into my left wrist while staring at the watch on his other arm.

"Yep," he said, dropping my wrist. "One-fifteen."

"My pulse?"

"The time," Dr. Seibert said. "What? You think people can accurately measure pulse rate by pressing fingers to your wrist? Jesus! That's why we have *technology*, dude!"

"Next time you're here, Doc," I croaked, "maybe you could bring your med school degree? I'm starting to have doubts."

"Yeah, I'm not too good at the whole icky-sticky-poopy-guts thing," he said. "Gives me *agita*. However, I *do* make this look good, huh?"

He stepped away from my bed, did a slow model's catwalk turn while gesturing to his crisp white lab coat. The one that held his

nameplate: DR. TIMOTHY SEIBERT, DETROIT
RECEIVING HOSPITAL, DIRECTOR, THO-
RACIC SURGERY.

I started to applaud, but Seibert pressed a
forefinger to his lips, then pointed to the
visitor's chair next to my bed: Tatina. Curled
up, asleep, her bloodstained silver bubble
coat draped over her.

"Been here for thirty-six hours," Seibert
said. "Had one of my meanest, most ornery
nurses — Nurse LaDelma Jackson — try to
get her the hell outta here after visiting
hours. Delma came back to me with her
dragon tail between her legs. Since then
we've brought your lady friend chicken
soup, sandwiches, coffee and cookies. When
she wakes up, apologize to her for the coffee, okay? It's always been shit here. Maybe
your next donation could take the form of a
cappuccino machine."

Tatina stirred.

"Your 'junk' suffered second-degree
burns," Dr. Seibert whispered. "But according to my ER assistant, Dr. Michelle Ozier,
your, quote, 'eight-pound trout' should be
swimming upstream in a couple weeks.
Would you like to know about your other
injuries or just about your bath buddy?"

Cracked ribs, fractured jaw, fractured right
orbital, collapsed lung (reinflated), cardiac

258

arrest and laceration trauma. He'd stitched the lacerations so there would be minimal scarring. "Instead of a B and an M, when it heals it'll just look like a small E and a V. Which could simply mean you're a guy committed to electric vehicles. Did you know chicks dig guys with scars? Clinical fact!"

Tatina, slowly awakening, mumbled something in German.

"I'll let you two get reacquainted," Dr. Seibert said with a nod to Tatina. "By the way — considering the kind of life I'm pretty sure you sometimes lead and the friends I'm sure you *don't* make — I've registered you here as a homeless John Doe found under the Warren overpass last Tuesday. You've been generous to the hospital, Mr. Snow. Seemed the least I could do. I mean besides saving your life through unparalleled surgical skills."

"Thanks, Doc."

Tatina stood over me. Even with swollen and bloodshot eyes, she was transcendently beautiful.

"I'll let you two catch up," Dr. Seibert said, walking to the door of my room.

"Hey, gorgeous," I said to Tatina.

Considering I was lying in a hospital bed with tubes snaking into my arms and nose

259

and half of my body mummy wrapped in white gauze, the last thing I expected from her was a stinging slap across my already-fractured chops.

Then, with equal ferocity, she kissed me.

"You need to be quiet and listen to me very carefully, Mr. August Octavio Snow," she finally said, fighting back tears. "I know this is part of you: throwing yourself into fires to help someone or prove something. And I am in love with this part of you. I also know there's a — darkness in you that keeps you from me. What I will not accept — from you or anyone else — is using silence and distance to do your lying for you. If we are to be together — here or with an ocean between us — you need to be truthful with me. And you must *trust* me. *Always.* I've been wearing my big-girl panties since I was seven and living in Mogadishu. So, I can handle myself. In daylight and in darkness." She showed me her ring, then said, "Do I keep it on? Or do I take it off?"

"Keep it on," I said.

It might have been the industrial-grade painkillers kaleidoscoping into my bloodstream, but looking into Tatina's eyes, I could have sworn I saw a reflection of my mother and father dancing like young lovers with a bright, self-made world ahead of them in the kitchen as Marvin Gaye and Tammi Terrell sang "Ain't no mountain high enough . . ."

"Thanks for saving my bacon," I finally said.

"Your 'bacon'?" she said. "You mean like your ass?"

"Yes."

"Isn't that why we're all put here?" she said, pressing my hand in hers. "To save each other's 'bacon'?"

"What about Elena?" I said. "She's not a fan of guns."

"All she needed was the right motivation," Tatina said. "The possibility of losing her godson qualified as that."

"How did you find me?"

"That, my love, I'm not sure I should tell you," Tatina said, smiling.

After a moment, I said, "Lucy? Jesus! She put GPS trackers in my clothes?"

"Maybe a year ago she told me. And just your shoes," Tatina said softly. "She worries about you."

"I don't know if I should take her over my knee or buy her a dozen shiny new laptops."

"Buy her the laptops," Tatina said. "Save the knee for me."

"Wow," I said, feeling myself tumble into

the gravity of her eyes. "Smart, tough and sexy. We'll make a Detroiter out of you yet."

With the defiance of an *adalwulf*'s daughter, Tatina said, "And like a Detroiter would, it's time to take the fight to those who did this to you. Finish them. Because you and me, Mr. Snow? *We* are just starting."

26

Considering I was listed as a John Doe at Detroit Receiving, I hadn't quite anticipated the number of visitors I got in my hospital room: Jimmy Radmon, Carlos Rodriguez, Lucy Three Rivers, Carmela and Sylvia and, of course, Tomás and Elena.

Everyone brought food — carne asada tacos, hot tamale pie, chorizo and beef chimichangas, cinnamon-sugar churros, zesty orange custard flan and sopapilla cheesecake. Dr. Seibert allowed the influx of visitor food only after certain confiscations were made for further examination and analysis at the nurses' station.

Of the food, I managed to choke down half of a taco and, courtesy of a stealthy Tomás, a life-affirming sip of Don Julio tequila from his flask.

"You look good, padrino," I said to Tomás. "Getting shot seems to agree with you."

"And you look like shit," he said. He tried

to maintain a tough guy's stoicism, but his bottom lip occasionally trembled, and he frequently looked away from me.

Tomás had been getting back into fighting shape at Club Brutus, which sure as hell beat the dusty free weights in his basement next to his gun locker. Before winter, I'd given Tomás and Elena memberships at Club Brutus. Elena had been enthusiastic about the membership, seeing it as both an opportunity to stay in shape and an activity she and Tomás could do together without actually having to *be* together at the gym. The further convolutions of marriage, I suspect.

Tomás hadn't been as receptive to the membership. At least initially.

"Ain't that where the snooty patooties go to get their sweat on?" he'd said. "I ain't about frontin' with no jelly-ass socialites in ugly designer tracksuits."

"Tell you what," I'd told him. "How 'bout one boxing session?"

He agreed.

A black eye, bruised rib and split lip later, Tomás was a convert. "I get there and Brutus puts me in the ring with a *girl*! A *freakin'* girl! I told him, 'I ain't fightin' no girl!'"

"You mean 'young woman.' "

"Any woman whose half my age and

weight is a girl," Tomás said.

I knew the boxer he was talking about: Abby Cosi, a twentysomething electrical engineer who was drop-dead gorgeous. A lethal beauty with lightning in her feet and thunder in her fists, the latter delivering punishment through hot-pink gloves. Brutus always put new light-to-middleweight boxing students — men and women — to the test with Abby. Part psychology, part physiology. Abby loved the sport and respected its history. Most important, she'd even rung Brutus's bell a couple times. And that's a hard feat for anybody, including me.

"Okay, so this Abby chick — I'm sorry, 'young woman' — she's got a sledgehammer right cross! But I showed her a trick or two. She said my stance was a bit off and I'm dropping my shoulder. Jesus! She even said I danced like an old, arthritic lady! I get pissed, try to pop her with a lead-left combo, and before I know what the hell's going on, she's hammered me *twice* in the solar plexus! I'm bouncin' off the ropes, and she says, 'You always get mad this easy?' Listen, Octavio, can I go again?"

"You've got a membership, Tomás," I told him. "Go whenever you want."

One visitor I had not counted on was Detective Captain Leo Cowling.

"Hard man to track down," Cowling said, taking a chair and crossing his legs. "Any reason for that?"

Outside my room a uniformed patrolman stood sentry.

"Stalkers on Tinder," I said.

"Them the ones put your mummy-wrapped ass in here?"

"No," I said. "Yo momma did that. She likes it rough."

Cowling proceeded to tell me why I was lucky to have been lying busted in a hospital bed for the past four days:

Seems four young professionals had been celebrating the year-end holiday season a bit too much at an office party. After their bellies were full of free jumbo shrimp, craft beer and shots of peppermint schnapps, they had decided to take selfies wearing furry red-and-white Santa hats in front of Robert Graham's Joe Louis fist sculpture on Jefferson Avenue. The large white box with a bright red bow on top of the fist was *begging* for a selfie!

As the drunk revelers struck a variety of poses in front of Joe Louis's giant bronze fist, the box managed to fall and land with a thud in front of the drunk professionals.

Detroit City Council President Lincoln Quinn's severed head, bagged in plastic, rolled out.

"Only reason you ain't in shackles cooling your heels in an eight-by-eight right now," Cowling said, "is because yo buddy at the coroner's office said the decapitation couldn't have happened more than forty-eight hours ago. You been here four days. Leastwise that's what these hospital folk say. Am I gonna have to roast me some nurse ass to get to solid bottom?"

"Contributions to the DR's emergency pediatrics unit and their homeless-vet outreach program buy me a lot of goodwill, Leo," I said. "So far it hasn't bought me any souls. Their records are true."

"Save for the fact you ain't no homeless vet sleeping under no overpass."

"There but for the grace of God," I said. "Have you talked to Jackie Ochoa?"

"In the wind," Cowling said. "Checked out of the Westin three days ago. Card wouldn't go through so she paid cash."

"That's a lot of cash," I said. "CCTV pick up who put Quinn's head on the fist?"

"Just looked like part of the city crew out getting festive shit up on Jefferson and Woodward for the holidays."

"And *you*, Leo?" I said. "What about you?"

"What about me?"

267

"Any reason *you* might have wanted to see Quinn's head separated from his neck?"

Cowling's eyebrows furrowed as he came closer to my bedside.

"I know what you think of me, Snow," he said in a low voice. "And I really don't care. I may have strayed from the blue line a while ago. Maybe even pimped for the old mayor. But Danbury put me right. The captain set me back on the path of the reborn righteous. I'll bleed DPD blue long before I bleed red. Hell, I might even save yo Tex-Mex ass one day in the performance of my sworn duties. As to Lincoln Quinn and my association with him — that died the day Danbury died. Which means that recording you sent me means nothing. To either of us. You feel me?"

Cowling turned to walk to the door of my room. "Forgot to ask. Know anything about a fire and a crispy critter near the Russell Street Industries ruins? Dude got fried by a work-light that fell over on a gas power generator."

"Why would I know anything?" I said.

"How 'bout some young, crazy-ass Jersey trigger-niggah we got in lock-up," Cowling said. "Says you put a beat-down on him."

"Mistaken identity," I said. "Didn't the academy teach you we all look alike?"

"Thought I'd ask," Cowling said. "Get some rest, Snow. I got the damnedest feeling you gonna need it."

As much of a surprise as it was having Detective Captain Leo Cowling visit, it was even more alarming when, an hour later, a "Dr. Enrique Manfredo" entered my room, closed and locked the door, then pointed a suppressed Chinese Type 06 9mm handgun at my nose.

"Let me guess," I said to the young Asian man standing over me. "You're not really Dr. Enrique Manfredo."

Without a word, he took a phone out of his white lab coat, pressed two digits and handed the phone to me.

"Am I speaking with Mr. Snow?" a voice said.

"Speaking," I answered brightly. "Hey, listen, if this is about me renewing my cable service, forget it. Cable's *so* twentieth century."

The man on the other end issued a sincere and robust laugh.

Nothing like killing with an audience that truly wants you dead.

"No," the man said. "I assure you — this is not a solicitation for renewing your cable service. This is an inquiry about thirty million dollars of my money, or rather, my *employer's* money —"

"Wait a minute. Hold on, pal," I said. "When did it become *thirty* million?"

"Ten million cash, twenty million negotiable barrow bonds," the man said. "Indications are *you* took possession of these funds after killing Mr. Sloane. Is this true? And before you answer, Mr. Snow, let me assure you, my associate is nowhere near as patient or forgiving as me. If you have the money and agree to turn it over to me, my associate leaves you to heal peacefully. If, however, you lie to me — things will get very final very fast. Am I understood?"

"Perfectly," I said. "And without further delay or adieu, I declare my innocence."

"Meaning?"

"I don't have your goddamn money," I said. "I never did."

"You killed Mr. Sloane for —"

"Hey, no offense, but are you as deaf, dumb and blind as my swinging dick?" I said. "*Sloane's* got your money. The body in the morgue is a cutout. Some poor homeless vet who mostly fit Sloane's description. Sloane is probably somewhere rolling in a bed of your money and drinking piña coladas. Jesus! Are you telling me I'm *smarter* than some international consortium of brigands and ne'er-do-wells? 'Cause that's really kind of sad."

The other end of the line was quiet for a minute. Then the man said, "Why have you persistently interfered with business that isn't remotely yours to be interested in?"

"An old man I'd known since I was a kid died because of people of questionable moral character that you dangled your money in front of," I said. "This city — *my* motherfucking city! — has gone through enough shit without you importing rich criminals, building luxury apartments and cheating tax rolls that already bleed the poor to death. And the Jersey boys you sent to cap me? The ex-cop, ex-con you paid that put me in the ground? Listen to me very carefully: I didn't take your money — not a fucking dime — but you have for *damned* sure motivated me to snatch the breath out of your fucking lungs."

Silence on the end of the line.

The killer in my room moved the suppressed gun a quarter inch closer to my nose.

"I will, of course, investigate your story, Mr. Snow," the man on the phone finally said. "If you are lying —"

"Let me guess," I said. "You'll put me in the hospital. Did you put Lincoln Quinn's head in a box?"

271

"Sometimes, the wayward enthusiasm of my young associate overextends itself. I hope Mr. Quinn wasn't a friend?"

"He was an asshole," I said. "That doesn't mean I approve of you going around my city lopping heads off."

"Of course not," he said.

"Since we're old pals now, what do I call you?"

"Mr. A," he said. "Or the Albino."

"Seriously?" I said. "Isn't that a little —"

"Goodbye for now, Mr. Snow."

He disconnected.

I tossed the phone back to the young Asian man holding the gun on me. He caught the phone. I said, "Your mom wants you home no later than nine. And pick up some rocky road ice cream on the way."

"You're not funny at all," the young man said. His accent was Australian, not British. A rookie mistake some folks make. "You're just a sad, old beat-to-shit punter. Jesus! Look at you!"

"And you look like this so-called Albino's delivery boy," I said. "So, fuck off."

Slowly, he pressed the supressed barrel of his 9mm to my forehead for a second or two. Smiled. Said, "Trust me, mate; Bob's *not* your uncle. Be seein' ya."

Then he left.

All I could do was lie physically dimin-
ished in my hospital bed and hope the real
Dr. Enrique Manfredo was in a doctors'
lounge somewhere nursing a bump on the
back of his head.

All I could do was lie physically dimin-
ished in my hospital bed and hope the real
Dr. Enrique Machado was in a doctors
lounge somewhere nursing a bump on the
back of his head.

27

There was a shooting at the House of Peace
and Gratitude Mosque in Oslo.

One Somali worshipper badly wounded.

A community in shock.

And a Scandinavian nation stunned,
embarrassed and angered that it had, if only
through the choice of its government-
regulated compassion, joined a bloody
worldwide fraternity of weaponized xeno-
phobia.

Two days after my release from the hospital and return to Markham Street, Tatina
flew home.

It didn't help that countries that once
looked to America for moral leadership saw
only a quicksand empire piling its Black,
brown, red, yellow, Muslim and Jewish
citizens on the AR-15 pyre of "white nation-
alism" led by a depraved former game-show
host.

"I think I know the answer," I said to

Tatina as we sat in my SUV outside of the Delta Air Lines gate at Detroit Metro Airport, "but are you okay?"

"I will be," she said. "This is why you do what you do, August. You have what some might call 'survivorship bias.' Maybe the same is true of me. Violence for you is a fulcrum. Maybe it doesn't solve problems, but it brings a measure of terrifying equilibrium."

"Funny," I said. "I just thought of myself as God's back-alley thug. The guy who'll break your legs then light a novena candle and pray for your speedy recovery. You're not gonna do anything stupid when you get home, are you?"

She kissed me.

Smiled.

"I'm not going to do anything stupid," she said before issuing a tepid laugh. "That's *your* department. What I *am* going to do is get everyone back on schedule. I'm going to begin teaching at the university. I'm going to go shopping. I'm going to go to the farmer's market and buy vegetables and flowers. I'm going to go to the movies. To restaurants. And I'm going — for the first time in a long time — to mosque."

I knew what she was saying.

"Escúchame como se escucha la lluvia," I said.

"Yes," Tatina said. "Listen to me as one listens to the rain." Then she kissed me and whispered, "Soon, my love."

"Soon."

Then she was gone.

When I got home, Jimmy Radmon was seated in the middle of my sofa. "Hey, Mr. Snow," he said. "I figure maybe you can help me with this."

On the coffee table in front of him was a box.

Inside the box was a gun.

I went blind with rage, grabbing the back of Jimmy's shirt collar, lifting him off the sofa and slamming him hard into a wall near the downstairs bathroom.

"What the fuck do you need a gun for?" I said.

"I — I know were you in a ruckus," Jimmy said, apparently as shocked as I was that I'd pinned him against the wall. "Put you in the hospital. You ain't askin' for no help, so I thought —"

"So, you thought you'd help me out by learning how to shoot?" I said. "How to kill? Jesus, kid! What the — You're fucking *better* than that, Jimmy. Better than *me* —"

"Friends help each other out —"

"I don't need your goddamn help!" I said. "I don't need *any*body's fucking help! Go home! Go home and pull your head outta your ass, okay?"

I pushed him toward the door.

"Ain't nobody on this street wouldn't hesitate to help you, boss man," he said. "Least of all me. You done gimme what ain't nobody else in this whole dang world *ever* gimme: a chance. That don't come around to too many folk in this world."

"Jimmy, I —"

"Let me have my say; then you can talk," he said with a defiant power in his voice I'd never heard before. " 'A friend loves at all times, and a brother is born for adversity.' Proverbs 17:17. I'm yo friend and yo brother. You took a chance on me when the world had written me off. See what I'm sayin'?"

I was speechless. Something I hadn't been in a long time.

"Grown man do what a grown man gotta do," Jimmy said as he slipped on his parka. "Y'all need to know that — I'm a grown dang man, Mr. Snow. Whatever child I may have been went gone when I was eight."

Then he left.

My wounds were still tender, and the stitches tugged at the rejoined flesh. My ribs throbbed and my groin burned from the antibiotic salve they'd given me at the hospital. If not for an additional notch in my belt, my pants would have fallen to the floor. All of this in addition to the silence of a house that had recently held Tatina's laugh.

In the kitchen I grabbed the bottle of Old Forester bourbon whiskey from a lower cabinet. There was a sticky note on the bottle, and in Tatina's handwriting it read, "A glass. Not a bottle." Instead of a tumbler, I grabbed an eight-ounce water glass and filled it halfway.

A glass.

Not a bottle.

28

"You remind me of me," Apollonius "Brutus" Jefferies said upon seeing me walk into his downtown fitness club. "A long time and three bullets ago."

"Nice to see you, too, old man," I said. I was wearing my exclusive Club Brutus sweats and Club Brutus–branded Nikes. The shoes fit fine. The sweats bagged on me a bit more than they should have.

Brutus and I clasped hands and gently bumped shoulders.

"Came to see you in the hospital," Brutus said as we walked to his office. "You was out like a light."

"So that's where that rusty precinct boxing medal came from." I laughed.

"Middleweight match I had with your daddy back in the day," Brutus said. "Went a straight ten, both of us wobbling around the ring with double vision, busted lips and aching ribs. I won, but it sure as heck didn't feel like it. That man had some mean Alabama timber rattler in him."

After the glass door to his office closed behind us, he handed me a smoothie — lemongrass, whey protein, banana, blueberries, Vitamin-E oil and coconut oil — and invited me to sit. I did. The walk had winded me.

"Whatchu done got yourself into, young-blood?" Brutus said.

"I don't know what you're —"

"Aw, don't BS me, son," Brutus said. "I didn't get to be a sixty-five-year-old Black man in the United States of Lynchin' Black Folk by not knowin' what BS smelled like from a hundred miles away. Now tell me what's goin' on and why I got four of my members ready to lock 'n' load for you, or you can pick yo sickly butt up and walk on outta here last time right now."

"Four members?" I said.

"Two confidential," Brutus said. "One's a cop, other works at City Hall's as far as I'll go. The third one is K — and K don't have a mean, violent or vindictive bone in his ripped-and-shredded body. Yeah, August! Even K's ready to tear the planet a new one if it would lead to who messed you up!"

K was one of Detroit's many assorted strays I'd picked up over the past few years.

A gentle giant of a man I'd, purely by happenstance, forced to quit two really bad security jobs — one at a crooked bank, the other at a ramshackle strip club that smelled like salmonella and unflushed toilets. I'd recommended him to Brutus as a weight trainer. Last thing in the world I wanted was to be the cause of him leaving *that* job.

"One wouldn't happen to be Jimmy Radmon, would it?" I said.

"You mean the boy hasn't told you?"

"Told me what?" I said feeling a rise in my heart rate and blood pressure.

"I ain't talked to him for a couple weeks," Brutus said as he walked the floor-flush treadmill under his desk. "Wasn't nothin' left I could teach him in karate. That boy just took it all in. Took it all in right to his bones. Never seen anything like it! Since this place is a full-service fitness club and not just a dojo, me and my staff could only take him up to his second-degree black. He's been over at the Detroit Martial Arts Academy on Michigan Avenue for a while now. Sifu Yang ain't taken an apprentice in five years!"

"I had no idea —"

"Okay, enough stalling, August," Brutus said. "You tell me what's going on, or swear to my loving Lord Jesus, I will boot you through the uprights."

For fifteen minutes I told Brutus what I was involved with, what I knew and what I didn't know. I told him about Vic Bronson, the mysterious Mr. Sloane and the thirty million dollars in missing dirty money, my tête-à-tête with City Council President Lincoln Quinn and a young gun Aussie named Xiang. I chose not to tell him about my dark partnership with another assassin called the Cleaner. Or my conflicted relationship with a man who had chosen the moniker Albino.

When I finished, Brutus brought the treadmill to a stop and gave me a hard look. He picked up the receiver of his desk phone and said through the club's PA system, "Abby and K to my office, please."

Ten seconds later, Abby Cosi and K were standing in Brutus's office. K looked fit, happy and dashing in his blue-and-gold Club Brutus sweats, shoes and jacket. We shook hands and I refrained from saying, "Ow!" from his grip. Abby looked healthy, happy and beautiful in short pink shorts, CrossFit athletic shoes and a fashionably ripped T-shirt that read, "Fight Like A Girl." We embraced.

"Doggone it, Abby," Brutus said. "How many times I got to remind you of the dress code?"

"Wait a minute," she said. "There's a *dress code* here?"

K stifled a laugh.

Brutus lowered and shook his head before he got to business. "K? I need you to put ten, twelve pounds of furious muscle on this man." He pointed to me. "Abby? I know you got your day job and everything, but I need you to up this man's boxing game — speed and dexterity. Don't worry about his footing. Footing's good. And I need all this in short order. Can we do this?"

Abby and K agreed they could.

Brutus dismissed the two.

Then he said to me, "I ain't held a weapon in ten years. But as I recall I was a dead-eye shot."

"You've already served the call, Brutus," I said. "But thanks."

"Figured you'd say something like that," Brutus said. "But what youth don't tell you about the truth is friends — *real* friends — are few and far between. Half of 'em are going to disappear when the sun goes down and the monsters come out. Another quarter of 'em gonna screw you for the sheer easy pleasure of violating your trust. And that leaves one-quarter of the folks you been callin' yo 'friends' who actually stand shoulder to shoulder with you when darkness hits the pavement and the beasts come out to play. I stood with yo daddy, boy. I stand with you. And ain't a gosh-dang thing you can do 'bout that. Now, what that smart mouth of yours got to say to *that,* boy?"

I struggled to my feet, snapped a crisp salute and said, "Sir, yes, *sir!*"

My physical rebirth began with K.

"How's your appetite been?" he said. We were in the weight room where a few of the city's movers and shakers were attempting to lift twenty-pound weights.

"All right," I lied. Truth was, I didn't have much of an appetite. Near-death experiences kind of take the joy out of eating since they make you realize everything turns to shit anyway. Tortillas, Kung pao chicken, KFC, it all just becomes fuel for a machine that's bound to fail.

Instead of putting me to work on the machines or free weights, K got both his coat and mine, and we set out for a quick trip to Greektown. Once we returned to the club, we sat in the employee lounge, each of us with a full five-pound rotisserie chicken.

"Weight training is protein training," K said, ripping a leg off his chicken. "It's eating with nothing else in mind but building, fueling and maintaining muscle mass."

"Yeah," I said, "but come on, K — a

whole fucking chicken?"

"Put down half," K said. "That'll be a good start."

And so we began.

After a week of aches and pains courtesy of Abby's squared-circle finesse and the protein-and-weights regimen K had me on, I began feeling my body and mind coming back to me.

"Do you realize how humiliating it is getting hit with pink boxing gloves?" I said to Abby after a strenuous forty minutes in the ring with her. She'd rung my bell at least twice with a lightning-fast left cross and a straight jab that had nearly knocked my mouth guard down my throat.

"Do you realize how hilarious it is to see tough guys like you wobble on your knees after getting hit with pink gloves?"

"Fair enough," I said.

After changing into my street clothes, I planned to forego protein stacking in favor of a Cobb salad at Schmear's Deli. Something that would help move out the pesky remains of four whole rotisserie chickens consumed that week.

As I walked through the first floor of Club Brutus toward the door, members had stopped lifting, running, stretching and cycling. They were all staring up at TVs suspended from the club's ceiling or hung on walls. Vic Bronson, Detroit real estate billionaire, had just suffered a life-threatening heart attack.

29

Time was, all you needed for good sleuthing was snappy banter, a wink and a nod with the ladies, comfortable shoes, an assortment of fake business cards, a high tolerance for whiskey, a few extra bucks you could slip a bent maître d' and maybe a Burberry trench coat with a "gat" stuffed in the deep pocket of thread-bare Brooks Brothers wool slacks.

Nowadays all you need is Hot Pockets Pepperoni Pizza microwave sandwiches to pay a kid with a laptop. In my case, a twenty-year-old Michigan Upper Peninsula Native girl with a bad attitude.

"Why should I help *you*?" Lucy said, sitting on my kitchen counter, arms folded defiantly across her chest. "You hurt Jimmy's feelings."

"How'd you know about Jimmy and me?"

"We're mostly pals. We talk. *And* play video games."

"Okay, listen," I said. "Jimmy and I just had a disagreement about what it means to help a friend —"

"You know he could've taken your face off, right?" she said. "He's, like, this Bruce Lee/Jackie Chan martial arts monster!"

"Lucy!" I said. "Focus! Are you gonna help me or not?"

She stared at me hard for a moment.

"Reimburse Jimmy for the gun," she said, "and apologize to him. And not in that macho-guy kind of 'Hey, bro, we cool 'n' shit? Wanna get some buffalo wings and beers?' way. *No!* I mean a real, honest-to-goodness *apology*!"

After establishing that Jimmy's gun wasn't registered and there was no background check trail that could double back on him (welcome to the Land of the Free and Home of the Well-Armed!), I agreed to buy it from him and lock it away. And I promised Lucy that next time I saw Jimmy I would sincerely apologize. No buffalo wings or beer.

"Seriously?"

"Scout's honor."

"Scouts are like Jesuits, dude," Lucy said. "They *have* no honor. Just promise like yourself. Like a marine."

The security around Vic Bronson at Henry

Ford Hospital was near-impenetrable, and I'm sure every nurse, doctor and orderly within his orbit wasn't only bound by the rules of HIPAA but also NDAs. It probably didn't hurt that while Bronson was being wheeled into Emergency, a couple new state-of-the-art heart-lung machines were being unloaded at the hospital's receiving dock courtesy of a generous donation from Bronson's empire.

Iron fist.

Velvet glove.

Lucy sat on my sofa, eating Twizzlers while two of her laptop screens flickered and flashed with what looked like greetings from Alpha Centauri. I still had ambiguous feelings about using the services of a hacker. I'd had these feeling since first employing the young man who was Lucy's dark-web mentor, Skittles. Both as a marine and a police detective, I had been trained to believe engaging various human "assets" was the quickest way to the truth or a target or both. Something about using backdoor technology as a surgical tool to cut into and extract the heuristically algorithmic data humans had become made me uncomfortable. It felt invasive, cynical and boorish. Then again, I'd recently given the Internet my full name, credit card number, address and clicked "Yes" to Terms of Service I didn't read for the purchase a Pendleton "Sea Chief" wool blanket online, absolutely giddy at the promise of next-day delivery.

Lucy demanded I make veggie tacos while she surfed the black waves of the dark net.

Since my kitchen was my sanctuary and cooking my way of attempting to achieve serenity, I obliged her.

Rough-chopped Vidalia onion, red and green pepper, jalapeño and roasted corn sizzling in unsalted butter. I added porcini mushrooms and cut two avocadoes into chunks. I chopped romaine and butter-crunch lettuce and mixed them together. Finally, I rough chopped Roma tomatoes. I'd long ago given up on stopping Lucy from defacing the culinary art of my tacos with big, messy scoops of sour cream; I set out a tub of the vile stuff for her, and while she worked, she dipped each of four tacos at least twice in the foul glop. I suppose I should have been grateful she didn't eat them the old-school Mexicantown way, like I did when I was growing up; back then ketchup was our salsa.

After an hour, Lucy said, "Bingo, bango, Big Jim's dango."

"Got something?"

"I *always* get something, slick."

I couldn't disagree with her.

On her screens were two hospital admission records, both for Victor Michael Bronson.

"Why are there two admission forms?" I said.

"Because the one on the left was deleted," Lucy said. "Ejected into the airless void of cyberspace. Look at the initial assessment."

I did: three groupings of two red subdural penetrations around the left pectoral muscle.

Jesus.

He'd been tased.

"They were interrogating him," I heard myself say.

"Now look at the form on the right," Lucy said. "Submitted twenty-seven seconds later to Admissions Records Server 898-3C."

No mention of the red marks. Simply, *Male Caucasian, 48. Suspected cardiac arrest.*

Whoever had done this had to have been part of Bronson's security team and, I suspected, in the employ of the man calling himself the Albino.

"Anything else?" I said.

"Holy minestrone," Lucy said, "that's not enough?"

"Don't make me beg, Lucy."

291

"Why not? It's *fun*!" I gave her a look that was far from begging. "Oh, all right," she said. Lucy typed in a string of numbers and letters and hit ENTER. Both screens became live-feed CCTV monitors. "I figured hospital personnel were blocked from making any notation of which room he was in, so I checked the schematic of the hospital and found where their hoity-toity private rooms were located. Then I checked the security CCTV feeds, and wouldn't you know it, the feeds were down on the sixth floor, hall four, rooms three through seven. They physically disconnected most of the cameras, but they missed two. Not the best angles but enough to see Bronson's security huddled around room six seventeen. I figure the other rooms are for his gestapo — three teams, eight-hour shifts. Are you getting married?"

"What?" I said.

Lucy nodded to the ring on my right-hand ring finger. The "commitment" finger. Not the "married."

For whatever reason, I felt my cheeks flush. "No, it's — uh — you know, just friendship rings."

"Wow," Lucy said. "Did you make them yourselves at Bible camp just before the square dance?"

I chose not to answer.

As I got my coat on, Lucy said, "You should marry Tatina, Sherlock. You're in your *thirties,* for God's sakes! Time is not your friend, dude."

Camped out in the expansive lobby of the Henry Ford Hospital were four print reporters, an AM news radio crew and two local TV news teams. I recognized one of the print reporters: Anna Rayling. Anna used to work for one of the big daily newspapers until they weren't so big anymore. She was a good reporter with twenty-five respected years of hard news experience and a couple regional and national awards behind her. Now she was a stringer for several small out-of-state papers and online news organizations.

"How's tricks, Anna?" I said to the short, round Black woman with impossibly large brown eyes.

"If *only* I was turning tricks, big guy," she said, giving me a hug. "Maybe then I could afford healthcare instead of waiting around another six fucking years for Medicare to kick in." She brought up her digital recorder, turned it on and said, "Anything you'd like to say for the record about the rather gruesome death of City Council

President Lincoln Quinn?"

I gently took the recorder from her, turned it off and handed it back to her.

"He was a sorry sack of shit who should have died from embarrassment," I said. "Not beheading."

"He was a bloviating cocksucker," Anna said. "Pardon my newsroom language."

"Anything on Bronson?" I said.

"Zip," she said. "When I got here, they told us there was supposed to be a press conference in a half hour, but that was forty minutes ago. Sure you got nothing for me, August?"

"I got no stories for you, Anna," I lied. "Just a private citizen living a quiet life come to check on an uncle. Spastic colon. Not worth a column inch." I laughed and said, "You just can't quit the game, can you?"

"Taking an online class in medical billing," she said. "And I got a book manuscript out to a couple New York agents."

"Hard-hitting journalism stuff?"

"Romantic time travel."

"Oh."

By eleven that evening, the press conference hadn't materialized.

The print reporters, including Anna, grumbled as they left for the bars along West

294

Grand Boulevard. The radio guys traded swigs from a flask before heading out. The TV news people gave their audience a compelling and thought-provoking live report on the likely reasons the news conference didn't happen. Then they, too, left for a bar.

I told the pretty young receptionist wearing a white burka that I needed to talk to one of Vic Bronson's security guards.

One of Bronson's *smaller* security guards.

She asked my name. I smiled and said, "Elwood Singer. People call me Lockjaw."

After five minutes, the security guard I'd gone toe to toe with at Bronson's office — and Bronson's part-time playmate — entered the lobby.

"Oh, for fuck's sakes," he said upon seeing me. "You want me to call five-oh on you *again,* homeboy?"

"No, *homeboy,*" I said. "I want you to call your boss."

"Maybe you ain't heard, bro, but my boss is lying upstairs —"

"No," I said. "Your *other* boss. The so-called Albino."

He stared at me for a long, hard moment before taking a step into me and harshly whispering, "You, my friend, are a dead man."

"Make the fucking call — bro," I said. "Or they'll be mopping your ball-sack off the lobby floor in about five seconds."

30

As is often the case during a Michigan winter — especially in this, the disconcerting age of climate change — the weather had gone from near-cryogenic with four-foot-high hardened snowdrifts to forty-two degrees, sunshine and the imminent threat of flooding in a day. While most folks chose to complain about Michigan's weather being bipolar, I saw it in a much more positive light: since climate change continues at its current disastrous rate, a humid, 95-degree summer day in Detroit would likely be a skin-shearing 123-degree melanoma factory in LA, Phoenix, Vegas, Dallas and a host of other western and southern cities.

Oh, and Michigan will *still* have a fifth of the world's fresh water.

A large part of my moderately renewed spirit came from the fact that I'd gained back the weight I'd lost due to my torture injuries, and thanks to K at Club Brutus, most of that weight gain was pure muscle. My boxing coach, had mentored me to a faster, more accurate delivery of punches.

"I know Brutus said your footwork was okay," Abby had said to me after our fourth workout, "and for the most part, he's right. But you could — how do I say this? — unclench a little."

" 'Unclench'?"

"Yeah," she said, uncharacteristically embarrassed. "You know. *Unclench.*"

"I'll see what I can do."

Then, of course, there had been the Skype calls with Tatina, which always put a little more testosterone pep in my step.

"You look *fantastic!*" she'd said during one. "And you're feeling healed? Body, mind and spirit?"

"Body, yes. Got a ways to go with mind and spirit," I admitted.

On such a bright and hopeful day, I'd decided to take lunch at Schmear's Deli. I'd invited Jimmy along so that I could offer my sincere apologies to him over good food.

"How'd things go in Windsor with Carlos?" I said as we slid into the third booth, across from the end of the lunch counter.

"Good," Jimmy said. "He ain't making a

lot of money. Yet. But his clientele's expanding, and people seem to like him and his work. I only took half what he was gonna pay me. Didn't seem right to take it all what with him and his family."

"Generosity will be the death of you, Jimmy."

He flashed a big, bright grin and said, "Look who's talkin'."

I felt the warm prickle of embarrassment fan out over my cheeks. Good to know I could at least feel *some*thing besides anger these days, even if it was simple modesty.

"Why didn't you tell me you were over at Detroit Martial Arts Academy?" I said. The lunch crowd was clearing out; it was time for all the kids wearing Kenneth Cole and Donna Karan suits or expensive preshredded jeans and imported plaid shirts to buzz back to their hives to make semibig decisions. I had sucked lungs full of sand and shot Afghan people in the head in order to make the world safe for them to get degrees in marketing communication and international finance, so you'll pardon my rather acerbic assessment of these wastes of space.

"You been busy with other stuff, boss," Jimmy said. "Plus, I wanted to make this decision on my own. No sense botherin' you all the time."

"You've never been a bother to me, Jimmy."

"Mr. Jefferies — Brutus — he introduced me to Sifu Yang over at the academy," Jimmy said. "Mr. Yang, he's — I mean *dang*! He's, like, in his seventies, and I wouldn't bet against him in a fight! But you know what's really cool?"

"What's that, Jimmy?" I said, feeling a genuine familial warmth for the kid.

"Sometimes, after my group lesson, Sifu Yang, me and him, we just meditate, you know?" Jimmy said. "Sometimes he tells me stories about martial-arts masters from a hundred, two hundred years ago. Chinese, Japanese, Korean, Filipino — all these dudes! And it ain't all about fighting and stuff. It's spiritual. Directing the soul's energy. I like that. And I like spending time with Sifu Yang. Drinkin' that oolong tea. It's like being around a grandpa who can't wait to tell you his stories and can't hardly wait to hear yours."

"Listen," I said. "Jimmy. I, uh — I invited you to lunch —"

"Yeah, I know," he said. "So you could apologize to me."

"Video game chat between you and Lucy?"

"Yeah, we — you know — talk sometimes," Jimmy said. "But seriously, ain't nothin' in this world you got to be apologizing to me for. Not a gosh-dang thing. I — That gun? I just wanted you to know they's people — folk like me and Carlos and Lucy and more — that will step up for you. Anytime, anywhere."

"I appreciate that, Jimmy —"

A burst of cold air rushed over the table as the front door of the restaurant opened. My eyes target locked two men who had entered the restaurant. One of the men had threatened me at gunpoint while I lay in my hospital bed. Xiang. The man who had more than likely taken City Council President Lincoln Quinn's head.

The other man was shorter, stoutly built and wearing sunglasses.

A man with albinism.

Both were well dressed.

They were staring at me.

Jimmy shot the men a look. "Trouble?"

"Could be," I said. "You have to leave, Jimmy. Now."

The kid smiled at me. "Ain't always about what *you* want, boss man."

The two new restaurant customers walked to our booth.

The Albino smiled down at Jimmy, gestured to Jimmy's booth seat and said,

"Would you mind, young man?"

"No, sir, not at all," Jimmy said, standing and gesturing for the man to take his seat.

The tall, lean man accompanying his boss gave Jimmy the slow once-over. Jimmy smiled again and slowly took a stool at the counter.

"You may have guessed," the man seated across from me said, "I'm the Albino."

"And I'm the Blaxican," I said. "Tell you the truth, I'm not a real big fan of addressing people based solely on which chromosome got added or subtracted. You got a name, or should I just make one up — like Mookie or Chad?"

The man calling himself the Albino laughed.

"I don't think you're funny," the accomplice said in his thick Aussie accent, staring at me with dead eyes. "I just think you're an asshole."

"You might be right, Crocodile Dundee," I said to the young killer. "But unless or until you're called upon in class, you're on mute."

"Oh, don't pay him any attention," the Albino said. "He takes his work too seriously. I had no interest in sending those three men from New Jersey after you. It was overkill. Literally. Unfortunately, my associate went ahead with the order."

"Some might call that 'initiative,' " I said. "Where I come from, it's called 'insubord-ination.' "

"Ah, well — the help one gets these days, right?" The Albino smiled and glanced at Jimmy.

"He's not 'the help,' " I said. "He's a friend who has nothing to do with this. He walks or I do both you and Bondi Beach fast and ugly."

"I abhor violence," the Albino said. "Your friend is free to leave."

"Think I'll stay," Jimmy said. "I hear they make a really good bacon cheeseburger."

"A man should be free to follow his own path," the Albino said with a decisive nod to Jimmy. "So. You're not uncomfortable with or intimidated by my albinism?"

"I'm uncomfortable with people who chew with their mouth open," I said. "Or people who say 'awesome' for anything that doesn't involve the cosmos or Lupita Nyong'o. And I'm intimidated by really smart people. You're none of those, so I'm good. Far as I can tell, you're just another shitty human being making consistently bad life choices." I jabbed my thumb toward his young killer associate. "And him I'd get a leash for."

Ben Breitler approached our table.

"Why don't we do this?" the Albino said. "Let's have this gentleman decide if I keep my moniker or if I give you what you might call my 'Christian' name."

Ben greeted us and took out his order pad.

"What's it gonna be today, gents?" he said.

I ordered the turkey Reuben special with buffalo seasoned fries and coffee. The man seated across from me — the Albino ordered a small salad with French dressing (on the side) and sweet iced tea.

Before Ben left, the Albino said, "Pardon me, sir. May I ask if you notice anything unusual or unsettling about me?"

Ben scanned the Albino with narrowed eyes, thought for a moment, then said, "I probably wouldn't have worn *that* tie with *that* shirt."

Ben left for the kitchen to put our orders in.

The Albino reached across the table, and reluctantly I shook his hand.

"You may call me Bojing," he said. "Bo for short."

"August," I said. "August Snow. But I'm sure you already knew that."

"You'll pardon me for the nickname," Bojing said. "I am considered something of a

304

dangerous genetic anomaly where I was born."

"Like being born Black in 'Bama."

"Precisely!" He laughed. "I've learned to embrace my anomalies — the unwanted offspring of a Chinese naval officer and a native Djiboutian nurse. *Plus,* my albinism. The yellow man in me hates the Black man I am and vice versa. A grotesque reflection of conflicting and misunderstood cultures. Then again, I've grown to trust my white skin. As I'm sure you already know, white doesn't give a shit about yellow or Black. Only debts that are repaid."

It was then we heard the rising voices of Bo's accomplice and Jimmy. Apparently, under the impression Jimmy was my gun-hand, the accomplice had decided to goad him.

"This guy's going to be a problem for any discussion we have, Bo," I said. "Control him or I will." Xiang had the one thing he needed to be a quick, efficient killer: complete and indiscriminate disregard for human life. Jimmy on the other hand . . .

Bojing spoke in emphatic Chinese to his accomplice, but the young killer would have none of it; he produced a six-inch switch-blade and laughingly jabbed it at Jimmy. I started to get up from my chair, but Jimmy shook his head. Instead, he unraveled silverware from a rolled napkin, took out a fork and held it up.

"You taking the piss, mate? You think I'm a joke?" Xiang said.

"No," Jimmy said. "But you bringin' dishonor on your boss."

"Put that away, Xiang!" Bo commanded in English.

Instead, Xiang thrust the blade at Jimmy's midsection.

Jimmy caught the blade in the tines of the fork and redirected the knife — and Xiang — away from him.

I took out my Glock. Bo took out his Type 06 9mm.

Bo yelled again at Xiang, again to no avail.

Ben came out from the kitchen carrying my sandwich and Bo's salad.

He casually set the salad on our table in front of Bo, walked up behind Xiang and hit the side of Xiang's head with the heavy ceramic plate holding my sandwich and fries. Xiang, banging his head on a booth table on the way down, fell sprawled on the floor covered in fries.

Ben turned to me and said, "I can remake that sandwich, five minutes, August."

"Yeah, no problem, Ben," I said.

31

Jimmy and I were was kneeling by the unconscious body of Xiang, clearing away the remains of broken plate and what was to have been my sandwich. His switchblade was near his right hand. I took it, retracted the blade and tossed the knife to Jimmy. He caught it.

"Souvenir," I said.

As I was preparing to give the unconscious killer a thorough pat down, his boss said, "Stop."

I looked at Bojing still seated in the booth; he was discreetly holding his 9mm on me.

"You can shoot me," I said to Bojing. Then I nodded toward Jimmy. "And you can shoot him. And when the owner comes out from the kitchen, you can shoot *him,* too. Then the cook. Then anybody who's coming in for a late lunch or early dinner. In five minutes you're gonna be neck deep in bodies, and thirty Detroit cops will shred you with a thousand rounds. Everybody dies. Nobody wins."

Just then, a professionally dressed man and woman opened the door of the deli. They saw Jimmy and me bent over the unconscious killer.

"Health inspectors," I said. "Bad salmon." The couple left.

I turned my attention back to Bojing.

"So what's it going to be, slick?" I said.

I didn't wait for an answer. I gave Xiang a thorough pat down and found a fifteen-round Heckler & Koch USP SP, an extra clip and a suppressor, another knife, a plastic baggie of blue and yellow pills and a small tin of what appeared to be cocaine. Then for good measure I broke his thumbs and index fingers. The pain brought him around, but briefly — a right cross to the jaw resolved that.

"How do you know I won't shoot you right now, Mr. Snow?" Bojing said.

"I don't," I said, standing. "I just know what I've got to do. And I'm fairly smart." I sat back down at the table across from Bo. "Was torturing Vic Bronson by Taser your idea?"

"I'm not a fan of torture, Mr. Snow," he said. "It rarely yields dependable, actionable results. Still, I am responsible for the miss-

308

ing thirty million dollars —"

"And if not me, you think a billionaire twenty times over nicked your thirty mil?"

"It's been my experience that most millionaires and billionaires are excessively overleveraged," Bojing said. "If you held a gun to any one of their inflated heads and demanded one hundred million dollars cash within thirty-six hours, most would soil themselves, having absolutely no idea where they could lay their hands on such cash. And we only deal in monetary liquidity —"

"And 'we deal in lead, friend,' " I said.

Bojing burst into laughter.

The Magnificent Seven!" he said through his laughter. "Steve McQueen as Vin Tanner! *Great* film! An American classic! I really do enjoy your company, Mr. Snow."

"Frankly, I'm not too keen on yours," I said. "My godfather almost died because of your disorganized organization. You sent three no-talent punks from Jersey for me, and you gave a cop I put in prison twenty-five hundred to punch my ticket. I ended up in the hospital for four days, but the *real* fucking insult is you gave him *twenty-five hundred.* I'm worth at least fifteen large, asshole! So stop being a pain in my ass and get smart: Sloane's got your money. You find him, you find your money. You keep coming after me, and swear to God, I'll dump separate pieces of you in sewers from here to Dearborn."

"You seem to forget," Bo said congenially. "I have a gun pointed at you, Mr. Snow."

"And you forget," I said. "I have a friend with a switchblade less than an inch from the base of your skull. Six inches in, a little shake and bake, and you're either dead or a vegetable."

Bo's face went slack.

I wasn't sure Jimmy had it in him to stick a knife into the brain stem of another man. But his look was one of someone quietly centered and clear about whatever his choice was. I hated putting the kid in that position, but it was the only card I had left to play.

Bojing's phone announced an incoming call: Elvis Presley's "Viva Las Vegas" covered by ZZ Top.

He slowly, cautiously stowed his gun away in his shoulder rig.

Ben brought my remade sandwich and fries out and set the plate in front of me.

"Everything cool?" Ben said. He nodded toward Xiang, who was sitting up against a counter stool but still out of it. "You want me to watch the kid?"

"With what?" I said. "A spatula?"

Ben reached into the wide pocket of his cargo pants and revealed a .357 Colt King Cobra revolver. "I call it my Holocaust denier denier."

"We're good, Ben."

He went back to the kitchen.

Bojing was speaking fluent French into his phone.

I don't speak French, but I know the look of someone getting reamed out by a superior. That sudden and confusing storm of anger, embarrassment and desperation. The call ended and Bo stared at me with a look that I've met numerous times before: barely restrained murderous contempt.

"It seems I've vastly underestimated you, Mr. Snow," Bo said.

He stood, buttoned his overcoat, gave Xiang on the floor a kick to his ribs and issued the semiconscious killer a command in Chinese.

"What's happening here?" I said.

"I thought we were coming to a gentleman's agreement," Bo said. "About the money and about your neighborhood. Apparently, I was wrong."

"Wait a minute —"

"Good day, Mr. Snow."

Xiang, nursing his broken fingers, gave Jimmy a bleary-eyed look and said, "Next

311

time, mate."

Bo pushed Xiang to the door, and the two men were gone.

Jimmy took the seat opposite me and issued a heavy sigh. "Is it always like this for you, Mr. Snow?"

"Like what?" I said after a gluttonous bite of my sandwich.

"Like — God Lord Jesus forgive me — a *rush*?"

"Sometimes," I said, shoving a fry in my mouth to join the bite of sandwich. "Most of the time it's just ugly work somebody has to do. Like cleaning the grease traps at McDonald's. Or voting. Thanks for having my six, Jimmy."

"Thanks for trusting me to have your six, boss."

My phone rang and I answered it.

"I think you'd better get back here," Lucy said breathlessly. "Now."

"Why?" I said. "What's going on?"

"I hate to use racist metaphors employing my people's incarceration on barren land," Lucy said. "But I think your pal in Switzerland? The, you know — *that* cleaning guy? Yeah, well, I think he just wandered off the reservation. *Big*-time."

32

I insisted Jimmy drive back home with me, leaving his Ford truck in the One Campus Martius parking garage. He'd just seen my hunter-killer dark side up close and very personal. I wasn't bothered so much by the fact that I'd called on him to participate in my sometimes-grim world but that he had been willing and able to commit to such night moves without question or hesitation. Quick converts to violence are just as troubling as nonviolent zealots.

I had to see which one of those was riding with me.

We didn't talk for a while, but his body language told me he was relaxed — no nervous tics or tells. No need for me to make a roadside stop so he could throw up. My gut told me Jimmy had seen enough violence in his young life.

The temperature had dropped considerably and cold melt-water was freezing again as it rushed to sewers. WDET public radio warned of freezing wind and a couple inches of snow heading our way.

For half the wind-whipped ride to my house, Jimmy stared at the passenger and cargo space of my new GMC Yukon.

"Yeah, I know," I finally said. "It's like a leather-upholstered barn."

"Drywall's up on the last house, taped and mudded," Jimmy said, introducing a conversation I was unprepared to have. "Another couple weeks and Miss Jesse can put it up for sale. I figure we should be able to clear two, maybe even three times what we done put into it the way property is going around here."

"Maybe you can just settle into school after this one, Jimmy," I said.

"I like getting my hands dirty and breakin' a sweat, Mr. Snow," he said.

A moment of silence passed between us as I dodged a freewheeling camo-painted Ford F-250 Super Duty truck with a tattered "Make America Great Again" bumper sticker. Finally, I said, "Just to be clear, would you have stuck that knife into the back of Bojing's head?"

Jimmy said, " 'But if anyone does not provide for his relatives, and especially for members of his household, he has denied the faith and is worse than an unbeliever.' Freedom from fear is what we most supposed to provide family. You my family, Mr. Snow. And I feared losing you."

"The Bible's been used to justify a lot of spilled blood, Jimmy," I said.

"And the devil's a regular at Sunday service, Mr. Snow," he said. "Meek as a lamb, quiet as a mouse."

To say Lucy was in a tizzy when Jimmy and I arrived at my house would be an understatement. Her eyes were red and unblinking. She was pacing back and forth, a shot glass in one hand, my sole bottle of Old Forester Bourbon in her other.

She saw Jimmy and froze.

"Wha'd you bring *him* for?" Lucy said, thrusting a forefinger at Jimmy. Her voice was quaking. "*Nobody* should have to see this shit. *Especially,* not him! Not Jimmy! This ain't your world, dude!" Then, aiming her *j'accuse* forefinger at me, she said, "This is *his* world. And *his* world is a freakin' horror show!"

"How many of those have you had?" I said, pointing to the bottle of whiskey.

"None," she said. "Just seemed like I should have it nearby considering what I've just seen."

"It's all right," Jimmy said. "I know who

he is, and I know what I'd do for Mr. Snow push come to shove."

"Oh, yeah?" Lucy said. "Would you do *this*?"

She plopped down in front of one of her laptops and hit a button.

A news report began to play: A long, lean, dark-haired woman with a large microphone stood in front of the more-than-a-century-old grand structure of the Casino de Montbenon in Lausanne, Switzerland. She was speaking rapid-fire German and occasionally pointing to two shimmering cylindrical structures in front of the casino.

Lucy's autointerpret program instantly translated the news-woman's feverish reportage into a robotic monotone: "As you can see behind me, standing freely in front of the main entrance to the legendary Casino de Montbenon are two shiny cylinders. Both cylinders are made of ice, measuring approximately three meters by two meters in diameter. Frozen inside each cylinder? The body of a man."

I stood, walked to the kitchen and brought back two more shot glasses.

I offered one to Jimmy, who shook his head.

I pried the bottle of bourbon from Lucy's death grip, poured myself a shot and knocked it back.

The news report showed a close-up of the two naked men suspended dead in their separate cylinders of ice — two men, post-mortem blue eyes barely open, frozen in their lost struggle against drowning and hypothermia.

"We thought they were sculptures," a man with round wire-rimmed glasses said. "Some new installation. That's not unusual for Lausanne, is it?"

"I thought it was new art installation," a woman wearing too much makeup and a load of dead animal skin said. "Something meant to be provocative and deliciously offensive. Like Mapplethorpe and Damien Hirst for more — how shall I say? — discerning, mature tastes."

When the captain of the Lausanne police was interviewed, he had very little to say that was in any way informative. It wasn't that he was being purposely obtuse; it was simply that bodies suspended in cylinders of ice happened to be new, uncharted territory for his department. Behind him, officers were throwing large tarps over the cylinders of ice.

"We are currently checking every frame, every angle of CCTV, as I'm sure you know —"

I think we all nearly hit the ceiling when Lucy's other laptop suddenly blurted alarm sounds and flashed red and white.

"It's *him*," Lucy growled. "He's been calling every twenty-three minutes and sixteen seconds since this story broke."

"Who's 'him'?" Jimmy said.

"The goddamn *boogeyman, that's* who!" Lucy said. Then she pointed a trembling forefinger at me and said, "*His* assassin freak-show buddy, Count Fuckula!"

33

"Tell me this wasn't you," I said to one of Lucy's two laptops.

"It was me."

It was the effete Eastern European accent of the man I'd come to know as the Cleaner.

"Jesus!" I yelled. *Why?*

"You asked me to keep a protective eye on the young Bronson girl," he said. "Non-lethal protection, you said. And I did as you asked: I watched the men watching her. Unfortunately, their simple assignment to shadow the young lady evolved into KRM."

"KRM?"

"Kidnap, rape, murder," he said. "Was I to simply stand by and allow this to happen?"

"You turned those guys into fucking popsicles!" Lucy blurted.

"Ms. Three Rivers?" the Cleaner said.

A chill snaked up my back.

"It's a pleasure to hear from you," he said.

"Your talents are renowned."

"You — *know* me?" Lucy said. In her voice was both pride and the terror that comes when a world-class killer drops your name.

"Of *course* I do," he said with a surprising giddiness. "Well within the top six percent of today's cyber black hats. Were it not for that unfortunate incident a few years ago, you might be completely off the grid. But you were seventeen. What were you supposed to do?"

Lucy's clay-red skin suddenly turned ashen and her eyes flooded.

She stood suddenly from her seat on the floor near my coffee table, ran past Jimmy to the downstairs bathroom, slammed the door and proceeded to vomit.

"You got somethin' on her, you gonna have to go through me, mister," Jimmy said.

"You misunderstand, Mr. Radmon," the Cleaner said. "I wouldn't *think* of hurting her. I wouldn't think of hurting *any* of you. But if we are to work together, we must have a rudimentary understanding and appreciation of each other, yes?"

"How you know me, man?" Jimmy said.

"Through me," I heard myself croak. For the first time in a very long time — since Kabul — I began feeling the high costs of making small deals with the devil. Debts where unsuspecting souls were used as currency to pay for my sins.

Lucy emerged from the bathroom looking stunned and frail. Jimmy went to her, whispered something comforting, then took her into his arms. She let him. Her eyes, wide and panicked, flitted between me and her laptops.

"Somebody tell me something," Jimmy said sternly. "Now."

"Lucy was fifteen when she got accepted to Michigan Tech," I said. "She was going to study theoretical computer architecture."

"*You,* Sherlock?" Lucy looked at me with wide, glassy eyes. "*You* sold me out?"

"I'm a cop," I said apologetically. "Ex-cop. Eventually I check everybody out. Force of habit."

Tears streamed down her cheeks as she stared at me in disbelief.

"So, what did you *do*?" Jimmy said to me. "What have you *done*?"

"After second year," Lucy said, a vacant look in her wet eyes, "I went home to visit my mom. There was this sheriff's deputy. He tried to — to my mom *and* me — I cut him. Bad. I ran. I've been running for three years. It's why I don't stay long anywhere. Coming back here was a mistake." After holding back a flood of tears, Lucy said, "But how — how does *he* know about me, Sherlock?"

"I paid a guy to delete your records," I said. "A guy who's good with computers. A hacker who used to live in Detroit. Nobody's after you, Lucy. There aren't any warrants. They're gone. And that deputy that attacked you and your mom? Drunk driving. He's dead, Lucy."

"And you didn't *tell* me?" Lucy said.

"I — like having you around, kid," I said. "I didn't think —"

"No!" Lucy screamed. "You *didn't* think!"

I stood from the sofa, feeling my chest filling with dread, anger and the weight of my betrayal of Lucy's confidence. To the house, I shouted, "Come out, come out wherever you are, you sonuvabitch!"

The house was suddenly thrust into darkness.

Then the gas fireplace erupted with flames.

An exaggerated evil laugh erupted through my Bluetooth wireless speakers and bounced off the walls of the living room.

Lucy screamed.

"Not goddamn funny!" I yelled.

The evil, echoing laugh suddenly morphed into the regular laugh of a man genuinely amused with his joke. "Hey, yo, I'm sorry, y'all. I couldn't help myself. That shit's funny to me!"

"Skittles?" Lucy said.

"Sup, ma niggahs!" the voice of Skittles said with unfettered glee.

"You're working with — *him*?" I said through my anger and confusion.

"Funny thing, Snowman," Skittles said. "One minute I'm pullin' five a week, eight a day with D.C. Feebie" — his nickname for the FBI — "next minute, they done bounced my carotid with ten ccs of Special K, black bagged my dome, throwed me on a flight and tossed my ass in this really nice baroque-style hotel bed somewhere outside of Bratislava —"

"You — *told* that assassin dude about me? About that deputy trying to —" Lucy's voice broke off, emotion getting the better of her.

"I'm sorry, baby girl," Skittles said, "but y'all needed to know this shit was all the way for real —"

"You fucking ratted me out to *that* psycho maniac!" she screamed.

"Get her outta here!" I said to Jimmy. "Take her home! Now!"

Jimmy grabbed Lucy's coat and struggled to get her to the door. She would not go easy into that cold night. "I thought you were my *friend*! You *fucking bastard*!"

Once they were gone, I said, "I'm gonna take a wild guess here, and I don't want any bullshit. I even think you are bullshitting me, and we are fucking done, now and forevermore. Are you — *both* of you — company assets?"

Silence.

Then Skittles said, "Listen, man: I used to think all this shadow-world geopolitical shit and subterranean socioeconomics was just the one-half of one percent keepin' they collective foot on the neck of the collective poor. All them years back when you sold me out? That was the start of me seeing the *real* players behind the curtain, man. I could've taken my talents and easily disappeared a year after the FBI scooped me up. But having seen the shit I've seen — rigged elections, engineered viruses, fresh mass graves — I'da been playin' a clown prince dickin' around the edges of Armageddon. Am I an 'asset'? You damned skippy I'm an 'asset'! I ain't gonna bleed on the flag to keep the stripes red, but I'm doin' what I can with what I got to keep abandoned African babies from being emulsified for gene research. Doin' what I can to stop Great Lakes fresh water being sold on the black market. You was always good to me, Snowman, so whichever way you go with this, I'm cool. *We* cool."

I thought for a long, uncomfortable moment. Then I said, "No more human popsicles, okay? We clear?"

Skittles laughed. "That was some certifiably sick shit, right? Hey, man, we got our day jobs anyway, so no worries. But when it comes to my man Dieter? Hey, a dude's gotta do what a dude's gotta do."

"They were bad men, August," Dieter said in a soft, almost apologetic way. "Very bad." Then he said, "You're still in danger, August. Bojing does not react well to losing. And you've brought him to the brink of catastrophic failure."

"What can I expect?" I asked.

"Armageddon."

34

"I already got me a wife."

"Shuddup and hand me the spatula," I said.

"Which one's that?"

I was in the kitchen at Tomás and Elena's house cooking what I hoped would be a nice Sunday afternoon lunch for the three of us: roasted artichoke salad, salmon with fennel and mashed yellow turnips with crispy shallots. Recipes from my chef crush, Ina Garten.

Of course, I had an ulterior motive: gauging Tomás's appetite for helping me out of my upcoming Bojing jam. Since Elena was holding a late morning coffee confab with Councilwoman Rosado in an effort to convince her to run for the recently decapitated Lincoln Quinn's vacated position as council president, I had a better chance of recruiting Tomás to whatever lethal counterassault I might need to undertake.

Dishonest, yes.

I was fairly sure Elena had granted me 98.5 percent unconditional forgiveness for having contributed to getting Tomás shot a month earlier.

Still . . .

"I always knew you could cook," Tomás said, immersing his head in the roiling clouds of steam coming from the mashed yellow turnips, "but *damn,* jefe! You know that's mostly your momma, right?"

"I do."

"But your poppa?" Tomás said. "Oh, now, that man could throw down, too! He could make chicken-fried steak, collard greens with a ham bone or pepper bacon and rice and beans like nobody's damned business! And he did this thing with baked beans —"

"With ground beef, bacon, ham, pinto beans and maple syrup —"

"Oh, my *God!*" Tomás laughed.

He let me work for a minute before he said, "So what do you want?"

"How 'bout a little more sea salt?"

"No," Tomás said. "What. Do. You. *Want.*"

I stopped seasoning, stirring and sampling. "I need help."

"What kind of help?"

"The lethal kind."

Tomás nodded thoughtfully, then said,

327

"You finished cooking?"

I covered the roasted artichoke salad with plastic wrap and put it in their fridge. Then I loosely wrapped the salmon and mashed turnips in aluminum foil and placed them on the middle rack of the oven, which was set to warm. The salmon might dry out a bit, but I doubted Ina Garten would mind. She seemed an understanding lady.

Tomás briefly opened the kitchen back door and retrieved a bottle of Don Julio Añejo Tequila that had been chilling in a snowbank on his back porch.

"Aren't you afraid somebody could snatch it out there?" I asked.

"Fee-fi-fo-fum," Tomás said.

Then we went to the basement and sat in webbed lawn chairs in front of his gun locker. Elena had switched out the poster of Mexican-American comedians for a religious motivational poster: a heart made of flames in a bright blue sky, a set of praying hands holding a rosary and the words HIS LOVE FOR YOU. Draped over the top of the locker was a cream-colored lace runner.

"You remember Sister Luciarose Bonafusco at Ste. Anne's?" Tomás said.

"Yeah," I said. "You could've driven a Mack truck into her —"

"And the truck would've lost. I hated that

big self-righteous bitch," Tomás grumbled.

"What about her?"

"Doesn't my gun locker look like her now?"

"Holy cow," I said after nearly choking on a shot of tequila. "You're *right.*"

He poured me another shot of tequila. "You gotta stop this half steppin', Octavio. You got something to ask me, you ask. No more dickin' around."

"If you haven't already noticed, you're kind of a scary dude," I said.

"Yeah," Tomás said, knocking his shot of tequila back. "To everybody else I may be El Sepulturero —"

"Which you are not."

"But to you," Tomás continued unfazed, "I'm your godfather. And I made a blood oath with your papa to watch out for you like you was my own."

"A 'blood oath'?"

He held the open palm of his right hand up for me to see. A big, calloused steve-dore's hand I'd seen many times before, crosshatched with nature's lines and a faint four-inch white linear scar.

"Summer, five years ago," he said. " 'Bout two months before his heart and the diabe-tes got him, we was drunk, havin' a good time, talkin' shit. Which one of our women

329

had the best ass —"

"You can skip that part."

"So, anyway, he gets to talkin' 'bout you. How much he loves you. How he's scared for you in a world that seemed hell-bent on tearin' itself to shreds. Worried Black folk won't accept you. And worried brown folk won't take you in. I tell him ain't nothin' gonna happen to you as long as I got breath. I take out my huntin' knife and slice his right palm, my right palm, and we clasp hands. I swore on the graves of my folks that I'd look out for you." Tomás poured another shot. Then he laughed. "Your momma and Elena went apeshit when they saw us bleeding. Called us estúpidos y grandes cerdos idiotas. Bandaged us up. Took us home. Threw our drunk asses in bed. But your papa and me, we never forgot that pledge. That blood oath. To you."

"Thank you, gran papi."

"You're welcome," Tomás said. "Now tell me what's going on straight up."

I gave Tomás the lowdown on everything, starting with the fact that the drug dealers he'd put down were a setup to devalue Mexicantown property in general and Authentico's location specifically.

"I was the fly in the ointment: Old man Ochoa offered me the business that Jackie had been planning to take from him. She convinced the family lawyer, Danny Romero, to kill old man Ochoa. As the last blood relative she'd more than likely get Authentico Foods," I said. "She would inherit the business, fly off into the sunset with Sloane's ten mil and leave Danny hanging out to dry. Unfortunate for both of them, you busted in on old man Ochoa's murder and Danny, being the skittish type, put two in you."

"Ain't that Shakespeare kind of shit?"

"Yeah," I said. "The CliffsNotes version. Anyway, all of this in an effort to make a fast and big sale to the mysterious Mr. Sloane, who was using Vic Bronson as a front to set up ghost towns in Detroit. Luxury off-the-grid safe houses for very dangerous people."

"That's a goddamn shame about Jackie Ochoa," Tomás said. "She was a good kid. Smart as hell."

I told Tomás about my infiltration of Vic Bronson's compound and about his daughter — which led to the Cleaner.

Tomás went off like a Roman candle in a fireworks factory.

"That *hit-man* guy from the bank job?" Tomás bellowed. "You pulled in a favor from an *assassin*? Jesus, Octavio! Estás

331

loco?"

"I just may be crazy," I replied. "But he's really not too bad of a guy."

"He's a *contract killer* wanted by *governments*!" Tomás said. "Any *other* surprises I should know about?"

"He's currently employed by *our* government."

"Jesus Holy Christ," Tomás said, slapping a palm to his forehead. "*This* is why people don't vote."

I told him about Bojing — the Albino — and Xiang, Bojing's pathological assistant, who were the leading edge of all of this. How they suspected me of ripping off ten million of their cash and twenty million in negotiable barrow bonds. I skipped the parts that involved the letters *EM* embossed on a dead man's shoes and — as I'd learned thanks to Dr. Bobby Falconi's intrepid scientific investigation — the exclusive Ecuadorian shoemaker Ernesto Manta. If I told Tomás, that would make him an accessory to a murder I hoped to commit very soon.

"Them's the motherfuckers that desecrated Joe Louis's fist with Lincoln Quinn's head?"

"Them's the ones."

After a moment, Tomás burst out laughing. He slammed a hand on my shoulder and said, "Octavio, my boy, you live a seriously fucked-up life."

"Yeah," I said. "Don't I know it."

"I still want to send a bullet up Danny's ass," Tomás said.

"Unwise," I said. "And unnecessary. These days, popping Danny like a cherry tomato would be the relief he's begging for. His law firm's bankrupt, and he's under investigation by the state cops and FBI for malfeasance. Not to mention Jackie Ochoa gave his heart a dry hump, then split. Last I heard he started some online business just to make a few rent dollars."

"Online business?"

"BigWoodforYou.net."

"Porn?"

"Firewood."

Tomás went quiet for a moment. Then he said, "Octavio, I been beat to shit, carved up like a Thanksgiving turkey, shot three times and left for dead. If I didn't have no fight, I wouldn't have the woman I got, a beautiful daughter, the best grand baby girl in the world and you. According to my momma, God rest her soul, I came into this world with my fists up and punching. And I'm bettin' that's how I go out. So, do I have some fight left in me you can depend on?"

Tomás stood from his lawn chair and walked to a darker, cobwebbed corner of the basement behind the water heater.

After a moment of reaching between floor joists, he came back and stood in front of me holding a long custom black metal case. Gently, he laid the case on the floor in front of me, opened it and carefully took out the contents.

A Barrett MRAD bolt-action sniper rifle.

The former marine sniper in me said, "*Oorah.* God bless America."

"And goddamn the enemy," Tomás said.

35

Elena returned home at six that evening, and though half of Tomás's expensive bottle of tequila was floating our brains, we managed to look and sound like our sober selves.

At least that's what a couple of drunks thought.

Councilwoman Nadine Rosado was still justifiably freaked out by the beheading of her city council rival Lincoln Quinn, but under the friendly pressure of Elena and several other Mexicantown community activists, she had consented to run for his vacated seat. An enthusiastically supported proposal that had caught Elena completely off guard.

Lunch proved to be a hit.

After clearing the table and thoroughly handwashing the plates, serving dishes and silverware before putting them in the dishwasher (a tragicomic ritual observed by households across America), Elena made a carafe of slow-drip Mexican coffee and added Kahlúa, tequila and a splash of Mandarine Napoléon Liqueur for a nice orange, clove and cinnamon finish.

The perfect warm drink to fight off the swirling chills of a cold Michigan winter evening.

As we made ourselves comfortable in their living room, Elena narrowed her eyes at me and said to Tomás, "So. Did el bebé ask you to join him in any risky escapades thinking I wouldn't find out?"

Tomás laughed. "Sí."

I felt my cheeks warm and prickle — and not from the coffee drink.

Keeping her eyes locked on me, Elena continued to address her husband. "And, of course, you told el bebé I see everything, hear everything, know everything, sí, mi amor?"

"I did," Tomás said. He whispered to me, "She does. It's freaky."

"Listen, Elena —" I started.

"No, *you* listen, Octavio," Elena said. "When Tomás was still laid up with his injuries and Tatina asked me to help find you, I knew then — clearly and without question — what I had to do: I had to save my godson. I had to bring you home. Standing over your coffin or, worse, having no

336

body to bury was not an option." She took a moment to assess if her words were reaching me. They were. "It's always been there, Octavio. Like it is in everyone else. The darkness we fear and sometimes embrace. My need was — *is* for you to live. A mother's uncompromising force of will to keep you safe. The cost — *my* cost — was shooting a man twice. I don't regret it. In fact I've just enjoyed a wonderful meal because of it." Smiling at me, she said, "I abhor violence. But I'm not a fool, Octavio."

"I never thought you were, Elena," I said. "I just —"

"Wanted to protect me because I'm a woman?" she said. Then to Tomás she said, "Tell el bebé what my superpower is, mi amor."

Tomás rolled his eyes, then said, "She's a woman."

"Exactly," Elena said. "And next time say it without rolling your eyes, pig."

Elena brought more Mexican coffee in and filled our mugs.

"You know what I heard this afternoon at the restaurant?" Elena said as she resumed her seat next to her husband. "I heard some young white people refer to Mexicantown as 'West Corktown.' Can you imagine that? West *Corktown*! Over a hundred years of

Mexicans living and working and worship-
ping and having babies and baptisms in
southwest Detroit — and now we're the
browns of *Ireland*?"

"Naturally," Tomás said with a wink to
me, "you didn't say anything to them."

"I said to them, 'Excuse me — but this is
Mexicantown. Not "West Corktown." It
might be best if you learned the history of a
place before you decide to rewrite it.'
They're what I fear, Octavio: the nameless,
faceless pallbearers come to slowly bury the
still-warm body of Mexicantown." After a
moment, Elena stood and declared she was
tired and "slightly tipsy" and was going to
bed. At the foot of the staircase, she said,
"God forgive me, but I pray for the death of
the pallbearers."

She ascended the staircase like a noir film
queen who'd had her evening's fill of men,
money and champagne.

"When she's like this, I got maybe a ten-
minute window, jefe," Tomás said.

I took his one-ton brick of a hint and left.

The invitation came in the form of a postcard.

On the picture side of the card was the
expansive glass-domed Anna Scripps Whitcomb Conservatory on Belle Isle. On the

address side were my name and address executed in fancy script with a brief note: "Your attendance is requested Thursday evening for a very special dinner.–TA." Since I'd apparently worn out any friendly familiarity with Bojing, I assumed the "TA" represented his more deadly moniker — the Albino.

"I'm thinking this is his version of the Last Supper," Tomás said. "*Your* last supper."

"I'm thinking you're right," I said.

Tomás was sitting at my kitchen island on a December morning. Three inches of snow had fallen the night before, bringing the week's total to six inches with the promise of another two inches by week's end. Outside was the persistent whirling buzz of Jimmy Radmon's trusty Husqvarna ST 427T snowblower clearing the sidewalks of Markham Street. He didn't do it for extra money. He did it because this was the neighborhood he'd helped rebuild. The neighborhood he called home with love and pride. Folks offered to pay him. Jimmy, being Jimmy, refused payment. A few other neighbors even joined him in a kind of snow-blowing brigade.

I wasn't one of them.

I was warming six cinnamon-sugar churros in the oven. Both Tomás and I were drinking Mexican coffee, which, for the uninitiated, makes espresso taste like diluted herbal tea.

"You think he's been using the conservatory as a base?" Tomás asked.

"Unfortunately, I think this time of year people are more interested in staying warm, eating meat loaf and watching the Lions lose than venturing out to see thirteen acres of orchids, lily ponds and palm trees under a glass roof," I said. "Plus, it's been closed for reconstruction — the dome's glass panels are being replaced. That'll probably happen the first of the year — maybe later. Whatever security there is has to be minimal: a state patrol here and there, DPD drive-throughs every once in a while, a bored DNR officer in a booth at the entrance, maybe. Bojing could hole up with eight, ten guys for a week and nobody'd know."

"My guess?" Tomás began. "If he's as dangerous and well-funded as you say he is, he's probably got switch-out crews of four, five guys. South side, maybe in a Zodiac inflatable from Windsor. Tough to navigate ice floes on the river at night, though, even with HD night-vision goggles." Tomás paused to slurp some coffee and scrutinize the topographical map of Belle Isle that had unfolded in his head. "I gotta be honest,

Octavio — we might be punching way above our weight on this one."

"So, what's the solution?"

"Put on more muscle. Fast." Turning the postcard over like the ace of spades between his fingers, Tomás said, "How come you don't use your microwave?"

"Because it turns churros into molten dough," I said. "Or charcoal briquettes. I don't know why I have the damned thing in the first place."

"Can I have it if you die?" Tomás said. "And the 442?"

"Yeah, sure, why not?" I said. "Just so you know, Carlos and Jimmy secured a sawed-off shotgun under the back seat. I haven't figured how to get it out without blowing off the right-rear quarter panel. So what do I get if *you* die?"

"Monthly note on my regular truck," he said. "Plus the awesome responsibility of taking care of Elena, my daughter and grandbaby."

"Sounds fair. What are you thinking?" I said, donning one of my mother's old oven mitts and pulling the churros from the oven.

"What I'm thinking is you ain't gonna like what I'm thinking," Tomás said. He grabbed a hot churro and devoured half of it. Chewing, he said, "I don't half like it myself."

"So, surprise me."

He did.

I admitted to having serious doubts.

"You think you can pull that off?" I said.

"You mean can I swallow my pride long enough to keep your butt topside?" Tomás said, licking his fingers clean of sugar. "You and me been way enough for each other in tight spots. This time's different. We both got our asses handed to us on this one. Both of us done seen the faces of people we love from hospital beds — and that's a view I don't never want again."

"How's the coffee?" I said.

"Like suckin' a buffalo's wet balls, jefe."

"How would you even *know* that?"

36

"You *won't.*"

"But you have to admit — I *could.*"

"But you *won't.*"

"How do you know that?"

"My Somali great-grandfather Bashiir Cilmi told me in a dream."

"Wait a minute," I said. "Your *great-*grandfather? Isn't he, like, dead?"

"August." Tatina laughed dismissively. "If he were truly dead, how could he speak to me?"

Every once in a while — both in families and in politics — you are confronted by such glorious lunacy that it's simultaneously indefensible and unimpeachable.

Tatina and I had been going round-robin for ten minutes on the subject of my possible death at the hands of Bojing and his crew. It was a cold early evening in Mexicantown, a cold late night in Oslo. I was loading the remaining arsenal of Tomás's expansive cache of weapons into the back of my GMC Yukon. Tomás had already cleared out more than half of his gun locker and was in the process of distribution. I'd never seen his gun locker empty before; it was a strangely unsettling feeling staring at the now-vacant insulated steel walls, shelves and open and empty lockboxes.

The last thing to go from Tomás's gun locker was a box of flash-bang grenades. God only knows where he got them.

"Americans are funny," Tatina said with a sigh of disappointment as I loaded the grenades into my SUV. "You pretend to believe in magnificent, forgiving spiritual worlds beyond the flesh. But you morbidly worship and fear for that same flesh. You mourn its loss before it's even gone. Or you *deny* the spirit world — belittling it as a fairy tale and castigating those who *do* believe as indolent children — then you look up at the night sky and see nothing but an end without a narrative. Oh, my *God*. It must be *so* hard to be American!"

"You have no idea, toots," I said.

"After tonight," Tatina said in a tone that reminded me of my mother preparing to scold me, "we need to have a theoretical talk about what kind of spiritual life we wish for our children."

I felt myself swallow hard. "Our — children?"

"I said 'theoretical,' August." Tatina laughed. "No, I'm not. And yes, I would someday like to be. By you. We can make the discussion a drinking game if that's easier."

"I have to go."

"I know," Tatina said. "Just remember — my great-grandfather has never been wrong."

"From your lips to Great-Grandpa's ears."

As I drove back to my house, I thought about what fathers did: policemen and firemen, doctors and teachers, accountants and computer programmers and plumbers and carpenters. They volunteered as football coaches and soccer referees and took their families out for breakfast after church, synagogue or mosque. They suffered through tax season, played LEGOs with their kids when they were bone tired and spun their brains into aching balls trying to figure out how to save a dime on a dollar for their kids' education.

Me?

I was heading back to my house with six hundred pounds of guns, ammo and grenades in preparation for a dinner date with a madman.

In the life of a kid, what the hell kind of father would that be?

At home, I changed into a crisp white shirt, black silk tie and grey wool Emporio Armani two-piece suit.

Wearing the ensemble, I cut as fine a figure as Mr. James Bond, 007.

Unlike Mr. James Bond, 007, beneath my snappy dinner attire, I was wearing LAPASA merino wool thermal long johns and matching long-sleeve shirt because this wasn't summer in Ibiza. I was also wearing a pair of my father's old Carhartt black wool socks (perfect for walking a beat or midwinter stakeouts) and spit-shined all-weather tactical boots. In my left inside suit coat pocket was a wallet-sized photo of my mom and dad. In the right inside suit coat pocket was my Marine Scout Sniper medal, khaki uniform recon sniper Marine Forces Special Operations Command (MARSOC) patch ("From afar death") and first-place team citations from the United States Army Special Operations Command (USASOC) International Sniper Competition and the Mammoth Sniper Challenge. I also carried a small section of a bloodstained map given to me by a former British SAS officer.

If I was going to die that night, I wanted

those fuckers to take away a strange sense of honor, pride and shame in who they'd killed.

Then again, what I carried in my pockets was all that I was. All I would ever be.

The trinkets or talismans of a life lived briefly.

I took nothing from my days as a Detroit cop.

One or most likely two of Bojing's men would pat me down at the Belle Isle Park security booth. The booth where the folks from the Michigan Department of Natural Resources sporadically posted an officer who was highly trained at checking windshield park stickers, handing out maps and watching bass fishing competitions on an iPad. I had the feeling the regular DNR officers were off between the holidays or had been paid handsomely by Bojing to stay at home with families who had been threatened with gruesome deaths if they did otherwise. I would, of course, congenially submit to the entrance pat down, then not so congenially break the guard's neck before he searched the back of my munitions-loaded SUV. I would park a hundred yards away from the conservatory and, carrying only the dead guard's weapon, make my way to the conservatory hoping somewhere hidden in the thicket of old-growth pine and maple trees, the frozen-over ponds and fountains, were people who liked me enough to risk their lives for me.

I made one last call before heading off to Belle Isle.

"Leo?" I said.

"Snow?" Leo Cowling said in a sleepy voice. "What the hell you want? You know what time it is, niggah?"

"Late," I said. "*Very* late for some of us. Listen. I know we haven't exactly been pals —"

"You got that right."

"And I doubt we ever will be —"

"Is this a drunk dial?" Cowling said. " 'Cause if this is a damn drunk dial, swear to God Almighty, I'mo throw yo Tex-Mex ass in the tank for about a million mothafuckin' years."

"No drunk dial," I said. "I'm in the shit, Leo, and if I don't come out of this one, I just want you to know, yes, you're an asshole — but an asshole I've come to respect. I might even take a bullet for you."

There was a long pause. Then Leo said, "Talk to me, Snow. What's going on?

"See ya round, Leo," I said. "And remember: turquoise is not a man's color, so burn

348

half of your ties."

Then I disconnected.

37

Two of Bojing's men were stationed at the DNR security booth on Belle Isle. I could tell they were his men because frankly I'd never seen DNR officers that massive. Not to mention they were wearing bulletproof vests beneath DNR-emblem-embroidered shirts stretched to bursting. It was like looking at white versions of the Compton twins — they looked equally dumb, equally dangerous. Both men were equipped with 9mm handguns and hunting knives stowed in black sheaths.

"Colder than a congressman's pecker, eh, guys?" I said to the blond slab of guard-dog meat as I descended from the SUV. I raised my hands slowly and laced my fingers behind my head. He said nothing. Rather, he cut his eyes to his buzz-cut brunette partner. An indication he hadn't understood a word I'd said.

Buzz Cut translated what I'd said into

French for Blondie.

Not a laugh or smile between them, confirming my longstanding belief that psychopaths laugh or smile only when blood is spilled. That, or I'm not as funny as I like to think I am in *any* language.

"My name is —"

"We know who you are," Buzz Cut said, taking out a Ruger SR-9 from a shoulder rig and holding it casually at his side. He nodded to Blondie, who kept me in the sights of his own Ruger pistol while Buzz Cut methodically inspected the SUV from stem to stern.

When Buzz Cut reached the back window of the SUV, he peered at the tarp that covered all of Tomás's munitions.

"Holy shit!"

My cue . . .

I swung low and to the back of the Blondie guard near me, extracted his knife and buried it to the hilt in his left eye. I knelt behind Blondie's collapsing body, using him as a shield. Buzz Cut fired twice from behind the SUV, both shots thumping into Blondie's bulletproof vest. Blondie was trembling, slowly losing contact with motor skills because of the knife buried in his brain. I grabbed his Ruger pistol and waited for Buzz Cut to fire. He did, which meant he'd leaned or stepped out from behind the SUV. I quickly took two shots, hitting his left knee, then his hip. He fell sideways into a snowbank. He fired three more shots, his dying partner receiving one in the head. A spray of blood and brain in my face. I fired one more shot, taking out Buzz Cut's trachea.

Dead.

I washed my face and hands with snow, checked my suit for any blood or brains and took Blondie's walkie-talkie. I got back in the SUV and fired up the engine. Before shifting into drive, I clicked twice on the walkie-talkie's speak button.

"What's up?" a voice said, crackling through the walkie-talkie.

"Guess who's coming to dinner, motherfucker?" I said before tossing the walkie-talkie out of the driver's side window.

The roads on Belle Isle had barely been plowed since the conservatory was closed for major renovation. Mostly I followed the tracks of a couple snowmobiles and construction trucks. I parked eighty to a hundred yards from the conservatory, hoping the contingent of help I'd prayed for would make effective use of my payload. As I walked to the conservatory, I thought about how nice it might be to be buried next to my folks beneath an old-growth oak.

At the main entrance of the conservatory, I was met by three of Bojing's men — two big white guys and a trim Black guy — all of whom were pointing what looked to be heavy-duty Ruger AR-556 MPR rifles at me.

"Hi," I said brightly. "I have a dinner date with Bojing. Sorry I didn't bring flowers."

One of the white guys gestured for me to come closer.

I did.

He pressed the barrel of his rifle to my forehead while the other two men carefully patted me down, taking the gun I'd retrieved from one of the guards at the island's entrance. The Black guard picked something off the lapel of my suit coat and showed it to the guard holding his rifle to my forehead.

"Real soon," the man with his rifle to my head said, "that's gonna be *your* brains, asshole."

The Black man flicked the piece of his comrade's brains into a snow pile, then took up his rifle again.

All three men stood at my back, ready to shred me with their semi-automatic rifles.

"In you go," one of the white guys said.

It had been a while since I'd been to the Anna Scripps Whitcomb Conservatory, which proved once again people don't really know of or embrace the treasures surrounding them in their own hometowns.

The towering glass greenhouse conservatory fans out over thirteen acres and includes the Palm House, the Tropical House, the Cactus House, the sunken Fernery and the Show House, full to overflowing with all manner of exotic flora. And while most folks don't normally associate Detroit with the growth of oranges, bananas and figs, you can often find a few budding to life at the conservatory, which is the oldest continually running conservatory in America.

Unfortunately, the Albert Khan–designed conservatory, with its fogged-over glass, had begun showing its age. The low Palm House dome limited the growth of the collection of palm trees. In early November — while Detroit was battling snowstorms, subzero temperatures and high winds — the conservatory had been closed for major renovations, making it the perfect home away from home for a band of well-funded cutthroats.

As I followed the tree- and flower-lined path to the reconstructed central dome, two guards trailed me. I had no doubt they would lay waste to hundreds of thousands of dollars' worth of rare flowers and exotic trees to cut me in half with their semiautomatic rifles.

And there he was beneath the shimmering dome.

Bojing.

The Albino.

Dressed in a white tuxedo, he sat at one of three tables draped in white linen and laden with beautifully arranged flowers and a variety of what looked like expertly prepared foods. When he saw me, it was as if he were seeing a long-lost, beloved brother.

"August!" he said.

"Bojing," I said. "Nice spread you got going here."

"I never knew Detroit had such a fine variety of food!" Bojing said. "Our clientele will appreciate it. Look! Beet elote, seafood fideuà and Szechuan lamb sausage! Oxtail tacos and curry goat from Norma G's, blackened shrimp farro jambalaya from Savannahblue, fried bologna and waffles — whoever *heard* of such a thing? — from Grey Ghost, salted maple pie from Sister Pie and bacon barbeque blintzes from LaBelle's Soul Hole patisserie! Isn't this *amazing*?"

"What's the occasion?" I said. "My birthday?"

"Your *death*day!" Bojing held up a bottle of wine. "A Domaine du Comte Liger-Belair La Romanée Grand Cru Pinot Noir.

I hope you don't mind. I proceeded from the assumption you liked red."

"Love a nice Pinot," I said. "I think I'd enjoy it more without knowing it wasn't going to be my last."

Bojing gestured for me to join him at the table.

I did.

He opened the wine, poured two generous glasses and offered me one. I hesitated in taking it.

"Poison is a woman's thing, August," Bojing said. "And I believe an execution should come quickly after a good meal. You'll receive a single head shot — the least I can do out of my immense respect for you and your tenacity. With all the trouble you've caused me, I've come to realize something: I've established eight fully functioning and profitable 'ghost towns' around the world. Minor hiccups. Small inconveniences. To be expected. But it's been a very long time since I've faced a challenge like *you*. A challenge that took me back to my childhood in Djibouti, where survival was visceral. Primal. Adrenaline fueled. All while being intellectually invigorating. A game of chess played with increasingly explosive pieces. I finally realized such a challenge should be celebrated!"

"Sure you can't let me off with just a warning?"

"I'm fairly sure," Bojing said after a sip of wine.

"What about the missing cash and barrow bonds?"

"I have men on it," Bojing said. "Fried bologna?"

"Trying to quit," I said.

"Would you mind if another guest joined us, August?"

I felt the muscles in my stomach clench.

Before I could find words, Bojing yelled the name of his assistant, the young, lean psychopath Xiang.

Xiang appeared from a thicket of ferns; in one hand, he held a long ancient curved Chinese sword. In the other hand, he held the shirt collar of a badly beaten Jimmy Radmon.

"Let him go!" I said, standing.

"And what?" Bojing said. "You'll hand yourself over? You're already *here*! No, August. There are no more deals to be had."

"It's all right, Mr. Snow," Jimmy said with a wheeze. He tried to raise his head to look at me; his right eye was swollen shut, and his bottom lip was split open and bleeding. "I for real didn't really expect to make it past the age of eight, so, like, every year since has been a blessing. You and me? We cool, boss man. God gonna take real good care of you, Mr. Snow. Me, too, I hope."

Another of Bojing's men brought in a laptop and positioned it at the end of the dining table.

Bojing suddenly looked both angry and confused and started yelling at the guard in French. The guard turned the laptop on and a well-dressed, erudite-looking, grey-haired man with a dark and well-groomed mustache appeared. When the man's image appeared, Bojing suddenly came to attention.

"Well," the man said with a thick French accent. "Looks like even *more* of my money has been squandered. I, at the very least, hope the wine is French?"

"Oui!" Bojing said.

"And *you*?" the man said, looking at me. "You must be Monsieur Snow — the man who has cost my point man so much of my valuable time and money."

"Tha'd be me," I said. "You remind me of somebody. Pepe Le Pew?"

"In my business, I can afford to lose neither time nor money," the Frenchman said. "Let me show you what happens to those who cause me such grievous losses, Monsieur Snow. Xiang, if you please?"

"No, goddammit!" I yelled.

Xiang pushed Jimmy to his knees, then dramatically brought back his sword.

"Love you, Mr. Snow," Jimmy said.

Just before the length of blade went through Bojing's back, coming out through the middle of his chest.

I watched the Albino's red blood fan out across his white tuxedo before he fell face-down into the beet elote and seafood fideuà.

38

"Thirty million dollars in cash and barrow bonds," the Frenchman said. "Poof! Enough to warrant Bojing's demise. He had once been quite effective. Strange, isn't it, how success makes some men sloppy? His public displays of incompetence — mostly involving you, Mr. Snow — had become unforgivable."

"Is this where you bore the shit out of me with your grandiose super-villain plans?" I said. "If so, I'm gonna have a seat and eat some of this food. At least the stuff that hasn't been bled on."

"This is all about business, Mr. Snow. Nothing more, nothing less. A burgeoning seven-billion-dollar-a-year business providing high-end clientele with a worldwide assortment of convenient and luxurious properties that are simply off the grid. Away from prying legal eyes and governmental ears. Clientele like, say, Mr. Jeffrey Epstein?"

"Great retirement plan you've got," I said, jerking a thumb at Bojing's body. "Maybe you guys should consider a cruise line."

"A fine idea!" he said. "Now. To the point —"

A red dot appeared on the Frenchman's forehead. Suddenly his head jerked violently as a bullet found its target.

His livestreamed death was quickly followed by what appeared to be a bright, happy commercial sponsored by the Austrian National Tourist Office.

It took a second for Xiang to recover from his shock at seeing his former boss's boss assassinated. When he recovered, he raised an already bloodied sword above Jimmy's head.

That was as far as Xiang got before the conservatory filled with automatic-weapons fire. Xiang took three quick rounds to the chest and collapsed behind Jimmy. I jumped over the dining table and dragged Bojing's body with me as a line of bullets ripped into the table. I found Bojing's holstered semiauto pistol. Then I made my way to Jimmy and pulled him behind a collection of tropical ferns.

"You're gonna be okay, Jimmy," I said

361

against the deafening sounds of two flash-bang grenades exploding at opposite ends of the conservatory.

"Sure don't feel like it," he said. He glanced over my shoulder. I spun around, ready to unload Bojing's gun.

The short, round figure of Labelle's Soul Hole Donut Shop owner, Lady B. She was wearing her usual white chef's apron, and at her side she held her signature long-barrel revolver.

"I'll get the boy out," she said. "You do what you got to do."

"How many of us?" I said.

"Three of my people, Tomás, Duke Ducane and them crazy-ass Compton twins," Lady B said. "With you maybe seven against fifteen —" One of Bojing's men suddenly appeared and leveled his rifle at Lady B. She swung around and fired two killing .357 bullets into him. "Fourteen," she said.

Jimmy, halfway to the unconscious world, smiled up at Lady B and said, "You smell like warm donuts."

"Oh, I know, baby," Lady B said sweetly as she helped lift Jimmy up. "Soon as we outta here, I'mo get you some of them donuts. Hot chocolate, too." From the look of it, Lady B had carried the weary and the wounded before. She cut me a look and growled, "Mop up them motherfuckers!"

I saluted her.

Then I jumped into the fray.

A semi-automatic rifle chewed through exotic foliage as I made my way, low and fast, to a modestly higher collection of ferns. I got off three in the direction of the rifle fire before I leapt behind a large, thick-rooted fern. Just as I checked the clip of my weapon, one of Bojing's men stood over me, his finger poised on his trigger, his rifle barrel holding me at the center of its bull's-eye.

"Mine," he said.

Before he could pull the trigger, he took three rapid-fire bullets, two to the body, one to the head.

"Not today," DPD Detective Captain Leo Cowling said as he watched the man's body roll away from us.

Leo pulled me to my feet.

"Nice of you to join the party," I said. "How'd you find me?"

"The usual way," Leo said. "Followed the trail of blood and the smell of bullshit. How'd you convince Brutus Jefferies to get mixed up in this shit?"

"Brutus is here?"

"Snapped a guy's neck as I was making my way in," Leo said. "Brotha's like some kind of Incredible Shaka Zulu Hulk."

Automatic rifle fire splattered through the line of ferns Cowling and I were huddled behind. We ducked low, listening to the cascade of bullets chop the greenery and thud into the soil.

"Ever see *Butch Cassidy and the Sundance Kid*?" I said.

"Yeah," Cowling said. "On one of them classic-movie channels. Couple of blue-eyed white boys playin' cowboys on a bicycle with some dumbass music about raindrops. Never seen it all the way through. It ain't no *Buck and the Preacher*, that's for damn sure. Why?"

"Never mind."

We looked at each other; Cowling nodded to the countdown in his head.

On "three" we stood and began emptying our weapons in the direction of the automatic rifle fire.

One of Bojing's men fell while another to his left sprayed automatic rifle fire in our direction. Cowling dived right, I dived left, both of us barely managing to keep our skin intact.

A volley of pistol fire.

Then laughing. A brief but intense argument:

"He's *mine*!"

"No he's not! *I* got him first!"

"Oh, you are such a fucking liar!"

Cowling and I peeked above the tropical ferns.

"Oh, you are just bullshitting me," Cowling said. "The goddamn *Compton* twins?"

"Yeah," I said. "About that —"

"Jesus, Lord in heaven," Cowling said, shaking his head in disbelief. "Any more surprises I should know about, Snow?"

"I — am your *father.*"

"Fuck you, asshole."

A rustling of foliage. We rolled and leveled off, ready to drop the intruder.

Tomás!

"You lovers sandbaggin' while I do all the heavy lifting?" he said. He was dressed for war: green camo and desert khaki boots, two semi-auto pistols slung low on his hips and a quick-release shoulder rig holding a Smith & Wesson 686 .357 Magnum. Slung across his chest bandolero-style were three flash-bang grenades. In each hand he held a Ruger AR-556 MPR rifle.

"I'm sorry," Cowling said to me. "Remind me again who the good guys are and who the bad guys are? 'Cause I be sho 'nuff confused right now, Massa Snow."

"God, am I glad to see you," I said to Tomás.

365

"They're buggin' out," Tomás said. "Six of 'em."

"How?" I asked.

"Snowmobiles," Tomás said. "Heading to the fishing pier. Probably a Zodiac to cross into Canada, then God only knows where."

"A Zodiac? Up against ice floes and freighters?" Cowling said. "That's some crazy shit."

"Look around, hotshot," Tomás growled. "We ain't exactly dealing with very stable geniuses here."

"Stay here, Leo," I said. "DPD's gonna want to see one of their own on scene when they get here. Tell 'em what's going on."

"Mothafucka, *I* barely know what's goin' on!"

"We either giddyup and go now," Tomás said, "or they're gone."

"You know how to ride a snowmobile?" I asked Tomás. He gave me a look as if I'd just asked if he knew how to scratch his own ass.

There are very few straight lines of entrance and egress on Belle Isle, especially in the winter with mountains of plowed snow and roads closed for repaving. Nothing new for Belle Isle's occasional winter photographer, bird-watcher, iron-man jogger or dog walker. But when you're full throttle on a

165-horsepower snowmobile in pursuit of killers, the last thing you care about is the scenic route. I was in hot pursuit of revenge.

Three snowmobiles screamed to the northeast, following the curve of the narrow canal, probably on their way to the snow-covered soccer field and handball courts. They'd likely cut south across Woodside Drive to the fishing pier. At least that's where I'd moor a couple of Zodiac inflatable boats.

I signaled to Tomás, and he followed my lead south.

Brake lights.

Sixty yards away at the two-o'clock position.

Rooster tail of snow. One of the snowmobiles turned sharply and accelerated to meet Tomás and me.

A line of automatic rifle fire hammering into the snow six feet to my left.

Tomás and I skidded to a halt, nose to nose, and opened up our semi-automatic rifles.

The shooter took a hit. Lost control of his snowmobile. Crashed into a high drift of snow. Went airborne between Tomás and me. Tomás unpinned a flash-bang grenade and tossed it onto the pinwheeling snowmobile overhead . . .

Boom.

"Was that really necessary?" I yelled to Tomás as the shooter's body and the fireball wreckage tumbled away from us.

"No," he said in Spanish. "But it was sure as hell *fun*!"

Sometimes, you have to seriously wonder about the sanity of family and friends.

A DPD helicopter locked us in its spotlight.

I signaled to the pilot that it wasn't Tomás and me that he should be interested in — it was five guys boarding inflatable boats he should shine a light on. The fact that Tomás and I were holding semi-automatic rifles and not firing at him should have been a big clue we weren't the bad guys. Unfortunately, some folks are, as my father used to say, "slow on the uptake."

"Lower your weapons," boomed a voice from the helicopter. "You've got nowhere to go."

"Not us, dumb shit!" Tomás yelled. Pointing to the fishing pier, Tomás said, *"Them!"*

The helicopter banked and turned, putting the men at the pier in the spotlight.

Cockroaches and germs tend to hate intense light. These particular cockroaches were equipped with Ruger AR-556 MPR rifles and two Zodiac Bayrunner 500s.

The DPD helicopter came under fire. It banked hard left, lifted and hightailed it south along the Detroit River.

"Those guys get away, and there goes our alibi for this shit!" Tomás said.

"Not gonna happen," I said, gunning my snowmobile in the direction of the moored boats.

I kept low, closing the distance between myself and the pier, taking enemy fire. My windshield was blown away. I did a few quick S-turns to kick up a cloud of snow as cover. On the last turn, I managed to take off my belt, aim the snowmobile at one of the boats and wrap the belt around the accelerator handle. Following the fastest Hail Mary I've ever recited, I rolled off the snowmobile. It took flight and crashed into one of the boats, igniting a bright orange fireball.

One of Bojing's men crawled out of the freezing water and stood on wobbly legs.

The last man.

"Toss your weapons! Get on your knees —"

That's as far as I got before he pressed his sidearm just beneath his chin, fired and fell backward into the river.

Our alibi was literally dead in the water.

39

The well-dressed, middle-aged Black man behind the podium looked uncomfortable, as if his tie were choking him. Or maybe the white camera flashes were painfully distracting. It could have been the phalanx of men and women assembled tightly behind him: the mayor, the DPD chief of police, the police commissioner, the Michigan Director of Natural Resources and a host of other men and women who looked as if they'd rather be anywhere else except in front of rabid reporters and TV camera crews jockeying for the perfect shot.

"Some thirty to forty deer suffering from CWD — chronic wasting disease — were culled two nights ago on Belle Isle in a joint operation between the Michigan Department of Natural Resources and the Detroit Police Department —"

Tomás nearly shot beer through his nose

as we watched the press conference live on my TV.

"These deer are commonly, and perhaps apocryphally, referred to as 'zombie deer.' They posed a serious public health threat," the well-dressed Black man said with a straight face while reading from a prepared statement. "A night operation was deemed the most efficient way to cull this CWD herd without endangering public safety."

Tomás was nearly in tears as he laughed at the press conference.

"It was reported to have sounded like a war zone!" a reporter shouted, momentarily throwing the well-dressed Black man at the podium off his timing.

"The Michigan Department of Natural Resources," the Black man bravely continued, "along with some of the City of Detroit Police Department's finest sharpshooters and a DPD helicopter used as a spotter, cleared Belle Isle of all — repeat, *all* — deer suspected of carrying the fatal chronic wasting disease. We apologize for any disturbance this action may have caused —"

"A citizen from Windsor, Ontario, reported a fireball!" another reporter shouted.

Without finishing his prepared thoughts, the Black man introduced his portly white Michigan DNR public relations counterpart, who proceeded to educate the undulating crowd of reporters on the apocalyptic horrors of "zombie" deer.

And ticks.

Killer ticks.

Not unlike the reporters, I had a few questions of my own, like why none of us — Tomás, Lady B and her well-armed crew, Brutus Jefferies, Duke Ducane and the notorious Compton twins and me — were cooling our heels in a high-security lockdown. Or how an all-out bloody war on the island had become a DNR deer cull.

I took special notice of Police Commissioner Renard standing in the background. He looked as if he were seconds away from going thermonuclear. Renard had shown up at the Belle Isle scene in a black Lincoln Aviator SUV. Emerging from the back, over the din of sirens and people shouting, Renard had growled to a fellow passenger, "You fucking people are *ridiculous*! You'd sure as shit better have one big rug and a giant goddamn broom to sweep this shit under!" Then he'd slammed the rear door shut. Before the door closed, I'd seen a pair of long, shiny legs and white stiletto heels.

Tomás and I had been interviewed separately by DPD and someone I suspected was FBI (maybe the snappy suit and fifties high-and-tight haircut), but the interviews had been short and restrained — as if invisible strings were being remotely pulled and somebody else's hands were operating their mouths. We had finally been released by Commissioner Renard, who tersely told his men, "We're done here. Cut 'em loose." As I passed by Renard, he'd glared at me and gruffly mumbled, "Why am I not surprised?"

"You know I ain't got one damn weapon left," Tomás said after a finishing gulp of his beer. "Not one pistol, rifle, bullet, knife or grenade. No C-4, no flash-bangs, no —"

"Here," I said, reaching into the downstairs closet and pulling out one of Bojing's guards' Ruger AR-556 MPR rifles. "I managed to walk this out. Feel better?"

Tomás's eyes lit up.

"You *do* care!" he said, taking the lethal weapon and cradling it as if it were a newborn. "You sure about this?"

"The rifle? Yeah, sure, why not? You earned it."

"No," Tomás said. *"This."* He gestured toward my carry-on luggage by the door. "This ain't a part of you I've ever seen — and I ain't too sure I like it. I understand it. But I don't know if I agree with it. You're absolutely sure, Octavio?"

"Yes," I said. "I'm sure."

"Nobody's gonna have your six, compadre," he said. "*I'm* not gonna have your six."

I put a hand on Tomás's shoulder and said, "You've always got my six, padrino."

> But if I were you, I would appeal to God; I would lay my cause before him. He performs wonders that cannot be fathomed, miracles that cannot be counted.
>
> — Job 5:8–9

The Spanish.

The Portuguese.

The Dutch and Belgians.

The English.

Jesuits.

Republicans.

Democrats.

It's nothing short of a miracle that Black people are still topside and kicking on this spinning mass grave called Earth.

I stared with unabashed awe and unequaled sadness at the faces, postures and strides of slavery's children as they searched for their flights, ate sandwiches, swept floors, emptied garbage cans, embraced and kissed, laughed, talked and hailed taxis at Quito International Airport in Quito, Ecuador. Near-white, tan, golden-brown,

374

smooth-chocolate, cappuccino and black-coffee skin with kinky, curly, wavy, close-cropped and dreadlocked hair that was the legacy of a capsized slave ship sunk off the coast of Esmeraldas. The escaped slaves who built Ecuador's capital, Quito. The shackle-scarred and whip-lashed men, women and children who suffered noon heat as they worked the Jesuit cotton and sugarcane fields in the Chota Valley. Who thrived after having joined Simón Bolívar's fight for South American independence only to be abandoned after the fight was won.

I saw in their faces my own.

I felt their blends of blood in my own veins.

"Hey, hey, *hey*!" my young Black cabbie said. On his car's old CD player, he was playing a song called "No Weakness" by Hety and Zambo. "Where you in from today, my man?"

In Spanish I told him Detroit by way of a long layover in Miami.

"Detroit?" he said. "Motown? No shit?"

"No shit," I said as we quickly transitioned from Spanish to English.

"Aretha! Smokey! Marvin Gaye! Temptations!" he said. " 'Ain't No Mountain High Enough!' "

Like every other person who has lived in

375

Detroit for longer than five minutes, I felt the needle drop into an etched vinyl disclaimer groove. "Actually, Aretha never recorded with Motown," I said, "Aretha Franklin was mostly with Atlantic Records, not Motown."

"She's still *la Reina del Alma*!" The driver laughed. "The Queen of Soul!"

"You got that right, mi amigo."

"So, you coming home? Or what hotel you staying at, my man?"

"The Villa Colonna Quito," I said. "What's your name?"

"Remy," he said. "Reymundo, but friends, they call me Remy. *You* can call me Remy. And your name, sir?"

Over the back of the driver's seat, I held out fifty bucks American to him, which instantly turned on the money light in his eyes. "I don't have one, Remy. Comprendes?"

"Sí, señor," Remy said, snatching the fifty bucks from my fingers. "A ghost. A puff of smoke. Sure. I can dig that. Sí."

"There's more, Remy," I said. "And it involves very little of your time and hopefully no trouble, sí?"

"Sí, señor," Remy said. "Okay. I am down for that, yes. Whatever."

"I need a gun," I said. "No street-thug

piece of shit. Nothing with a history. Nothing with much of a future. Can you handle that, or should I find another driver?"

"No problem," Remy said. "Something clean. Acid-burned serial number. Semi-auto nine millimeter. Like un bebé."

40

Sunshine looks different in this part of the world. A deeper, more sweeping hue of yellow shimmering on the edge of Incan gold.

The air smells different, too. Muskier. Thicker. A tinge of cracked pepper filled with a history of zarapatoca stew, barbequed langostinos and a dash of trade-wind sea salt. In Quito these aromas live in symbiosis with the stench of men, their varied enterprises and the sweat from clenched fists, as do the aromas of any city of over two million people,.

As Remy drove the twists and turns at the outer edges of Quito, I gave brief thought to what life in an Ecuadorian prison might be like.

Maybe the food would be better than in an American one.

Maybe instead of fighting for a spit of idealized land called Mexicantown, I could simply bare-knuckle for cigarettes and rations of whiskey, finally get shivved and be done with it all.

As we reached the old town, navigating past the towering and perpetually unfinished Basílica del Voto Nacional, I wondered if the God of Spain and Rome would forgive me my murderous intentions or banish me to an obscure, smoldering corner of Dante's Inferno. Or worse, relegate my remains to the mountainous terrain of slave bones tossed and intertwined with the skeletons of long-dead cattle and donkeys.

It didn't take Remy long to find a weapon for me in the bright and bustling Otavalo Marketplace.

"She wants three hundred American," Remy said as he discreetly handed me a Beretta Px4 Storm Inox without a magazine. I sniffed it. Broke it down. Ratcheted the slide a couple times.

"Two clips?"

"Five hundred American with two clips," Remy said. "To be honest, señor, I think you could get her down to —"

"Pay her," I said, handing Remy the money in a compact roll.

Inconspicuously, he paid a middle-aged Incan-featured woman wearing a colorful skirt and brown fedora who sat placidly watching the crowd of shoppers walk past her handmade skirts, blouses and scarfs.

"Two clips," Remy said, handing them over the back of the driver's seat to me.

"You talked her down, didn't you, Remy?" I said, stowing away the gun and clips in my luggage. "You talked her down and pocketed two hundred, sí?"

It took a moment, but he finally answered, "Sí, Señor Ghost."

"I thought we were pals, Remy."

"She *still* made out like a bandit, señor!" Remy pleaded. "She could have sold the gun for *fifty* American and made in a day what it would have taken her a week to make from her crappy clothes and shit."

"I'm deducting two hundred from your tip —"

"Aw, come on! Is that really — That's not really fair! I got bills to pay —"

"And babies to feed," I said. "Yeah, I know the story. Listen. You can drop me off at the next corner, or we can continue our relationship for a couple more hours, and you can make two months' wages — maybe more. But our relationship has to be at a higher level of trust, comprendes?"

Two hours and fifteen high-end shoe and clothing stores later, I had the name and shop location of the shoemaker to the wealthy: Ernesto Manta — EM, the letters embossed on the inside sole of the shoes on a dead man purported to be the mysterious Mr. Sloane. The man with ten million in dirty and disappeared cash and twenty million in vanished barrow bonds. The man who had planted my name in the pocket of the suit he put on a homeless vet before tossing him into a water clarifying tank. The man whose finger had flicked every domino that had started a chain reaction that had threatened to kill my friends and me.

I had Remy take me to my hotel, where I had registered under the name Pumpsie Green, hoping no one at the front desk was a diehard Boston Red Sox baseball fan.

"Be here in an hour, Remy," I said. "If you decide not to show, it's been fun."

"I'll be here," he said. "But promise me one thing, señor."

"What's that?"

"My payment's not going to be a bullet from one of those clips."

"Your payment is going to be cash money," I said. "That's all and that's a promise."

"Cool," he said. "Una hora."

Traveling in Latin America is pitifully incomplete without a healthy sampling of the region's multitude of gastronomic pleasures. That being said, knowing I was here to kill a man purely out of spite did little to enhance my appetite. I managed to choke down half a plate of the hotel's gringo version of churrasco — thin grilled steak topped with fried egg, rice, plantains, fries, sliced avocado, salad and garlic ají sauce — but only for the protein and carbs murder sometimes requires. If I was right, the man who had set my hell in motion had been living the high life somewhere off the Ecuadorian coast. That was where his exclusive shoemaker was, and that was where a lot of new, luxurious and near-anonymous seaside residential developments had recently gone up. I briefly gave thought to a mid-20th century Black poet who wrote —

Where does the good man go after his
 blood has been taken
and his teeth are held in the palms of his
 hands?
He wanders deep into his own shadow,
where he no longer bleeds and where his
 bite
is reborn.

Maybe the assassin I'd come to know as the Cleaner was right after all.
Maybe we were two of a kind.

382

When Remy picked me up outside the hotel, I was dressed in a well-tailored cream-colored linen-and-viscose suit, a powder-blue Egyptian-cotton shirt, no socks and black velvet Ferragamo shoes. The waistband of my pants had just enough give to accommodate my newly acquired Berretta and extra clip.

"Damn, jefe, you looking killer!" Remy, realizing the cold irony of what he'd just said, stammered through a profuse apology until I excused him his transgression. This time I offered him two hundred American over the back of the driver's seat and gave him the address of Ernesto Manta's shop.

The "master," Señor Manta, was not in. And he was never available for an initial client interview, style consultation or measuring. It didn't matter if you were a Saudi prince, prime minister, drug lord or gunrunner. If you wanted to put your feet into his hands, you followed his rules. And his rules included a handwritten request accompanied by a thousand in US cash.

I was good with being a "walk-in."

In fact, that's how I preferred it.

Five hundred cash turned the key to the door, allowing for my entrance, though not an audience with Manta.

The display of shoes lining the softly lit

walnut shelves of the small shop was impressive. These were merely examples of his work. Models. None were meant for customers to try on. If you saw a design element, flourish or frill on one shoe that you'd like added to yours, the "master" would let you know if your detailing suggestions made sense or not. If not, then you were more than welcome to spend your money elsewhere. Perhaps you were more of a Thom McAn man than an Ernesto Manta client.

In this part of the world — not unlike in Washington, DC — loyalty and discretion are earned over years, while treachery and deceit can be purchased in mere minutes. I was sure one of Manta's employees took cash clients when the master wasn't in and altered his order records and accounts.

A little grease on the side.

Three middle-aged women — one with the handsome, snobbish look of an upperclass Spaniard, the other two with a working-class Andean look — and an austere man in his late sixties, who was dressed more fittingly for the work of funeral home director, examined my feet. Scrutinized them. Pressed and rubbed them in their gloved hands. The women spoke Spanish to one another in accents I was unfamiliar with. The austere man nodded and scribbled notes. At one point, one of the Andean-looking women rolled out a portable X-ray machine.

"Whoa! Hold on!" I said in Spanish. "What the hell is *that* for?"

"The master finds bone structure to be of utmost importance when it comes to podiatric comfort, performance and styling. It is the personalized foundation of an exquisite shoe," the humorless man said. "X-rays are held in the strictest of confidence, and should you not order from us again within two years, the films are shredded."

The austere man was not my mark.

No one wants to be around when focused beams of high-intensity radiation are being deployed. The austere man and two of the women — the snobby Spaniard and the younger Andean — left the showroom while the third woman donned a lead vest and prepared me for the machine.

She was my mark.

I discreetly took a fold of two hundred dollars American from my suit coat inner pocket, and while she set up my left foot for the X-ray machine, I inconspicuously showed her the money and whispered, "Información, por favor."

Without a word, she took the money.

Forty minutes later, I met the woman on

her lunch break. I gave her another three hundred, and she gave me Sloane's address.

It was during this transaction over a cold pork sandwich and warm Coke that I realized how mundane cold-blooded murder could be.

41

The company was Mirabella Property Development, a division of Kostler and Reinman, a high-end international German property management and development company. And this was one of their newest developments: Santuario del Sol — Sanctuary of the Sun. Twenty brightly colored detached luxury condos, each hidden from the others by ingenious man-made elevations, deceptive little switchbacks and dense tropical landscaping. There was a glorious clubhouse rising above all the condos, and for a five-figure fee, it could be reserved for engagement parties, wedding receptions, quinceañeras, bar mitzvahs, bat mitzvahs, wakes, family get-togethers and, one would assume, bacchanalian orgies — but bring your own lube. There was a guardhouse resembling a small-footprint whitewashed Spanish villa and, behind it, a ten-foot-high wrought-iron gate almost completely hidden by palm trees, tall grass and tropical ferns. The guardhouse, right next to the resident RF keycard stand, was manned 24-7 by two guards in simple black suits. There was one wide road in, the same road out. In the distance, a considerable cliff dropped to the roiling Pacific Ocean. There were no signs announcing the name or address of the place; if you had to ask what this place was, you clearly didn't belong there.

Santuario del Sol. An exclusive development designed for aggressive anonymity.

It was where I would disappear with thirty million in someone else's money.

On my third day, I had Remy slam on the brakes in front of the guardhouse.

I kicked open the rear passenger door and frantically unloaded two cases of Johnnie Walker Blue.

"Swear to *God*," I said, laughing and dramatically pointing to Remy. "If you hadn't come along, man, I'd *really* be in the shit! Okay, now! Bye-bye! Fucking lifesaver, this guy!" I handed Remy a bottle of the whisky. "Least I can do, compadre! Least I can do!"

"Excuse me," one of the guards said in English as he approached me. "Señor? Sir? May I ask —"

"Oh, geez Louise," I said, doing my best blustery American in paradise. "My rental broke down about — what? — four miles — kilometers? — from here. You guys use miles, right? Anyway, you wouldn't expect a new Beemer to break down, right? German engineering and all that. Yeah, so, anyway, that taxi guy comes along and saves my bacon, I'll tell you what! Sloane's been waiting for his booze for an hour now!"

"Sloane?" the guard said. "Who is this Sloane?"

"Who's Sloane?" I said. "He's *Sloane. Sloane*! White guy! Balding! Looks like a million other slightly balding white guys in their forties! Jesus! *Sloane!*"

The guard's eyes cut to the two cases of Johnnie Walker Blue.

Gotcha.

"Listen," I said, moving close to him and dropping my voice to a conspiratorial whisper. "*You* know the guy. I'm just dropping his booze. That's it. In and out, easy peasy. Motherfucker was half in the bag when he ordered it. I'm sure, you know, he won't even know if a bottle —"

"I have a partner."

"*Two* bottles go poof," I said. "As soon as I drop 'em at Number Ten, I'm gone, sí? And you guys can drink good whisky and sing 'Viva la revolución' or whatever. I'm begging you. This is my *job,* man."

One minute later, Remy was driving off twenty-eight hundred richer (minus the two hundred), and I was walking the private road with two cases of scotch whisky — shy three bottles. Halfway along the road, I ditched the booze behind a fern, extracted my weapon from my belt and continued on.

Number Ten Santuario del Sol was a key-lime-pie green two-story Spanish villa with a red clay tile roof, crowded in on all sides by giant ferns and several young palm trees. Hidden within the overgrowth were two security cameras and a laser trip wire twenty feet from the door. None of the modest security measures meant anything considering the tall cathedral arched front doors were open. It was a stagnant ninety degrees, so I doubted the door had been left open for a cooling breeze.

I entered, low and fast.

Nothing but the distant copper-penny taste of blood drifting in the sea salt air . . .

Winding staircase to the left.

No one.

Large open-concept dining room and expansive living room to my right.

Nothing.

Following the sound of the ocean . . .

. . . through to the balcony . . .

Bingo.

On the tiled balcony, reclining on a chaise with his back to me, fingertips resting on the rim of a glass of white wine, was the man I'd come to kill: Mr. Sloane. Relaxed. At ease. Taking in a small corner of the world's beauty while the rest of the world burned.

And someone else.

A crossed pair of long, shiny woman's legs, high arched feet in white stiletto heels. I turned my attention — and the barrel of my gun — to her.

I finally got a good view of the woman: a platinum blonde I'd seen before. The Flowers of Vietnam restaurant in Mexicantown. The one who dropped Renard off at Belle Isle.

The woman smiled at me — the kind of smile that draws a man inextricably into a woman's web. The last things he feels are elongated incisors piercing his jugular vein.

"Had a feeling we'd see each other again," she said.

I moved slowly around to face Sloane.

Eyes glaring open. Blue tongue jutted out. Throat cut. Red blood staining the front of his white terry robe.

"You?" I said to the woman.

"Oh, God, no," she said with a modicum of disgust. "That I leave to others. And even then, my people aren't so — sloppy."

"And your 'people' are?"

"Exactly that," she said. "*My* people. *My* assets. *Not* yours. *Ever.*"

"You're CIA."

"Let's just say a subsidiary of the company," she said. "For whatever reason — personally, I can't see it — you seem to inspire loyalty in people who should otherwise know and appreciate who truly butters their bread, Lieutenant Snow. Like Dieter and Mr. McKenny. *My* assets. I didn't mind the two thugs Dieter iced — for lack of a better term — in Switzerland. In this job, there's considerable downtime. And however they choose to amuse themselves during such downtime, I don't give a shit. But having Dieter kill the Frenchman was a bridge too far. You invited yourself to *my* party, put your cock in the punch bowl and stirred vigorously."

"You *want* these guys to build their ghost towns?"

"For the first time in five years, we would have known the locations of at least a sixth of the world's most well-financed and dangerous players," she said, standing and smoothing her form-fitting white dress. "I

can still salvage the deal they made with Vic
Bronson about the Detroit condos, but —"

"Leave Mexicantown out of this."

She laughed.

Then with furious power she grabbed the
body of Sloane by the lapels of his bloody
robe and heaved him over the balcony rail-
ing, watching him fall to the breakers two
hundred feet below.

"In two hours, he'll be shark shit," she
said, watching the breakers for a moment.
Then she cut her eyes back to me. "Your
worldview is adorably quaint, marine. That
being said, you have certain 'friends' who
prevent me from ripping your gigantic brass
balls off and stuffing them down your goddamn throat."

"Wow," I said. "And I thought *I* had anger
issues."

"See ya round, gunney," the blonde with
long, shiny legs said as she walked past me
toward the front door.

"If we meet again, what do I call you
before I shoot you?" I said.

"Ms. Soligney," she said. "And you've got
five minutes before my cleaning crew gets
here. I would suggest you take that time to
go upstairs, second bedroom on the right,
and say goodbye."

I ran past the blonde and took the staircase

two, three steps at a time.

At the foot of a king-size bed lay Jacqueline Ochoa, dressed in a blue bikini, bleeding profusely from three stab wounds to the stomach. Her breathing was quick and shallow. I sat beside her and took her into my arms.

"Jesus," I said. "Come on, Jackie. You can't —"

She looked up at me, attempted a smile and in a hoarse voice said, "August."

Then she was dead.

42

"What's this?" Jimmy Radmon asked after I handed him the folded pieces of legal-sized paper.

"The ownership papers for 87915 Vernor Highway," I said. "The old Authentico Foods building. It's yours."

Jimmy gaped at the papers for a stunned minute before saying, "I — I ain't got that kinda money, Mr. Snow."

"Yes, you do," I said, handing him another collection of legal-sized papers stating that he and Carlos Rodriguez were the free-and-clear owners of the property and the property taxes were paid for three years. I'd purchased the building from the city, which had held it in escrow since its rightful owners were now gone. Then I transferred ownership to Jimmy and Carlos.

I didn't tell Jimmy the money had come from a forged Wassily Kandinsky painting.

Before I'd left the late Mr. Sloane's Ecuadorian hideaway, I'd wrapped Jackie Ochoa's body in the silk bedspread and laid her carefully in the center of the bed. Then I'd said a Hail Mary over her. Considering the personality of Ms. Soligney, I'm sure this was the closest Jackie would come to a dignified burial. I was about to leave the bedroom when my mother's spirit whispered, "What's wrong with this picture?"

Above the bed hung an "expert copy" of Kandinsky's 1923 *Composition VIII*. Aside from the fact that the painting was a forgery, hung upside down and imprisoned in a vulgar gold-leaf frame, I couldn't see anything that was wrong with it.

I looked more closely at the frame — the bottom corners were hinged.

It only took a few seconds to find the release for one of the hinges. Once I triggered it, the bottom left side of the frame dropped. Inside the ugly hollow frame was a half million in cash and five million in negotiable barrow bonds. Bug-out money, I figured. In case things got a little too hot for Sloane in Ecuador.

Getting the money back to Detroit took some doing.

But isn't that why rich people have lawyers and accountants?

I have a *very* good lawyer and a *very* good

accountant who — though not altogether too happy about it — proved exceptional at doing a bit of laundry.

"But —"

"No buts, Jimmy," I said. "The building's paid for. You've got tax, repair, redesign and repurposing money in the bank. And I happen to know one of the major hospitals is looking for a community care presence in Mexicantown. Make sure they offer the folks who lost their Authentico jobs employment."

"I — I don't know what to say."

"Say, 'I deserve this, goddammit.' "

"I deserve this, gosh dang it."

"Close enough," I said. "Get to work."

When I came home after the second and last of my Afghanistan tours, I stayed at my folks' house. The same house I grew up in and took possession of after they passed away.

They knew something was off with me — you don't go to war and return unchanged. But unlike a number of vets, I was fairly good at hiding, controlling and commanding my damage. I enrolled at Wayne State University with the secret mission of getting a degree in sociology so that I could work with high-school-age Mexican-Americans and African-Americans, convincing both to stay the hell away from the meat grinder that was the military.

Back then, there was no Detroit Cristo Rey High School; if you had dreams of a college education, you were your dreams' sole advocate. You prayed the rosary for a scholarship that was unlikely to come, begged and borrowed from already strapped family or swept floors at the college you wanted to go to and hand over your check to the tuition office, studied by flashlight and slept in your car if you couldn't go home. If you were really lucky, you may have gone to school on an athletic scholarship, but even then you most likely wouldn't make it through the devouring university athletics gauntlet with your body and mind intact and a degree in your hands.

My father was convinced, as men of his generation often were, that the lingering nightmares of war could be resolved through clarity of purpose and hard work.

"You get into the academy," he once told me over breakfast, "you got a reason to get up in the morning. They would snatch you up in a heartbeat: decorated former marine, smart as hell, and you got *me* on the inside. Put you on the fast track. I know some of them boys over at the academy. Yessir. A man needs a reason to get up in the morning. I'll check it out for you, son."

"Thanks, Dad," I said, unconvinced of my promise as a cop.

Of course, my mother could see the ghosts performing un baile macabro inside me.

As with many men who return from war, I'd lost my faith in God.

It's a helluva thing to realize the fallacy of both God and country in one fell swoop.

I attended mass with my mom and dad only for the love of them.

God be damned.

Then my beloved mother intruded into my private hateful place by arranging a meeting between Father Grabowski and me.

Only for her did I keep the appointment.

He was old even back then, though his beard had not quite turned Santa Claus white yet.

"Let me guess," Grabowski said, escorting me up to his office at St. Al's. "You don't want to be here, right?"

"You're a good man, Father, and a family friend," I said. "But no. I don't want to be here."

"I get it," he said. "Just let me show you something. Then you can bug out if you want." Once we reached his office, he said, "You want a beer?"

"You keep beer on church property?" I said, sitting on his beat-up canary-yellow sofa.

"If the apostles could drink a cask of wine dry, I can have a beer now and again." He tossed me a well-chilled can of Molson Canadian from his minifridge. We popped the tops on our beers simultaneously and toasted each other's health. Then he took a photograph from his desk drawer and handed it to me: a young man, grinning, shirtless, muscular, holding an M16. There was a clunky necklace slung around his neck.

"Who's this?" I said.

"That, my dear boy, is me," Father Grabowski said. "Dong Hoi, Vietnam, 1972."

"You served?"

"Sure did," he said.

"What's with the funky necklace?"

"Those, son, are human ears," Grabowski said. "One from each kill I had." He let that sink in for a moment. I looked more closely at the photo; they were indeed human ears threaded together with twine. "I know a little bit about the monsters war can turn men into. The monsters that go bump in the night when we return from war. Me, Vietnam. You, Afghanistan. Lost causes, lost lives, lost souls. You hate God. Deny Jesus. Screw Abraham and Muhammad and Buddha and Miss America. I get it. When I got back in the world, I found my salvation in the Franciscan brotherhood first and God a distant second. And when I prayed — oh, you'd better believe it — I broke a sweat praying with anger. Like a monster exhausted from being a monster."

"So, you're telling me to pray away the monsters, Father?" I said. "Like a child with night terrors?"

He laughed. "I'm telling you if I didn't have my Franciscan brothers to talk to, I probably would be twenty years in my grave, August. They used to call it 'shell shock.' Now they call it PTSD. The difference between the two is at least now they know something about treating it. And it all begins by talking about it. It begins by seeking help." He finished his beer and asked if I wanted another. I said no. "Would I like for you to pray? Oh, heck yes! But you know what I'd like even more? I'd like for you to talk to somebody. A therapist. A veterans' group. People who know the monsters. You'll never quite get rid of them, August. But it's possible to put them in tiny boxes and stow them away."

I stood and offered his picture back to him.

"Keep it," he said.

With ambivalence, I kept the photo.

The picture was in my right pants pocket when I honored a promise I'd made to Tatina.

"August," the silver-haired man with wire-rimmed glasses said while shaking my hand, "I'm Dr. Sussman. Call me Alan."

"I don't want to be here," I said. "What makes an academic think he can even in the slightest know what I've been through?"

He lifted his right pant leg — a prosthetic.

"Tony Bennett may have left his heart in San Francisco," Sussman said. "But me? I got a right leg hobbling around somewhere in Baghdad looking for its owner."

"You got coffee?"

"*And* cookies!" Sussman said.

For that first of six sessions, all I could do was drink coffee and fucking cry.

I thought it might be Elena, Jimmy and Lucy who would have the hardest time with my going to Oslo for a month.

Maybe longer.

Turned out it was Tomás.

While Elena said she'd miss me, she quietly understood why I had to leave for longer than my usual two weeks in Oslo every few months: Too many ghosts crowding in on me, each one bellyaching. Too much violence brushing against my skin and humming in my bones. And a heart very much in need of healing.

I wanted Lucy to know a sense of normal. Something I hadn't quite given her the past several months. It took some doing to convince her to stay. I was willing to leave in an effort to let her have that peace and also prove to her that she had become part of the fabric of my heart.

"You let me down," she said. "I expect that from humans in general. But not you, Sherlock. Not you. Ever."

"I know," I said. "And I am so sorry."

"Just don't be such a dick."

"I've pretty much got this dick thing down to a science."

"Tell me about it," she said.

Then we hugged.

But Tomás . . .

"At least I don't have to worry about you going off to some godforsaken war zone," Elena said as she and Tomás dropped me at Detroit Metro Airport.

"He's going for a *woman*," Tomás said. "That's *always* a freakin' 'war zone'!"

"Don't mind him," Elena said. "He's feeling a bit abandoned."

"What?" Tomás said indignantly. "Because *this* pendejo is going on a trim hunt? Not a chance, woman! No way!"

As I sat in first class waiting for my flight to taxi to its runway, my phone pinged with one last text before I set it to airplane mode: I GOT YOUR SIX — TU PADRINO.

About a year ago, Tatina and I promised each other we'd stop making out in airports like horny teenagers. I, after all, was a trained killing machine who knew how to keep his cool under fire. And she was now a university professor, a profession that demanded at least a modicum of respectable behavior in public places.

But when Tatina saw me emerge through the Oslo Lufthavn arrival doors she leapt into my arms and wrapped her legs around me, and we kissed for what was apparently a long time. Long enough for a security guard to kindly suggest we move to the side of the doorway. It was then I noticed several people staring at us, smiling or laughing.

As we raced down the Lufthavnvegen highway in her MINI Cooper, Tatina said, "Okay, what's the second thing you want to do today?"

"You proceed from the false assumption,

Dr. Stadtmueller, that there will be enough of the day left over after the *first* thing for there to be a second thing."

"Okay then," she began. "Let's assume there *is* time for a second — how shall I say? — activity. What might that be?"

"How 'bout helping me find an apartment, furniture, that sort of stuff?"

Tatina nearly swerved off the highway.

"Seriously?" she said. "Don't tease, August!"

"I'm not," I said. "But the apartment's got to have a really nice kitchen, enough wall space for a large TV, a sizable leather sofa — forest green, preferably — and a big bed."

"*Huge* bed!" She laughed.

"*Gigantic* bed! Know any good lookin' babes who might like to share this gigantic bed with me?"

"I'll put a list together for you," she said, adding, "Idiot."

Frankly, I had no idea what I was doing.

Who the hell does?

ABOUT THE AUTHOR

Stephen Mack Jones is a published poet, an award-winning playwright, and a recipient of the prestigious Hammett Prize, Nero Award, and the Kresge Arts in Detroit Literary Fellowship. He was born in Lansing, Michigan, and currently lives in the suburbs of Detroit. *Dead of Winter* is his third novel.